ROMANCING HIS WIFE

The door opened behind her and she whirled around.

"You have the look of a doe at bay, Helena, or a princess tied to a rock awaiting the dragon," said Richard softly. The faintest of smiles played at the corners of his mouth. "I thought you were made of nobler stuff."

"But I'm not of noble blood!"

"Then mine will have to count for both of us, I suppose." Gently, he touched her lips with his own. She felt suddenly reassured; perhaps she could trust him. She closed her eyes as his hands gently smoothed over their lids. She could feel careful fingers pulling the pins out of her hair. As it fell around her shoulders, he smoothed it away from her face as if he were soothing a frightened horse.

"Your hair alone would be enticing enough to launch all the thousand ships," he whispered. "Helen of Troy would have been jealous." His mouth touched her temple and the lobe of her ear. When his lips closed once again over hers, she could not keep herself from responding. "There, you see. That wasn't so bad, was it?"

Her eyes flew open. She felt breathless and dizzy. "No," she said honestly. "It was lovely."

"Then would you mind if I did it again?"

"I think I might even like it."

"And I think, truthful Helena, that I am glad that I married you."

ZEBRA'S REGENCY ROMANCES
DAZZLE AND DELIGHT

A BEGUILING INTRIGUE (4441, $3.99)
by Olivia Sumner

Pretty as a picture Justine Riggs cared nothing for propriety. She dressed as a boy, sat on her horse like a jockey, and pondered the stars like a scientist. But when she tried to best the handsome Quenton Fletcher, Marquess of Devon, by proving that she was the better equestrian, he would try to prove Justine's antics were pure folly. The game he had in mind was seduction—never imagining that he might lose his heart in the process!

AN INCONVENIENT ENGAGEMENT (4442, $3.99)
by Joy Reed

Rebecca Wentworth was furious when she saw her betrothed waltzing with another. So she decides to make him jealous by flirting with the handsomest man at the ball, John Collinwood, Earl of Stanford. The "wicked" nobleman knew exactly what the enticing miss was up to—and he was only too happy to play along. But as Rebecca gazed into his magnificent eyes, her errant fiancé was soon utterly forgotten!

SCANDAL'S LADY (4472, $3.99)
by Mary Kingsley

Cassandra was shocked to learn that the new Earl of Lynton was her childhood friend, Nicholas St. John. After years at sea and mixed feelings Nicholas had come home to take the family title. And although Cassandra knew her place as a governess, she could not help the thrill that went through her each time he was near. Nicholas was pleased to find that his old friend Cassandra was his new next door neighbor, but after being near her, he wondered if mere friendship would be enough . . .

HIS LORDSHIP'S REWARD (4473, $3.99)
by Carola Dunn

As the daughter of a seasoned soldier, Fanny Ingram was accustomed to the vagaries of military life and cared not a whit about matters of rank and social standing. So she certainly never foresaw her *tendre* for handsome Viscount Roworth of Kent with whom she was forced to share lodgings, while he carried out his clandestine activities on behalf of the British Army. And though good sense told Roworth to keep his distance, he couldn't stop from taking Fanny in his arms for a kiss that made all hearts equal!

Available wherever paperbacks are sold, or order direct from the Publisher. Send cover price plus 50¢ per copy for mailing and handling to Penguin USA, P.O. Box 999, c/o Dept. 17109, Bergenfield, NJ 07621. Residents of New York and Tennessee must include sales tax. DO NOT SEND CASH.

Virtue's Reward

Jean R. Ewing

ZEBRA BOOKS
KENSINGTON PUBLISHING CORP.

For Mary and Naomi, with thanks

ZEBRA BOOKS are published by

Kensington Publishing Corp.
850 Third Avenue
New York, NY 10022

Copyright © 1995 by Jean R. Ewing

Zebra and the Z logo Reg. U.S. Pat. & TM Off.

First Printing: February, 1995

Printed in the United States of America

"Virtue is bold, and goodness never fearful."
—*Measure for Measure*

One

"By God, I've been hit!"

Captain Richard Acton whirled his mount at the cry. His fellow officer had sagged forward over the neck of his charger, and the horse, as the reins fell slack, jibbed and shied. At the violent movement, the rider slid heavily from the saddle and thudded to the ground, leaving a dreadful smear of scarlet across the animal's sweat-drenched shoulder. The frightened horse threw up its head and galloped away. Richard swore softly beneath his breath as he pulled up his bay and leapt to the ground. The men were momentarily alone, sheltered suddenly from the fury of the battle by a slight dip, where a stunted bush sent out the first green shoots of spring and the remains of a stone wall rose jaggedly from the lane. Just behind them a cluster of ancient French farm buildings lay in gaping ruins, then fruit trees and trampled vineyards seemed to stretch away to the far, white-capped peaks of the Pyrenees. Ignoring the acrid smoke-filled air and the thunder of the guns echoing through the damp orchard, Captain Acton knelt over his friend.

"So you have, sir," he said gently.

Edward's red coat was absorbing the blood as it was designed to do, without showing any stain, but it was becoming dark with moisture. Richard rapidly pulled off his sash and wadded the cloth into the wound; in moments it was the same color as their coats. Sir Edward Blake smiled wanly up at him.

"Don't waste your time, old fellow." He coughed weakly and blood spattered his chin. "I'm done for."

"Nonsense," replied Richard. "You'll live to win another hundred guineas from me yet."

"Lying don't suit you, sir. Not your style. Final wager to make now: Heaven or hell, what's it to be?" Blake grinned but clamped his teeth together as a spasm of pain shot through him and his fingers unwittingly crushed into his friend's muscled arm.

Richard cradled the dark head against the strength of his own body and smoothed back the limp wet hair. Edward had begun to shake. He was right, of course. A pretense would do nothing to help, not this time. He offered his flask of brandy: balm and sure death in one. "Then you don't want to meet your maker sober, do you?" he said quietly. But the wounded man pushed his hand away. His face was the color of the silver stopper.

"Richard, listen, there's—" He choked, and a fresh rush of sweat soaked his features.

"What is it, Edward? Name anything."

"My cousin," gasped Edward. "Helena. It's hers—" Another shudder shook his frame.

"Easy does it. What's hers, my friend?"

"Will—" His hand moved ineffectively toward his own brandy flask as he shut his eyes against the pain.

"Mine's as good as yours, sir, but if you prefer your own poison, you shall have it." Richard reached carefully for Edward's flask in its tightly stitched leather covering and pulled off the top.

"Helena," said Sir Edward Blake. "Trethaerin. Cornwall. Will—" His voice was filled with pleading.

Captain Richard Acton closed his lean fingers and gripped the dying man tightly by the hand. "Never fear, my friend. You have my word. I will take care of her."

Edward smiled faintly. "Brandy," he breathed. And died.

Richard ran his fingers thoughtfully over the silver monogram stamped in the leather before he replaced the stopper and thrust the flask into his own pocket. Laying the body of Sir Edward Blake softly into the mire, he said a single prayer, then swung back onto his restive horse. The noise of the guns and the shouts of men exploded around his head. Kicking the bay into a wild gallop, Captain Richard Acton burst out of the lane and swept a swath of merciless destruction through Napoleon's fleeing men.

"I am very sorry to tell you this, ma'am, so soon after your other loss." The solicitor coughed discreetly into his gloved hand. "But in the circumstance of your cousin having died intestate . . . It's very awkward, ma'am."

"I don't see any awkwardness at all, Mr. Marble," replied Helena Trethaerin calmly. Her blond hair shone like gold against her black dress. "I am sure that Mr. Garthwood will do right by me when he arrives. Poor Edward! I hope it was sudden. Had my father known before his own death . . ." She rose gracefully to her feet. "But there it is. I thank you very much for coming all this way—and in such dreadful weather—to explain things so clearly." She smiled and held out her hand. "There is no reason, surely, why I should not stay on here for now?"

"None at all, ma'am. Mr. Garthwood made that perfectly clear. You are to continue to treat Trethaerin House as your own. He will not be able to wrap up his other business, he tells me, for some months, and as you say, he will most certainly not see you turned from the door."

The solicitor left, and Helena gazed out at the steady rain pouring down past the windows. It was unusually wet for April. "Awkward!" she said aloud to the empty room. "Papa, now that poor Edward is killed, you have left me with a complete disaster!"

"Why does the summer sky of England smile on her children like a mother, when the sunshine of Spain sucks the soul of a man like a leech?"

Richard's charger flicked back an ear at his rider, then forward again when no further comment ensued. The bay could not fathom the difference, but the horse was also glad to be back on his native soil. Now, at last, the earth smelled green and lush again, the wholesome smell of the place of his birth. It was late summer in England, and the wheat stood ripe in the shook, promising the chill winds of autumn any day. The horse bent his glossy neck under his master's caress, then at the touch of his heel cantered away down the road.

Captain Acton did not speak to his horse again, but allowed the balm of the green trees, the rich fields, and the snug cottages to do their work. The Peninsular Campaign was long over. He would never see Spain again. Wellington's army had fought its way into France and won the final battle of the campaign at Toulouse in April. They learned later that Napoleon had already abdicated. But it made no difference to Edward; he had been over a month dead by then. The early part of the summer had passed quickly enough in Paris, and then Richard had been required to join Wellington in August, as he surveyed the defenses of the Low Countries.

The Iron Duke was now back in the French capital as ambassador and his captain could at last return to England.

He thought briefly of what he had discovered in Paris. It was one reason he had not returned to London in June and joined in the victory celebrations. The delay had been more than unwelcome, but at least he had done what he could. Now he was free to fulfill his own obligations rather than those of his government or his conscience. Secure in his saddlebags he carried Sir Edward Blake's leather brandy flask, all that was left of his friend. Somewhere in Cornwall was a place called Trethaerin and Edward's cousin Helena. He would find her and deliver the flask, and see that she wanted for nothing. No doubt he would have to make up some heroic tale about Edward's death. Ladies did not want to think that their relatives were victims of a slaughter as random and sordid as in an abattoir. There were not even any noble last sentiments to convey. Every simple word of that final conversation was engraved in his memory; would he also have to lie to her about that? A deep line appeared between his winged eyebrows as the nagging thought that had haunted him ever since made him frown. There had been something else, something important, that his friend had wanted to tell him. Whatever it was, he would never know, and neither would this cousin Helena. In any event, he was sworn to take care of her whether he found her in wealth or in poverty. He wondered fleetingly what she was like and what her situation was, before he forced his mind back to the road. The rise of Exmoor lay before him, and around the next bend was Fernbridge. He would get a room for the night with David Morris before continuing on down the coast to Cornwall.

* * *

"Good God, Acton! Welcome, welcome! To what do I owe this unexpected happiness?"

"To convenience, sir." Richard grinned at Morris and then at the antlered brass door knocker. "Stagshead is on my way; I could hardly pass by without paying my respects to a comrade-in-arms, could I? May I beg a room for the night?"

A groom took the bay, while David showed Richard into the study and poured them both a generous shot of brandy. Captain Acton threw himself into a wing chair and sprawled back against the squabs. David Morris turned to him, his face alight with pleasure above the folds of his cravat.

"Devil take you, Acton, but it's good to see you! How long can you stay?"

He did not have time to reply. Another gentleman had appeared in the doorway. He came in and leaned gracefully against the mantel.

"Long enough that we may all get thoroughly drunk reminiscing about our recent glorious, brave, and noble campaigns, I hope. How else should three old soldiers spend an afternoon together?"

Captain Acton looked up in astonishment, then sprang to his feet and shook the newcomer by the hand. "I would recognize that acid tongue anywhere. What on earth are you doing on Exmoor, Dagonet?"

"Je me jette dans l'eau de peur de la pluie."

"You leap into the water for fear of the rain?" Richard raised a brow, but his expression registered no annoyance when he continued. "I'm damned if I see why having a French father entitles you to speak nonsense in his infernal tongue, except when it was useful against Boney, of course."

Dagonet merely laughed and filled a glass for himself.

"You will get nothing more out of him, dear Acton," said

David. "He has come here for some sordid purpose of his own."

"And stays at Stagshead, imposing on the generosity of poor Morris and hiding his disgraceful presence from the locals. To be obliged to remain unseen in the place of one's birth is scandal's reward." Dagonet winked at the other man. "I'm undercover once again. You'll be discreet?"

"Of course." Richard sat back and relaxed. He and Dagonet had worked together on more than one covert mission in Spain. He knew better than to question further, and he had concerns of his own. "What particular part of our nasty military endeavors did you wish to recall?"

"Can't we talk about peace?" said David Morris a little wistfully.

Dagonet took a swallow of brandy. "If what we saw in Paris is what peace will bring, perhaps we're better off without it. Were you able do anything at all, Acton?"

"I've done what I can," said Richard quietly. An expression of disgust passed over his features. "Whatever a considerable sum of gold and the services of some damnably efficient fellows can accomplish."

"Do you think there is danger in becoming involved?" asked Dagonet casually.

Richard laughed. "To me? Hardly! But we shan't have much time to indulge ourselves in maudlin remembrances of either Paris or the glorious Peninsula. I'm for Cornwall in the morning."

Dagonet sat in the third chair, the sunlight from the window profiling his perfect features, and turned the glass of brandy in one elegant hand. "Why to Cornwall?"

"For Edward Blake's sake. If it were up to me, I would never travel again." Richard smiled. "All I want for myself is some quiet domesticity."

Dagonet closed his eyes. "Poor Blake. I'm sorry." He was about to go on, when there was a noise in the hallway. In the next instant he had sprung to his feet and made for the window. "Someone comes, dear Morris. I must leave like a thief." He nodded to Richard. "If I don't see you again before you leave, dear Captain Acton, bon voyage!"

He bowed and, throwing up the sash, stepped into the garden. Richard closed the window behind him, then grinned at Morris.

"Impossible as always," said David Morris simply. "It's what comes of being a spy. Such habits are hard to shake, I suppose." He laughed suddenly. "He grew up in Exmoor, you know. He's commonly known as Devil Dagonet in these parts."

"I never saw him here, certainly," replied Richard, an equally competent conspirator, and winked as two ladies walked into the room.

"It's the most awkward and annoying thing, David," cried the first. "Catherine may visit only when Lady Montagu allows her the day off. Can you imagine anything more mortifying? Oh, I'm sorry, I didn't see you, sir."

Richard had already risen, and he bowed over the hand that the speaker held out. She was a vision of English beauty: blue eyes, curling yellow hair.

"Don't linger too long over that pretty hand, Captain Acton," said Morris with a smile. "It belongs to my betrothed, Miss Amelia Hunter. She is my peace. May I present Amy's sister, Miss Catherine Hunter?"

Richard turned to the other lady. Taller, browner, she was regarding him with a look of considerable amusement. Catherine was used to men reacting to her younger sister's classic looks. "Pleased to make your acquaintance, sir," she said as they shook hands. "Do you visit Stagshead long?"

"Only for the night, ma'am," Richard replied. "With regret. I go down to Cornwall tomorrow."

Catherine Hunter looked at him. His hair, swept back carelessly from a tanned forehead, was bleached a more silver-blond than her sister's. There was a determined, controlled look to the fine straight nose and flared nostrils above the thin lips and strong chin. Yet the eyes had the same haunted anticipation as a man she had once seen being carried away to London to his hanging. Eyes that had looked death in the face without flinching, yet had lost their way back. For no reason she could name, Catherine's heart went out to him in something akin to pity.

"Where do you go in Cornwall, Captain Acton?" asked Amelia when they were all settled and the ladies had each been provided with a glass of Madeira. "It's a long way, isn't it, to the very tip?"

"A place called Trethaerin, ma'am. And to be honest, I have no idea exactly where it lies."

"Trethaerin? Good heavens! You're on the wrong coast, sir." The speaker was Catherine Hunter. "A Helena Trethaerin was at school with us in Exeter. She comes from Trethaerin House, and it's somewhere near Penzance. Could it be the same place? It's a very unusual name."

"Indeed, Miss Hunter." When he smiled, Catherine wondered if she had imagined the shadow she had glimpsed earlier. "I have no doubt it's the very same; Helena is the name of the lady I seek."

"You're going to visit Helena Trethaerin?" asked Amelia. Her pretty brow was wrinkled, as if with a slight distaste. "She was older than me, of course, so I didn't know her very well, but she and Catherine made friends. Didn't she write to you, Cathy, that she is in some kind of dire straits?"

Catherine gave her sister a quenching look. "Miss Trethaerin's affairs can interest no one else, Amy."

She was amazed when Captain Acton leaned forward and fixed her with his gaze. His eyes were very nearly black. "Miss Hunter, of course I should not want you to betray a friend's trust, but I would be very grateful if you could shed any light on her situation for me. I have never met Miss Trethaerin. I go only because it was her cousin Sir Edward Blake's dying wish that I should. If she is truly in dire straits, I might be in a position to aid her. You can see, I'm sure, that it would be immeasurably helpful to me to be forewarned of what I might find."

Catherine hesitated only a moment. There was something in his manner that assured her that Helena's confidences would be in safe hands. Indeed, the more he knew, the better; for Helena would undoubtedly be too proud to admit to any of it, and she would send this interesting man away empty-handed. "Miss Trethaerin wrote me that she has been effectively disinherited, sir. Her father was a widower and a rather formidable character, I understand. Anyway, when he died last spring, he left his entire estate to Helena's cousin, Sir Edward Blake."

"Good God! And did Edward know of this?"

"I've no idea. But when the news came some time afterward of Edward's death, both the Blake property and Trethaerin House then passed to some other relative, by the name of Garthwood. He did not arrive to take possession until last month, but now Miss Trethaerin is reduced to being a dependent poor relation in her own house."

Richard had steepled his fingers together and was looking down between them at the floor. It was impossible to know what he was thinking. "Why would her father leave his estates to Sir Edward Blake and not to his own daughter?" he said at last.

Catherine plunged on. In for a penny, in for a pound! "Since they were small children, I understand, he had planned that they should make a match. Helena and Sir Edward Blake were to marry."

Richard closed his eyes. "I feared as much," he said quietly.

Catherine instantly wanted to justify Simon Trethaerin's action. "Helena's father was leaving his estates, as he saw it, to his daughter's fiancé. He probably didn't believe in ladies handling their own affairs and wanted everything in a gentleman's hands."

"Then he got it!" announced Amy. "For now this Garthwood has everything and Helena Trethaerin has lost not only her betrothed, but her dignity and security at the same time. She has nothing in the world. It is quite dreadful!"

"Is there anything you could really do to help her, sir?" asked Catherine.

Captain Richard Acton dropped his hands and looked up at her and smiled. Sunlight blazed like a fire on his fair hair. "I can marry her," he said.

Two

Helena walked rapidly up through the home wood, the now-empty basket that she carried swinging against her black skirts. As she turned the last corner and caught sight of Trethaerin House, it was inevitable that she should stop for a moment and catch her breath. A tangle of roses, phlox, and wallflowers scented the heavy afternoon air. Three stories above them, dormer windows fancifully framed by curlicues of carved stone capped an otherwise simple façade of gray granite. The small, old-fashioned mullioned windows reflected a multitude of twinkles of blue from the sky. By listening hard above the lazy hum of honeybees and the occasional trill of a bird from the woods, she could hear the sea, pounding and pounding on the rocks of Trethaerin Cove below. Damnation! It was no use at all to get weepy about a house! She picked up her basket and stepped out onto the driveway. A lone horseman was trotting up the gravel toward her on a tall bay. As he drew level, he pulled to a halt and touched his hat.

"Miss Helena Trethaerin?"

"I am she, sir."

The rider swung instantly from his horse and held out his hand. "Captain Richard Acton, at your service, ma'am."

Helena unwittingly took a step backward and put a hand to her heart. Instantly she stopped, and forced herself to shake hands instead. "I am sorry, Captain Acton, you startled me! I didn't anticipate . . . oh, goodness! You must come to the house for some refreshment."

"You weren't expecting me, surely?" His brows had come together, causing a deep vertical line to appear between them.

"Oh, no! Of course not. But I do know who you are. Edward mentioned you in letters; though he didn't exactly write often, and letters took anywhere from one to six months to arrive here. You were friends, weren't you? I'm so sorry."

The midnight eyes opened in astonishment. "Sorry?"

"About Edward's death. It must have been a blow to lose a comrade."

"But it is I who came to offer my condolences to you, ma'am."

"Thank you. It's very kind of you. Now, please, won't you come up to the house? You must have ridden a long way."

Richard fell into step beside her, leading his charger by the bridle. This encounter was not going at all as he had imagined. Firstly, Miss Helena Trethaerin looked nothing like Edward. Why he had expected that she should, he had no idea. Edward Blake had been a typical dark, thick-set Cornishman with black eyes and a shock of dark hair. The tendrils escaping beneath Miss Trethaerin's bonnet were as blond as his own, and her skin was very white against the black fabric of her dress. It made her gray eyes look enormous. And then she had offered *her* sympathy to him!

"Poor fellow," Helena said suddenly.

Richard stopped short. "What?" he said.

"Your horse." She smiled and ran her hand down the animal's neck. "He was your *cheval de bataille,* wasn't he?"

Richard swallowed his astonishment and forced himself to reply casually. "Though that expression translates literally as 'warhorse,' it is generally used to mean anything one primarily relies on. Yes, I suppose he was, on both counts."

"And he has faithfully served you through it all. How can a creature like him possibly understand the dreadful things he is asked to witness? Cavalry chargers do their duty all the same, yet they must spend much of their life in a state of terror."

Without thinking, he replied, "And so do their masters, Miss Trethaerin."

He had never admitted it before. Not to his fellow officers, not to himself. But it was true, of course. Bravery in battle did not mean lack of fear; it meant carrying on even when the fear was overwhelming. How could this frail-looking woman know that?

A groom ran forward from the house and took the horse by the bridle. Helena led Richard inside, and they handed their hats and gloves to a footman. Her hair was almost silver in the dim light.

"Now," said Miss Helena Trethaerin once they were comfortably seated in the withdrawing room. "Won't you tell me why you have really come?"

"Edward asked it," Richard replied simply. "I don't really know why, except that he was thinking of you when he died."

"Oh, Lord! You were there!"

"We were cutting around the field together to direct a new flank attack and he was shot. He died almost instantly."

"It's a horrible waste, isn't it?"

Richard looked at her in shock. Didn't she care? You might say as much about a tree that fell in a storm! The idea that he would be obliged to make up a heroic tale for her fell in instant ruins.

"Yes, it is," he said. And suddenly it was his own feelings that threatened to overwhelm him. A wave of anger at the sheer wastefulness of war—all those young lives! He leapt to his feet and crossed to the window.

"I'll make this as short and simple as possible, Miss Trethaerin. Edward died of a major wound to the chest. He couldn't say much, but he wanted you to be safe. I think he also wanted you to have his brandy flask." He came back to her and held out the battered leather-clad bottle.

Helena took it and turned it over. "I can't imagine why," she said slowly.

"You were to be married, weren't you? There was nothing else that he had to send you!"

"Oh, dear. Please, Captain Acton, forgive me. It's more than kind of you to come. But, please, take it back. I think that you should keep it!"

She thrust the flask toward him. Richard could not do other than put it back in his own pocket. She was heartless! He knew suddenly quite clearly what he had expected to find: a woman as dark and passionate as Edward suffering an inconsolable grief, who would have treasured with tremulous emotion any memento of her beloved. Instead, this cool blonde was gazing at him perfectly calmly.

"Listen," said Helena. "Perhaps we should go for a walk."

"A walk?" Was she mad, perhaps?

"Yes, do you mind? It's still a lovely afternoon, after all."

"As you say, ma'am."

"Then humor me, please."

She rose gracefully to her feet and they went back into the dark hallway to collect their hats. Fifteen minutes later, Helena was leading him up through the woods behind the house, until the trees suddenly thinned and they came out onto a gorse-covered headland. Salt-laden wind buffeted at her black skirts. They walked quickly up a narrow path through the golden shrubs, until they stood overlooking the black sand of a small beach and there was a sudden screeching of wheeling sea gulls.

"Trethaerin Cove," said Helena. "Edward and I played there together as children. We used to act out the Battle of Trafalgar, though he would always insist on being Admiral Lord Nelson. It wasn't fair at all!" She laughed and clutched at her black bonnet as the wind threatened to carry it away. "Come on!"

Richard followed her as she crossed the headland on the cliff path. She had lost her betrothed barely six months before, but could still laugh! Suddenly they were looking down into fertile fields. A gracious whitewashed house nestled against a thick stand of oak and birch at the far side of the broad valley. Through the center ran a small stream, which eventually cut its channel across a long stretch of yellow sand. The beach must have been a mile wide.

"That's Friarswell, Edward's home."

"I see smoke from the chimneys. Who lives there now?"

"His heir, Mr. Garthwood."

Of course, the cousin who had inherited from Edward and thus also from Helena's father. Richard silently blessed Catherine Hunter for her information.

Helena went on quickly. "Friarswell has all the good productive valley land. My father coveted it for years. I'm afraid that Trethaerin has nothing but the cove, some moorland, and the tin that used to lie under it. When the mines began to fail, it was hard for my father to make ends meet, though we were comfortable enough. Papa refused to countenance smuggling, the mainstay of many a Cornish family! Of course, Friarswell and Trethaerin march together. Papa thought it was the perfect answer to everything that I should marry Edward and unite the two places."

"And what did you think about it?"

"Well, I hardly knew, to be honest."

"And you are always honest?"

She gave him a perfectly open look. "Of course. What on earth would be the use of pretending anything?"

Richard felt his hands clench. Her name had been on Edward's dying breath! "For God's sake, didn't you care for Blake at all?"

"Dear Captain Acton, I do apologize if I have upset you. But I hadn't seen my cousin for more than a few hours in seven years! I was a child when we were last together. Each of us was sent away to school, then Edward went to the war. Of course I honor his memory, but if you think I should pretend to be going into a decline over him, then I cannot oblige you! Please don't allow yourself to imagine any pitiful tragic romance!"

"I could not imagine anything of the kind, madam," he snapped. His eyes were like coal. "You have explained admirably. Shall we go back?"

They walked rapidly back to Trethaerin House in silence. As they entered the hallway once again, a gentleman stepped from the drawing room to greet them.

"Ah, Miss Trethaerin. You have a visitor?" he said softly.

"Captain Acton was a friend of Sir Edward Blake's, Mr. Garthwood."

"A pleasure, sir. Poor Cousin Edward! A sad loss."

"Not so sad for you, of course," said Helena calmly. "So there is no need to be unctuous. Captain Acton stopped by to pay his respects. He is just leaving."

"Then let me call for your horse, Captain. The rather fine bay I saw in the stable, I imagine?"

"Indeed, sir. Thank you."

Richard was used to sizing up men. Thank goodness he had never had anyone like Garthwood in his command! He felt an instinctive dislike: something about the way the man's eyes seemed to be unable meet another's, but slid away to focus on the wall or a window; or the way his hands clutched and fondled at each other as he talked. Richard took up his hat and shook Helena by the hand. He was about to make her a polite farewell, when he heard himself speak instead to Garthwood.

"You will have no objection, sir, if I should stop by to say good-bye to Miss Trethaerin tomorrow before I leave Cornwall?"

Garthwood smiled. "None at all, of course."

Richard bowed and stepped back out of the house into the sunshine. Now, why on earth had he promised to visit again? Obviously, he and Helena Trethaerin had nothing further to say to each other. In a foul mood, he swung up onto his charger and trotted away down the driveway without a backward glance. The sunken lanes with their stunted hedgerows and bulky stone walls passed by unnoticed. Within an hour he had ridden into the inn yard of the Anchor in the fishing village of Blacksands, and in another hour he was in a state that he had not experienced since his salad days. He was comfortably drunk.

Helena turned to face her nemesis. Bravery was indeed facing one's fear and carrying on regardless, and she was determined to be brave. "To what do I owe this visit, Mr. Garthwood?"

"May I not visit, dear Miss Trethaerin? This is my house, after all."

"The fact never leaves me, sir. Mr. Marble explained it all very well. Everything from Friarswell to Trethaerin is all rightfully yours. I am in your power; I don't dispute it."

"Then I wish that you would not take provisions to the Coopers. They are wastrels! I fear for your safety."

"I have known Rob Cooper and his family all my life, Mr. Garthwood. Your concern is totally unnecessary."

"And you must recognize that you cannot stay on here alone like this, in my house and dependent on me for your very bread, a young, single—and, may I say, attractive— young woman. It breaks every rule of propriety. Yet you know I will not turn you out to beg your living. Have you considered my offer?"

"I should like a few more days, sir, if you would be so gracious."

"Please, my dear, you may have all the time you require. I should want you to give it all due consideration."

"Thank you, sir. I shall."

She had seen birds once at the market, beating frantically against the wicker bars of their cages. Had those creatures been any more trapped than she? Why had her father been so stubborn about leaving Trethaerin to Edward? And why, oh, why, had poor Edward had to die?

Captain Acton woke the next morning with a pounding head and a foul taste in his mouth. Edward's brandy flask sat on the small table beside the bed, but it was only indirectly the cause of his headache. Several empty bottles stood beside it, mute witness to his incredible behavior of the previous night. Why on earth had he decided to get drunk? Devil take this whole place and especially Helena Trethaerin! If it had not been for what he had learned from Catherine Hunter at Stagshead about her situation he would start out for London that instant and never see Cornwall again. But he had given his word to a dying comrade. He would see it through.

He flung back the covers and plunged his head into a basin of cold water, then he stripped and flung the rest of the water over every lean inch of his body. Rapidly drying himself on the inn's threadbare towel, he pulled on a clean cambric shirt and buckskin breeches, then thrust his arms into the sleeves of a plain brown coat. He tied his cravat in a simple knot and finally plunged his feet into the loose-fitting tall boots made popular by the Iron Duke himself. Richard had no patience with a wardrobe that required the services of a valet in order to get dressed. It was simpler to travel alone and see to one's own needs.

His head still felt as if it were encased in an iron band as he followed the winding lane to Trethaerin. His horse was feeling fresh and, prancing under his hand, was looking for any excuse to shy. Richard cursed. He was in no mood to put up with anyone's high spirits, not even Bayard's. Sensing his master's impatience, the charger humped his back a little, but he knew better than to offer further disobedience. Richard's hand had tightened imperceptibly on the reins and the bay quietly trotted on.

Helena was in the garden, cutting the heads off the dying roses. She looked up as Richard came striding down the path toward her. *He looks so vital,* she thought to herself, *like a free creature of the sky! How can he possibly justify that frown?* Then she laughed at herself. Anyone with an independence would seem free as a sea gull to her! And he could certainly frown if he felt like it. Everyone was entitled to their demons. *Well, she must send this man away with a kind word and face her own problems by herself.*

"Good morning, Captain Acton. I trust you found comfortable accommodation in the village?"

"Comfortable enough, Miss Trethaerin."

"But you have the headache?"

Richard looked at her. Good God! Was he so transparent?

"Perhaps we should say our good-byes out of the sun?" said Helena calmly. "There's a summerhouse under the willows."

She turned and walked quickly through the rose beds and across the lawn. Richard was forced to follow. Indeed, the little gazebo was refreshingly cool and shady. They sat formally opposite each other in the wrought iron chairs and he leaned back. A breeze ruffled the frill around Helena's bonnet and lifted the bright hair a little off Richard's forehead. Something about Miss Trethaerin was very tranquil. He could feel his headache beginning to go away.

"I fear I was a little abrupt yesterday, sir," Helena began. "If you would like to talk about Edward, I should be perfectly willing."

Richard sat up and looked straight at her. "Edward? I came here this morning, ma'am, to talk about you."

It was Helena's turn to look astonished. "Me? But what possible concern am I to you, sir?"

"I know how you are situated, Miss Trethaerin. Miss Catherine Hunter of Fernbridge told me. You were at school together in Exeter?"

"Catherine? Yes, we were friends. But why should she tell you about me?"

"Because I asked her. You had written to her recently?"

Helena leapt to her feet and began to pace back and forth across the stone floor of the summerhouse. "What earthly business is it of yours! How dare she? I wrote to her in confidence. I cannot think that Catherine Hunter, of all people, would have so little honor!"

"You are completely disinherited by the terms of your father's will. Though you led me to believe by your manner yesterday that Trethaerin House is still yours, in fact it has become the property of Mr. Nigel Garthwood, who inherited it from Edward. You said, ma'am, that you believed in honesty, but you were not entirely honest with me."

"Because I did not launch into a pitiful tale of my situation? I remember nothing that I said that would have led you to believe that I was mistress of Trethaerin. Nothing! If my manner said otherwise—for heaven's sake, I was born and grew up here! Besides, it is not your concern, sir!"

"I am making it my concern."

She whirled around, making her black skirts eddy around her legs. There was an extremely becoming pink flush highlighting her cheeks. "Captain Acton. It is very kind of you to come down here to tell me about Edward's death. I am grateful. Perhaps I don't display the overwrought grief that you seem to feel I should, but he was my childhood friend and I am glad that you were there so that he didn't die alone. But there is no need for you to concern yourself further. In fact, I think that you had better go!"

"I can't go."

"Why not?" Her eyes were the color of storm-tossed waves at sea.

Richard also stood, and in a stride he was towering over her and had taken her by the elbows. "Because I promised Edward that I would see that you were not in want! What is your future here? You have nothing! What do you plan to do?"

Helena gazed frankly back up at him. The vertical line was incised deeply between his brows, and his nostrils were flared like a carving.

"Mr. Garthwood has asked for my hand, sir!"

His grip tightened on her arms. "Have you given him your answer?"

"Please, Captain Acton, you are bruising me!"

Richard flushed and dropped his hands. "Forgive me, Miss Trethaerin. I am not usually so precipitate."

Her voice was edged with anger. "No, you were Edward's idol: a model of all that was most controlled, correct, and gentlemanly, while all the time striking fear into the hearts of the enemy with your prowess on the battlefield. When you were not so employed, I understand you could play a mean hand at any game of chance and keep the camp in an uproar of hilarity with your facility at indelicate limericks. A very paragon of manly virtue, in fact."

"Good God!" Richard stepped away from Helena and spread his fingers on the back of one of the iron chairs. He looked totally astonished. "I had no idea!" he said, and then he bent his head forward on his hands and began to laugh.

Helena watched his shoulders as they shook in silent mirth. The breeze was dancing like a demon in his sun-bleached hair. At last, he straightened. "Miss Trethaerin, forgive me! Tell me truthfully that Mr. Garthwood has your heart and that you will marry him in gladness, and I shall be gone this instant. I promise you that I shall never think of you again—except to question your judgment." The laughter had still not entirely left his eyes.

Helena longed to relax into the warmth of his mood. "Then you are not impressed with the new owner of Trethaerin and Friarswell?"

"I don't believe I ever met a more odious creature!"

"Nevertheless, I shall marry him."

"What? Do you have windmills in your head, Miss Trethaerin?"

Helena looked down at her kid boots. Her anger had melted like ice in the sun. Captain Richard Acton had been Edward's anchor, and now his warmth and strength beckoned to her like the light in a window calls to the traveler lost in a storm. She would not be so weak!

"I assure you I am quite sane, sir. So you needn't be concerned anymore." She sat back down in her chair and folded her hands so that he should not see them shake. "My mind is made up as of this instant. As Mrs. Garthwood my future will be perfectly secure. Your promise to Edward is fulfilled."

Richard spun the other chair and straddled it, his arms along the back. "You did not answer my question, ma'am."

"What question?" She was determined to avoid his eyes.

"Do you hold Mr. Garthwood in affection?"

"You have absolutely no right to ask such a thing!"

"I have my answer. Obviously you do not."

"Captain Acton! I pray, do not continue this. I shall marry Mr. Garthwood, and that's an end of it."

"In fact, you are afraid of him."

Helena's head flew up and she found herself gazing straight into his eyes. It gave her a most uncomfortable sensation.

"You will not marry Nigel Garthwood," he said decisively.

"What else do you suggest that I do, sir?"

"You could marry me."

Helena leapt once again from her chair. She could feel the heat rising in her face. "Is this a jest? How can you? I did not ask you to come here with your pity and your sorrow. We are strangers! I suggest that we both forget that you said such a thing. Good day, sir."

And in a flurry of skirts, Helena swept from the summerhouse and disappeared.

Three

Richard leaned back in the chair and looked up into the white-painted rafters of the gazebo. Well, he had certainly made a mess of that! Maybe he was taking his promise to Edward too seriously. They had been comrades and friends, but they had not been particularly close. Why should it matter what became of the cousin of a fallen officer? Thousands had died, leaving their dependents in want. Should he offer marriage to every young widow and destitute daughter? He closed his eyes, and Edward's white face appeared clearly before him. The man had died in his arms and he had given his word. He must fulfill his obligation to Helena Trethaerin or know himself forsworn.

He stood and went to the door of the summerhouse. The sun gleamed on the surface of the close-mown lawn. If she were a respectable widow, he could just set her up in a house of her own with an income. But she was unmarried, young, and a lady. Gentlemen did not provide keep for young ladies, except in particular circumstances. Even the appearance of such an arrangement was sufficient to ruin her. In fact, if it ever became known in the wider world that she was living alone like this in a house belonging to Garthwood, tongues would chatter quickly enough. No wonder she was prepared to accept Garthwood's offer. He sighed and started walking slowly down a path that led through the trees. She could not marry Nigel Garthwood! The thought revolted him as clearly as what he had found at Madame Relet's in Paris. So why not marry her himself? If he was to achieve his dream of domestic tranquillity, he had to marry someone.

At the first bend, he met Helena coming steadily toward him. She had taken off her bonnet and was swinging it in her hand. Wisps of pale hair blew around her face.

She gave him a rueful smile. "I'm sorry, Captain Acton. I know you meant nothing but kindness. I was ungracious. But you are constantly springing the most extraordinary statements on me. I am honored by your proposal, but you must see that it's impossible."

Richard turned and fell into step beside her. "I see that it's impossible that you marry Garthwood." He gave her a genuine smile. Helena was amazed at how it transformed his face.

"Yes, I know. I admit I don't like him. But I can hardly accept an offer from you when it is based on nothing more than charity. In fact, it would be villainous to do so."

"Why?"

"Captain Acton, surely you're not serious?"

"I have never been more serious in my life. Listen, Miss Trethaerin. I have spent the last seven or eight years in constant turmoil and it's time that I settled down. I want to live a normal life, here in England. I need to marry. My father wishes it strongly, among other things. There is no other lady who has engaged my affections. You are eligible, you require escape from a situation that is intolerable, and I am sworn to provide for you. We can help each other. I need a bride; you need security. We are both reasonably well-mannered, I trust, and you seem intelligent and level-headed. Why shouldn't we form an alliance?"

"But I know nothing about you."

His eyes shone with humor. "I thought you knew that I was a paragon of virtue?"

"You're not the only officer that Edward wrote to me about!"

"Yes, but I'm the one that's here and offering you my hand and heart. Don't you trust me?"

Helena blushed. From the impression that her cousin had given her, there was no man on earth more deserving of trust. All the more reason she could not accept his extraordinary charity. "Edward was rather impetuous as a boy and easily impressed. You knew him these last years better than I. You think I should credit his judgment?"

"I shan't beat you, at least not with a stick thicker than my thumb."

As he smiled at her, she felt her heart turn over. When he forgot his shadows for a moment, there was something overwhelmingly attractive about him. Something beyond the obvious good looks.

"I'm to be reassured by that?"

"I trust that you will not have too much reason to complain, though obviously I have my faults. And neither of us can claim that it would be anything other than a marriage of convenience. I have never expected anything else, and if your relationship with Edward was as you have described, neither have you. I see no reason why we shouldn't be able to rub along."

"You know nothing about me."

"What is there to know? You were educated in Exeter at a young ladies' seminary. I may assume that you have the usual accomplishments. Isn't one young lady much like another?" There was a distinct quirk at the corner of his mouth. Was he teasing? She had no way of telling. "Of course, you were Edward's cousin. He was a good soldier and an honorable man. That surely is enough?"

Helena glanced around at the trunks of the trees. Every one was as dear to her as a friend. "Do you have a home, sir?"

"Of course. And I have sufficient funds." Helena blushed scarlet. Richard stopped and turned her to face him. "I can keep you in perfect comfort."

"This whole conversation is absurd, Captain Acton." Helena pulled away from him and walked on. What on earth had made her weaken for a moment? "However much I may have heard about you from Edward, we are still total strangers."

They had come out onto the grass and were approaching the house. A gentleman came out to meet them; it was Nigel Garthwood. His long mouth seemed to be curved into a secret smile, but he bowed politely.

"Captain Acton. I'm so glad to see you again, sir, before you leave."

"My pleasure, sir."

Nigel Garthwood reached a hand toward Helena, as if to usher her back into the house. "May I wish you a safe journey back to town, Captain?"

And then, to Richard's astonishment, Helena slipped her hand through his arm. She had not known until that moment what she was about to do. Helena did not think herself normally an impulsive type, but to stay one more day under Garthwood's power was intolerable, and somehow that had just been made very clear. Captain Acton had offered for her for all the wrong reasons, but the drowning don't question motives when clutching at straws. "You may wish me a pleasant journey also, if you would be so kind, Mr. Garthwood," she heard herself say. "I shall be accompanying Captain Acton to London."

She felt Richard's body go rigid next to hers, and she fought to keep her hand from shaking. Garthwood paled and clenched his fists. "Am I to have no other reply to my offer, ma'am?"

Helena took a deep breath. "I am very sensible of the honor you have extended to me, sir. It pains me to reply so precipitately and when we are not private, but I have just accepted Captain Acton's proposal. He and I are to be married."

The muscles in Richard's arm flexed hard under her fingers, as if ready for action. She glanced up at his profile. His nostrils were flared like those of a warhorse.

Garthwood merely smiled and bowed. "Then please accept my felicitations." The men shook hands. "I wish you both very happy. Let us go in and drink to your health."

Helena followed the two men inside. She looked around at the familiar room with its faded rugs and solid furniture. She would never see this house again! Garthwood went to the fireplace and rang the bell.

"Champagne, I think?" he said as the footman entered.

They duly partook of a ritual drink, of superb quality. Richard, for the first time, seemed totally bereft of words, so Helena filled the silence with a dutiful chatter. At last Garthwood rose. "When do you leave, sir?"

"I must order a carriage and Miss Trethaerin will need to pack some things. I thought perhaps tomorrow morning?"

"I can be packed in three hours, sir," said Helena firmly. She had been lost all summer, it seemed, in a haze of uncertainty, refusing to think about the future, but now that her decision was made, she didn't dare allow time for reflection.

"And there's a chaise for hire in Penzance. We can send Rogers for it. So there's no reason we can't leave this afternoon."

"Of course," said Richard. Good God! Was she afraid to be left alone here, even for one more night?

Garthwood shook him by the hand, then he raised Helena's to his lips and kissed her fingers briefly. "Then this is goodbye, ma'am," he said, and was gone.

Helena sat suddenly on the sofa. "Oh, heavens," she said. "A lady probably never either turned down nor accepted a proposal of marriage in such a ramshackle way. You will think I am wanting most dreadfully in decorum."

"Not at all," said Richard. "I think you didn't want to face him alone with a refusal. I don't blame you."

"He has never given me the least cause to fear him, Captain Acton. Since he arrived at Trethaerin, Mr. Garthwood has been nothing but generous and correct. His offer of marriage can hardly be blamed. It's not his fault that Edward didn't leave a will and that he was the closer heir."

And to Richard's astonishment, she burst into tears. He wanted desperately to sit next to her and take her in his arms. The violence of the feeling left him shaken. Instead, he walked to the window and looked out onto the roses. "The man is cruel," he said calmly. "Every instinct can tell you that!"

Helena wiped her eyes and smiled at him. "Yes, and I am an abject coward, to use you for protection and force you to be witness to my rejection of his offer. Even Nigel Garthwood did not deserve that humiliation. You really don't need to marry me, you know."

"But I want to." Richard was surprised by how strongly he felt it. "Are you sure of your decision?"

"If you really mean it, I most gratefully accept your proposal, sir."

"Of course. I don't go back on my word."

"Then it would seem that we have agreed to marry each other."

Richard smiled. "If we're to leave today, you had better pack."

Helena stood up. "Captain Acton. I must thank you!"

He came over to her and took her hands. "No, ma'am. It is you who have honored me with your acceptance. Now, let's send a man for that carriage."

The chaise was stuffy inside and smelled faintly of fish. Helena leaned back against the red velvet cushions and closed her eyes. There was a thump and the ancient carriage swayed as the hired men strapped on her box. She could not even bring a maid with her. All the staff at Trethaerin were local people with family in the village and the surrounding countryside, and none of those fresh-faced girls would make much of a London lady's maid. What had she done? She had just agreed to marry a perfect stranger! What possible reason could he have to go through with a marriage to a woman he had known for only two days? Perhaps he would ravish or abandon her? The door to the chaise opened.

"Good heavens," said Richard lightly. "It's like being Jonah in the belly of the whale. I thought I would join you. Bayard will follow tied on behind willingly enough."

"Of course." Helena did her best to match her tone to his. "But never having been on the sea, I can't say whether Jonah would have felt at home in our distinctly piscine equipage or not."

Richard stepped athletically into the carriage and took the

seat opposite her. "You mean to tell me that you spent your life in Cornwall and never ventured out on a boat?"

"I had a very uninteresting upbringing, Captain."

"Yet if the books in your father's library are anything to go by, you did not lack for mental stimulation." He smiled as she gave him a surprised look. "Forgive me," he said. "I nosed around shamelessly while you were packing. Did you read all that stuff?"

Helena was forced to laugh. "Most of it. There was nothing else on long winter evenings."

"Good God!" he said with a grin. "I'm marrying a bluestocking!"

"I refuse to believe you haven't read the classics yourself, sir."

"Yet I ran away from school several times, and a knowledge of Ovid and Homer wasn't in the least used in my later career."

At last, the opening she wanted. "Have you always been a soldier?"

The black eyes surveyed her with considerable amusement. "Like Jonah, fishing? No, I have not, but I have always retained an appreciation for Homer." And he adroitly turned the subject to a discussion of poetry.

As they traveled into the long summer twilight, Helena discovered that Captain Acton could be an extremely fascinating companion. Little by little, she became more entranced. He was more than widely read—he put her own knowledge of literature to shame. They were debating the merits of Lord Byron's work, when Richard suddenly leaned forward and rapped on the panel. Instantly the carriage swayed to a halt.

"Why are we stopping?" asked Helena.

"Because the sun is setting, dear Miss Trethaerin."

He leapt from the coach and held open the door for her. Helena stepped down. Their road ran along the high central spine of Cornwall. Open moor and stone-fenced fields dropped away beneath them to each side, and in the west behind them, in a glory of blazing color, the sun was sinking over the horizon.

Richard laughed. It was a sound of pure delight, with no hint of that underlying shadow. He grasped the brass handles at the side of the carriage and swung himself up past the astonished coachman and onto the roof. He stood for a moment, silhouetted against the sky, the slight breeze ruffling his bright hair. Helena gazed up at him. Something strange and dangerous twisted at her heart.

"Come," he said, kneeling and reaching a hand to her. "It's stunning from up here!"

The clean, strong bones of his wrist beneath his white shirt cuff showed clear shadows in the fading light. Their pure beauty surprised her. She hesitated. "I told you I had a very staid upbringing, Captain Acton. I'm not used to climbing on carriages."

He laughed. "You will be quite safe. No harm will come to you in my hands, I assure you. Do you know I could never resist such a sunset," he added with a sudden wicked smile. "Once in Africa . . ."

"You were in Africa?" asked Helena, astonished.

"Come up and I'll tell you."

She held up her hands and Richard grasped them. His strong hands and arms easily took her weight, and in the next instant she was beside him on the coach roof. He put an arm about her waist to steady her.

"North Africa. I thought it would improve my education if I traveled all around the Mediterranean."

"And did it?"

"It certainly improved my appreciation for my homeland!"

"But you have been away for so long—seven or eight years, you told me."

"The education took a while to sink in. I'm a dreadfully slow learner, you see. Africa was the first lesson." And then he created a compelling, shining picture of that year of his life: of camels, of bedouin, of pyramids. Yet she had no clear idea of what he was doing there, and the fact that it had been a dangerous mission was one she had to glean between the words. As Richard told it, North Africa was only a charming, amusing adventure. "It was a great disadvantage to be fair," he finished with a grin. "Now, hush, and let the sunset do its work."

They stood together as the colors deepened and streamed across the sky. His breathing was steady and reassuring at her back. His arm tightened just a little, holding her against his chest. Helena had never felt so safe. She wanted desperately to lean into his strength. Yet she wasn't used to being touched. It had been years, hadn't it, since her childhood nurse had held her on a warm lap? Her father had never hugged or kissed her.

"There. It goes," said Richard. "Now we must hurry or we'll not reach Bodmin before dark. I have told you one of my adventures. Now you must tell me tales of Cornwall. Were there ever smugglers at Trethaerin House?"

The spell was broken. Helena was helped down off the carriage and back to her seat. Half an hour later they rattled into the inn yard at the Dog and Raven. The innkeeper showed her to a room and she was sent up supper on a tray. Of her prospective bridegroom she saw no further sign. Restlessly, she paced about for a while. Captain Richard Acton was undeniably attractive, yet what had she learned? He liked books; he had traveled. Helena was uncomfortably aware that she had been gently but thoroughly manipulated. She had been so entertained that she had not had time to grieve for her childhood home nor to give a moment's thought to what she was about to do, but he had revealed nothing more of himself than was exactly calculated to reassure her. The realization of quite how skillfully he had managed to prevent her finding out more about him, however, had quite the opposite effect. What would her future bring if she married him? Would she be a pawn in the hands of this brilliant, fascinating man while he kept himself forever safeguarded against her? What could she offer him in return? She knew nothing of the world and less of marriage! Surely there were other alternatives? Of course, she admitted at last to herself, had she not been so loath to leave Trethaerin, she would already be working as a governess and guaranteed a bleak future of humiliation and hard work. Instead, she had impulsively committed herself to a life with a man she didn't know. Now she wanted beyond anything to discover more about him. It's hard to say, she thought ruefully, where bravery stops and folly starts. She fell into bed at last, only to dream of Trethaerin Cove. Edward stood far out on the rocks, dressed as Admiral Lord Nelson, and was smiling and waving to her as if he had a message. The roar of the surf drowned out his words. She thought about it when she awoke in the morning. Dear Edward! In truth she couldn't remember what her cousin had looked like. Yet she was prepared to marry Captain Richard Acton because Edward had worshiped him.

* * *

The next day they reached Exeter. At a major posting house Helena was installed in a private suite. She had a suspicion that it might be the best in the house. Perhaps Captain Acton was fairly well-heeled, if he could afford such accommodation. It was more than extraordinary that she still didn't know! After she finished her light meal, there was a knock on the door. Richard came in, and sat down at the table opposite her.

"Are you fatigued?" he asked simply.

"Not particularly, why?"

"Because I think we should marry right away. I set about procuring a special license before I came to Trethaerin."

Helena blanched. Could she really go through with it? "You were very sure of yourself, sir."

He smiled. "Just a contingency. It didn't have to be acted upon."

"But now you think that it should?"

"What do you take me for? We can hardly continue to travel together unless we are man and wife."

"Of course. I didn't mean to suggest otherwise." Suddenly she felt a rising panic. What was she about to do? "Captain Acton. If you wish to change your mind, it isn't too late!"

"You think I should abandon you in Exeter, after bringing you up from Cornwall alone?"

"I was at school here. Perhaps they would give me a post as a teacher!"

"When you turn up unchaperoned at the door? It won't wash, my dear."

"But I wouldn't hold you to such a Banbury arrangement as this marriage, Captain Acton, if you should wish otherwise."

He grinned. "I do not wish otherwise. I thought Edward had told you all my faults? Changing my mind isn't one of them; limericks are." His laugh seemed filled with a light-hearted good humor. It was better than any testimonial. "Good Lord! Relax, dear lady. I thought you knew that I was a renowned buffoon and completely harmless. Must I prove it? 'There once was a soldier who sighed/To the lady he took as his bride/They will never believe' . . . I can't tell you the rest! Until after we're married, of course."

Helena was forced to laugh. "You think I should marry you to hear the end of a shocking limerick, Captain?"

"It's not sufficient incentive? Then how about this one? 'The lady who came up from Bath' . . . No, that's even worse. I am lost to decent society. Unless you save me, Miss Trethaerin, I shall be forever confined to a soldier's barren life."

"Then you are determined on this match, Captain?" Her heart was unaccountably in her throat. What if he should say no? Where could she go? In the next moment, she was able to breathe again.

"Of course, or I would never have suggested it. Miss Trethaerin, we are both rational people. We expect nothing more from each other than courtesy. It seems to me to be a far sounder basis for a marriage than blind passion. You're the one who has second thoughts. Very well, sleep on it. We can be wed in the morning; but if you truly can't go through with it, I can send you back with the chaise to Trethaerin."

And Nigel Garthwood. The following morning Helena dressed in her best blue and white sprigged muslin, and married Captain Richard Acton in St. George's parish church. As soon as the vicar finished the simple service, Richard led her out onto the porch. She turned to him and held out her hand.

"I feel that I should at least offer you some acknowledgment, sir, for rescuing me from the lion's den."

"It is more customary, my dear, to kiss the bride, than it is to shake hands."

Very gently he pulled her to him and cupped her chin in his fingers. His index finger traced the line of her upper lip before he lowered his mouth and let his lips move briefly against hers. The touch was fleeting, courteous, and flooded her body with honey. She had never felt anything like it before. Oh, Lord! She had been more than naive! It had not occurred to her until that instant that he might expect her to be more than a platonic companion. But of course he would require her to do her duty in the marriage bed and provide him with children. Helena had no idea what such duties entailed, but she knew they were supposed to be unpleasant. How could she have been so foolish as to not get this delicate issue clear? Now it was too late. They were man and wife.

Four

Nigel Garthwood leaned back in the comfortable chair by the fireplace at Friarswell and gazed up at the portrait on the wall. It was that of Sir Edmund Blake, grandfather of the late Edward and brother to his own grandmother. He understood that when Clara Blake had run off with John Garthwood, Sir Edmund had struck her name from the family Bible. There was not a portrait of her in the house.

"Well, Sir Edmund," he said aloud with a smile. "The Garthwoods have their own back. It is Clara's progeny who rules the roost now. A toast to Clara and John Garthwood."

It had been a younger sister who had married a Trethaerin and thus Helena had lost out. He thought about her fleetingly. It had both surprised and annoyed him when she had announced her intention to marry that Acton fellow, who had sprung apparently from nowhere, but he was not unduly distressed. In fact, it was perhaps more convenient than marrying her himself. Either way, she was now out of his way at Trethaerin House and he could pursue his own plans for the place. He turned the glass of fine French brandy in his hand and smiled. Yes, it was undoubtedly better this way. Helena Trethaerin had possessed far too sharp a tongue and too precious a sensibility. She would have been appalled to find out how he intended to use her childhood home. Nigel Garthwood took a long swallow of wine and winked crudely at the portrait.

Helena looked at the well-sprung curricle in amazement. A beautiful pair of matched grays were harnessed and ready to go. From somewhere, two tigers had been hired. One stood at the horses' heads and the other was standing at attention, ready to let down the steps for her.

"Where did all this come from?" she asked.

Richard looked at her and raised a brow. "I bought it."

"You bought it? But how?"

"With money, dear wife. I can hardly bring you to King's Acton in a hired chaise with job horses."

She blushed uncomfortably. "King's Acton?"

"My father's place. It's on our way. We should stop there and pay our respects, don't you think?"

"I'm to meet your parents? Today?"

"Of course, what did you imagine? That I would hide you away? I do have a family, you know."

He must have, of course! In her hurry at Trethaerin, she hadn't even thought to ask him. And then Richard had not been exactly forthcoming about himself after that. "Aren't we going to London?" she said faintly.

Richard looked mildly surprised. "First I intend to show my father that I have done my duty and entered holy wedlock."

He handed her up into the curricle, then swung in beside her and took the ribbons. Bayard was tied on behind, and they set off. It was a clear, beautiful day. As they left Devon and crossed into Somerset, she was entering a part of England that she had never seen before. The landscape was steadily becoming softer and greener. The village houses that they passed began to be roofed in thatch instead of the gray slate of her native Cornwall. And there was no hint of the sea in these mellow lanes and snug cottages. The fields boasted thick thorn hedges; there were no more drystone walls and windblown gorse bushes. Just after Ilminster, they left the turnpike and began to travel due south. Then the road took another sharp turn east and Richard swept the curricle through a huge pair of iron gates flanked by stone pillars; the gatekeeper gave them a gap-toothed grin and doffed his cap as they passed. The gatehouse alone was large enough to serve as any respectable gentleman's country seat. The horses trotted on up a driveway that passed between rows of perfectly manicured laurel and rhododendron.

"For heaven's sake, sir," said Helena. "What on earth is this place? Is your father some kind of potentate?"

"Of course not; he's the Earl of Acton."

"What? Your father is an earl?" Helena's hand had gone to her heart in a vain attempt to steady its wild beating. "How could you not have told me!"

He gave her an odd smile. "Would you have turned me down if you had known?"

"Good heavens, sir! I thought we were to be honest with each other! Don't you think I had the right to know?"

She knew he was prevaricating when he replied. "To be truthful, I didn't even think of it. I suppose I owe you an apology. Does the thought discompose you?"

"It strikes terror into my very soul! How dared you not make this clear? You are a younger son, I trust?"

"I'm sorry to disabuse you. I am, alas, the heir. You will be a countess someday."

Helena did her best to steady her voice. "Are you also an only child?"

Richard was gazing straight ahead over the horses' ears.

"I have a gaggle of younger siblings who are variously scattered among schools and colleges. Should anything happen to me, Henry could come down from Oxford and make a perfectly good earl, if he ever gets sober enough. Should he also be struck down before his time, however, then John will do just fine. There are also enough little sisters to rattle anybody. They attend a select academy for young ladies near London." His voice was perfectly controlled. Was it just her imagination that she detected some trace of bitterness or sarcasm there?

The shrubbery opened up and King's Acton lay before her. Helena had to crush an uprising of panic. Row upon row of tall windows marched across the endless white façade. A battalion of ornamental stone spires punctuated the skyline in matching order, and carved stone medallions paraded below them, each engraved with some heraldic symbol. The front entrance would have been dwarfed by its crenelated portico had there not been an equally imposing flight of stone steps leading up to the door. Surely they were not going to live here?

"My grandfather had delusions of grandeur," said Richard dryly. "What do you think of his fantasy?"

"I suppose it's magnificent," answered Helena.

"You are trying without success to be tactful, my dear. When it becomes mine, I might well burn it down."

"You can't be serious?"

She was to have no reply. They had pulled up before the sweep of steps, and bewigged servants in livery appeared like ants from a disturbed mound. Richard handed her down, and the curricle was efficiently whisked away. The double doors opened and closed behind them and, as soon as they had removed them, their hats and gloves silently disappeared from view. Helena glanced around. The ceiling of the hallway arched away above her head. It was all in white stone. Marble statues of Greek gods stood on tall stone platforms, and classical urns graced a row of niches at each side of the room. In front of her, two branches of a grand stairway swept in graceful arcs to the floor above. She must not appear to be gawking, but she felt like a child at the circus. A footman was still hovering at her elbow.

"This is my wife, Manners. Please have her shown to the appropriate suite." The charming companion of the journey was gone. Richard's face was set as still and hard as that of Apollo on his dais. It chilled her like a frost. He turned absently to Helena. "We eat at nine. Put on whatever is the grandest thing that you have."

And leaving her standing alone with the servant in the hallway, he strode away.

Moments later a maid appeared and Helena was ushered up the right-hand staircase and into a huge, echoing chamber. It was dominated by a four-poster with blue velvet drapes. Instantly, a row of maids in starched caps and aprons bustled into the room. Her luggage was delivered and unpacked, and several of her things whisked away to the laundry to be washed or pressed. She was brought a tray of tea. A copper tub followed and was filled with steaming water. She was undressed and bathed without mercy for her modesty, and dried in a capacious towel. One of the maids sorted through the handful of dresses she had brought from Trethaerin. Helena knew without looking at the woman's face that she had nothing grand enough.

"Have you nothing but this?" said the maid, holding up Helena's best blue silk with the silver flounce. "I suppose it will have to do."

An older woman in a black dress had entered the room. "I am Lady Acton's personal dresser, ma'am," she said stiffly. "I usually touch no one's head but her ladyship's, but she asked me if I would attend you. The curling iron, if you please."

This last comment was addressed to one of the maids, who scurried to obey.

"You are most kind. But please leave it!" Helena stood and took up her own old brush and comb. "I am content to dress my hair in my usual way."

"But it is positively countrified!" exclaimed the woman in horror.

"Yes, indeed," said Helena. "And so am I!"

The woman merely nodded and dropped a small curtsy before sailing back out of the room and leaving Helena alone. How could Richard have sprung all this on her with no warning? She had married a stranger, indeed! Good heavens, she could never be a satisfactory countess!

At that moment she heard a gong, and a servant appeared to show her to the drawing room. She was about to meet Richard's family. If the thought had seemed enough to strip him of all his good humor, what on earth could she expect? Helena threw up her chin. Whatever his reasons, Richard Acton had married her and rescued her from Garthwood. She wouldn't disgrace him!

"Come, Helena," she said aloud in front of the startled maid. "Strike a blow for Cornwall!"

She was left by the girl in front of a white-painted doorway, where a footman stood rigidly at attention. Beyond must be the drawing room. She gave the servant a small nod and he began to open the door. She stepped forward as if to enter, when she heard Richard's voice. Instantly, she was rooted to the spot. The footman froze also, with the door cracked and his hand still on the knob.

"Yes, you heard me correctly the first time, my lord. I am married."

"For God's sake, sir! Who the devil is she? Trethaerin? I've never heard of it!"

"Pray, calm down, Acton." They were the tones of a woman. "Richard has married only to please us. Heaven knows you have been after him to wed for long enough."

"Yes, into a suitable lineage! Not to some unknown girl. What the hell was wrong with the Salisbury daughters? Does this creature have a family? Did she bring property? A dowry? Answer me, by God!"

Richard's voice was the only one that was calm. "The answer is no on all counts, sir."

There was the sound of the rapid fluttering of the woman's fan. It must be Richard's mother. There was an edge to her voice that almost expressed amusement. "You must admit the unknown bride is a clever one, Acton, to ensnare the eldest son of an earl."

"God's teeth, sir! Don't tell me you have been caught by a fortune hunter?"

"Miss Trethaerin did not know who I was, my lord. She thought herself wed to plain Captain Acton until today."

"She has cozened you, Richard!" The sound of the fan stopped as its owner spoke again. "Is it appropriate that I have hysterics?"

"Mama, I pray that you will not. Helena comes from a perfectly respectable home, but is orphaned. It is only through an accident of fate that she is left without property."

"Not an entail?" said the Countess of Acton with considerable sarcasm.

The older man's voice cut her off. He was almost shouting. "Damn your entails, ma'am. How could she be left without fortune? The girl is obviously a brazen hussy. What on earth possessed you to marry the wench, sir? Why not set her up in a place in London like your other mistresses?"

"Acton! Pray, remember the presence of your lady wife! I declare, I shall have the vapors!" The fan began to vibrate again.

"She is the cousin of Sir Edward Blake, my lord, of Friarswell in Cornwall," said Richard, his tones like ice. "A fellow officer who died in France for his country. She is a lady."

"Devil take me if I ever thought you would be carried away by a seductive smile attached to an empty purse, sir. Am I to have no control over your precipitate actions? You have set yourself against me ever since you were in leading strings. In every godforsaken corner of the world you have exposed yourself recklessly to danger and vice. When travel palled, you went into the cavalry, risking your worthless neck as if you were a younger son instead of my heir. You have responsibilities to England, sir, and to your name! Is this what your mother and I deserve? Damn me if I wouldn't strike you out in favor of Henry, if it wasn't for the entail."

Richard's voice seemed entirely unconcerned. "I am well aware of your feelings, sir. However, I am of age. I have married Helena Trethaerin. I would ask that you treat her with the courtesy due the future Countess of Acton."

And the footman opened the door.

Richard spun around, and she saw his eyes widen into dark pools as he gazed at her. He looked splendid and completely unruffled. His tall frame was clothed in the most impeccable and sober of evening clothes that fit his broad shoulders like a second skin. The golden hair caught the firelight and shone like brass. Had he not at that moment given her a smile, her courage might have failed her. The two other occupants of the room fixed her with hostile intensity.

"Lady Lenwood," announced the servant.

Helena felt her feet step forward and she was in the room. Richard was instantly at her side and had taken her hand in his.

"Mama, Father, this is my wife, Helena. My dear, I would like you to meet the Earl and Countess of Acton."

Speechless, she sank into a curtsy.

"You are late, young lady," said the earl. "We dine at nine o'clock sharp. Please remember in future."

There was no time for further conversation. Dinner was announced and they filed into the dining room. Richard escorted his mother, and Helena was obliged to lay her hand on the earl's arm and allow him to lead her to her seat. The dining room was vast and paneled in oak. A table long enough to accommodate thirty held court over two long ranks of chairs emblazoned with what must be the Acton crest in the back of each. Silver candlesticks, exquisite plate, fine linen napkins, innumerable sets of cutlery, rosewater-filled fingerbowls; all were ranked like soldiers on the cloth. Thank goodness she had attended the young ladies' seminary in Exeter and practiced everything that was considered correct. She did not speak a word as the courses were served and removed, since not a word was addressed to her. Instead, she surreptitiously studied her host and hostess. The countess was small and dark and drowning in jewels. Helena immediately surmised that she must once have been a great beauty. Her skin was still flawless and her black eyes magnificent: Richard's eyes. The earl, on the other hand, was a typical big, rawboned Englishman, his face florid beneath a thatch of pepper and salt. He made Helena think of a portrait she had once seen of Henry VIII. From him must have come the fair hair, but she could see nothing else of Richard in his father. She watched Richard as he talked calmly and politely with the earl, while Lady Acton added the occasional acid comment. The candlelight warmed his coloring to honey. Helena had known it, she supposed, since she had first seen him, but this was the first time that it had consciously sunk in. She was married to a man who was extraordinarily good-looking. For some reason, that was a distinctly uncomfortable thought.

At last the countess gave her a small nod and rose, and Helena followed Richard's mother from the room. When the excuse was offered that she must be fatigued from the journey and would perhaps wish to retire early, she happily took it and went up to her bedroom. The stream of maids instantly reappeared to remove her blue silk, comb out and braid her hair, put her into her plain muslin night rail, and fold back the covers. Had she not climbed into bed herself, no doubt they would have bodily picked her up and put her between the sheets. There were still two maids in the room, efficiently putting everything exactly to rights, when a door at the side of the chamber opened and with blushes and curtsies the girls made a sudden exit. Richard stood in the doorway. He had already removed his dinner jacket, and the fine silk shirt glowed amber in the dim light. Helena instantly pulled the covers up to her chin with both hands.

"Am I disturbing you?" he asked blandly.

Helena gulped. Surely he didn't intend . . . ? "No, of course not," she said.

He came into the room and pulled at his cravat. The elaborate folds collapsed into single strip of cloth, and he opened up his shirt and rubbed at the back of his neck. His skin gleamed smoothly in the firelight.

"Who is Lady Lenwood?" asked Helena. She must make some ordinary conversation! "The footman announced her."

Richard stopped, and suddenly the black eyes were filled with amusement. "I only want to talk to you. So you may relax and let go of the covers."

"You didn't answer my question."

"I have treated you shabbily, haven't I? You are, my dear. I am Viscount Lenwood in my own right. It's a title always given to the oldest son." He reached for her dressing gown. "Here, let's sit by the fire. It's distinctly uncomfortable to talk to a lady who is lying in bed."

Helena thrust her arms into the robe and slipped from the four-poster. She didn't know how to tell him, but it was also distinctly uncomfortable to talk to a gentleman dressed in nothing but night attire. But, of course, he was her husband; he had a right to be there. She joined him at the fireside and he pulled a chair close to the flames.

"I hope I didn't disgrace you this evening," she said calmly as she sat down.

He gave her a surprised look, and began to pace back and forth on the Oriental rug. "No, of course not. You have a natural dignity and, in spite of refusing the services of my mother's dresser, you looked more beautiful than I had any right to expect."

It was small comfort. "Thank you, my lord."

He stopped and turned to her. "My name is Richard."

Helena gave a wry smile. "I already knew that, Captain Acton. It is the rest of the name that I am discovering in bits and pieces that disturbs me."

"You know it all now, or very nearly: Richard Arthur Lysander Acton, Viscount Lenwood, heir to King's Acton and the accompanying earldom. Isn't that enough?"

"More than sufficient. I just wish it had occurred to you that it would have been only kind to forewarn me."

He shrugged. "You had no problem and coped admirably. I knew that you would."

She choked back her emotions. How could he be so casual about it? There was no reason for him not to have told her his true identity. Yet perhaps if she had known, she would not have married him. And that had been a risk he was not prepared to take. One day he would be an earl! One of the handful of men who directed the nation. Was an oath to a dying comrade enough to make him marry a nobody? "I did not exactly feel welcome," she said.

"Nobody ever feels welcome at King's Acton. It is more like attendance at an inquest and a visit to a mausoleum in one."

Helena tried to regain the light tone that had somehow slipped away. In this mood he seemed almost dangerous. "At least I didn't drink the water out of the fingerbowl or drop butter on my unfashionable skirts."

She was relieved when he smiled, but it was the polite smile of the drawing room. Something had occurred since dinner to upset him. "You will have to get some dresses eventually, of course, but the blue silk became you very well."

At least he had noticed her dress. Should she be pleased? "Surely you didn't get me from my bed to talk about gowns?"

He crossed over to her and leaned against the mantel, his hair a bright halo above the strong lines of his throat. "No, I didn't. I came to tell you that we aren't going to London."

She thought for a moment. Of course, he had never said that they were. She had just assumed that a bachelor would have lodgings in town. "Whatever you say." She looked down at her hands. Pray that they weren't going to stay here! Anxiety made her voice a little sharper than she intended. "If there are dreadful skeletons in the family closet, I should like it if you would tell me that, too. You seem to know my complete family history; I think you owe me a little of yours."

"My father fancies himself as a bully, and he prefers my brother Henry to me. My mother has been more proficient at producing children than in caring for them. I should say we are a very commonplace family." His tone was quite casual.

Helena looked up. "Why, really, did you marry me? I had no idea you were other than an ordinary gentleman, but you're an earl's son! Surely any number of more suitable young ladies would have been only too happy to wed the heir to all this!" She waved her hand around the sumptuous chamber.

"Exactly," he said. "But it is you I have married, so now we must both live with the consequences."

Her heart turned over. Oh, Lord. Was this it? Had he come to demand his marital rights? She felt her color rise and her pulse start pounding. "And what are those consequences? I am to be kept in the dark of every circumstance of our lives, while you continue to spring surprises on me as it suits you? If you had not insisted, I would never have done it, but I am your wife! Don't you think you owe me common courtesy, at least?"

"I don't believe I have shown you anything else. For God's sake, I plucked you from disaster!"

"And I am to be grateful for ever?"

"You seemed agreeable enough at the time!"

"You were able to rid yourself of an obligation to Edward, but it wasn't a bargain for which he had thought to consult me." She knew it was cruel and unappreciative, but the full significance of what she had done was only just beginning to sink in. And he must have had other motives! What were they?

"Damnation, Helena! I thought we understood each other?"

Helena gulped. She understood nothing! Why on earth had he kept all this secret from her? "Then where do we go next? Surely you don't live here?"

He looked as remote as the moon. "I do have a place in London; but now that I am wed, I have come into a house at Acton Mead that belonged to my grandmother. We go there tomorrow."

She felt the breath stick in her throat. "Acton Mead?"

"It's in the Chilterns. Quite respectable."

"What do you mean, now that you are wed?"

"Grandmama left it to me in her will to become mine the day that I married."

Helena leapt to her feet. "So you married me for a house?"

"If you like. Isn't that why you married me? For a roof over your head?" Suddenly, the vertical line marred his forehead as his brows flew together. "For God's sake, Lady Lenwood, please don't pretend that we married for affection!"

And with a curse, he strode from the room.

Five

The letter arrived at Trethaerin House the next morning as Helena and Richard set off for Acton Mead. Nigel Garthwood had no hesitation at all in opening it, although the battered cover was clearly addressed to Helena. It had apparently lain in some officer's effects that had only now arrived in England. Out of idle curiosity, he turned to the signature at the end. As he suspected, it was from Sir Edward Blake, written all those months ago, before his pitiable cousin had breathed his impetuous last. No doubt a pathetic love letter from beyond the grave; he almost tossed it aside unread. But it was not an amorous missive: in fact the tone was light, almost brotherly. But after a couple of pages of scattered news, Edward had turned serious.

"I wonder sometimes," read Garthwood, "if I shall ever see dear old Cornwall again. Although we all believe the war is nearly over and Boney stares defeat in the face, there are too many mishaps here waiting to trap a fellow. If anything should happen to me, dear cousin, I surely shouldn't want old Garthwood to get his hands on Friarswell."

Garthwood looked up and smiled like a snake before taking a delicate sip of his wine. It was no surprise to him that poor Edward had held him in dislike, even though their meetings had been few and far between. It was rather amusing to read the proof. The next few sentences, however, made him suddenly blanch and leap to his feet. His glass of wine spilled unnoticed on the floor. For God's sake! This could ruin everything! Nigel read the words again. A brandy flask! Had it survived the campaign? Or had it been buried with his cousin, somewhere in France? He cursed heavily and began to stalk the room, unconsciously twisting one hand against the other. It was essential that he find out immediately! Essential! Or all was lost!

In a moment Garthwood calmed down and began to write out some instructions. Everything he had planned here in Cornwall must go on without him. He could leave things in Jones's hands. First he must ascertain the status of the flask. If it existed, Helena and Richard Acton should not be too hard to trace. Had they not said they were going to London?

The Earl and Countess of Acton did not stand on the steps and wave them off. Of course, Helena had not expected for a moment that they would. She had, in fact, already had a very uncomfortable conversation with the countess in the breakfast room.

"I am given to understand by my son that you bring no competence of your own to this match, Lady Lenwood."

"That is correct, my lady." Helena continued to calmly butter her finger of toast.

"I hope that you will not think to batten on to him for funds. I'm sure he will give you an allowance for pin money, but gentlemen do not expect to have to furnish their wives with the necessary for serious purchases."

"I am aware of that, Lady Acton."

"Humph! Are you? I can imagine nothing but constant humiliation for you in this match. Richard will live a life of his own, you know. He is used to travel and adventure. Don't think for a moment that he will be the dutiful husband. Had you property, of course, things would be entirely different. You might have been able to hold up your head in Society with a modicum of dignity."

"But I do not, my lady. So I shall have to hope that my head will stand up by itself."

Lady Acton gave her an extremely sharp look from her beautiful eyes. "Yes, you have no family to turn to when things go wrong, do you? I suppose you are used to being alone. My son has always been a proud man. Can you give me the slightest reason why he felt obliged to offer for you? It seems to me to be entirely contrary to his nature. You're not increasing, are you?"

To her annoyance, Helena felt herself flush. "Certainly not!"

The countess laughed suddenly. It made her seem years younger. "I see that it is possible, after all, to discompose you. Well, I don't wish you ill of this match. It's done and there's an end of it. I only warn you again: Do not expect plain sailing."

And with that the countess rose and walked gracefully from the room.

As the curricle bowled along the turnpike, Helena wondered what on earth she had expected. Not to marry a lord, certainly! She had thought of nothing except to escape from Nigel Garthwood. Yet Mr. Garthwood had allowed her to stay on at Trethaerin House for all those months, after the solicitor had explained to her how affairs stood, and he had never once harassed her. Anyone else would interpret his offer of marriage to be only generous and correct. Why, then, had she been so afraid to put herself in Garthwood's hands? In spite of the bright sunshine, she shuddered. It was as if instinct had been telling her that beneath the polished exterior lay a cruel outlaw. So instead, she had put herself completely in the firm hands of Richard Arthur Lysander Acton, who would one day be an earl. How could she have done such a thing? Of course, Edward had hero-worshipped him. From her cousin's letters, she had already built up a picture of Captain Acton as a man of honor and admirable capabilities. She glanced at him. He certainly sat his horse like a centaur.

For Viscount Lenwood did not share the curricle with his wife. One of the tigers was at the reins and Richard rode Bayard alongside. Her husband's fine nostrils were set rigid above the thin mouth. His face had been locked into a frown ever since they left King's Acton. It darkened his eyes to pitch. Richard had spent a good part of the morning closeted with his father in the study before the earl had come out and bid Helena and his son a clipped farewell. She had not thought for a moment to question him about it; and she was not surprised when he curtly told the tiger to drive the grays and swung himself onto his charger. He did not appear to be aware of her. He was remote but courteous when they paused for lunch at Shaftesbury, and it was not until they stopped for the night at Salisbury that he was forced to take notice of her.

"I'm very sorry, my lord," said the innkeeper. "But I don't have a suite left that's suitable for yourself and her ladyship. There's to be a mill tomorrow, see, and everything's taken."

"Then two simple rooms will suffice, my man."

"I've the double chamber at the front of the house, my lord. Why don't I just go and check for a moment?"

Were they to be trapped together for the night in a room with only one bed? Helena decided instantly to take the bull by the horns. "If there is nothing but a double room," she said quietly, "perhaps there might be a trundle bed?"

To her amazement, Richard laughed. "Our marriage must eventually be consummated, dear Helena. I know the thought has been terrifying you since Exeter. I would not have dreamed of making love to you under my father's roof, but please relax and rest assured that neither do I intend to ravish you in this sorry establishment. I won't share a room with you."

Why must she blush like a silky milkmaid? "But if there is nothing else?"

"I prefer to be private. You may have the room alone. I don't share my sleep with anyone."

It was a simple statement of fact. "Why not?" she said without thinking.

His face set like marble. "I don't think that's any of your concern."

Helena was instantly silenced. A few moments later the innkeeper returned. It was soon arranged that her ladyship should have the front room and the viscount would take a simple chamber at the back of the house. The landlord sighed and scratched his head as they were led away. There was no accounting for the ways of the Quality. She was a right pretty little thing. Why on earth wouldn't her husband want to share her bed?

The next day Richard once again drove the curricle as they trotted on through Hampshire.

"What was it that my mother had to say?" he asked suddenly.

"Actually, it was more of a warning."

He raised a brow. "Really? Does she think I'm so dangerous?" The sun danced off his yellow head as he laughed. "I know I've been an ogre ever since King's Acton. The place has that effect on me, in spite of my best efforts. Will you forgive me? I promise reform as of this moment."

Helena's frank gaze met his. "I'm not sure whose behavior was worse. I had no right to accuse you. I accept your apology if you'll accept mine."

Richard was forced to look back at the road for a moment, but he smiled. "Extraordinary Helena! If there was any bad behavior, it was entirely mine, but very well."

"Your mother's concern was for my self-respect."

"Because you have no money of your own?"

Her eyes flew up again to meet his. They were filled with amusement. "Are you always so perceptive, Richard?"

"No, I just know my mother. She brought as much to her marriage with my father as he had himself and she has never let him forget it. I pray you won't regret that you couldn't do the same. You'll have an allowance of your own. I shan't question how you spend it."

"Lady Acton didn't doubt that you would give me pin money."

"I was thinking of more than pin money." And he named a sum that made Helena gasp. It would be sufficient to set her up in her own household if she wished.

"A fraction of that would be sufficient!"

"No, it would not. I don't intend to do your shopping for you, and you will need more than you think. Give the rest to charity if you wish."

"Richard, I can't take it! For heaven's sake, leave me some dignity."

"To leave you without funds would be worse, I assure you. Had your father been alive, there would have been marriage settlements. He wouldn't have sold you for any less."

"Yes, but as my husband, you would have gained Trethaerin. Do you think it would have been a fair exchange? Under the circumstances, how can I even the score?"

He smiled. "You think that I can't drive a decent bargain, like poor Esau who sold his birthright for a pottage of lentils?"

" 'And Esau was a cunning hunter, a man of the field,' " she quoted.

"Not cunning enough," said Richard with a laugh. "He let himself be outwitted and replaced in his father's affections by his younger brother, Jacob. Hardly a reasonable exchange."

"How can I know? Do you care for your birthright?"

"Passionately, as it happens."

So it meant a great deal to him to be earl one day. Could she live up to it? He was offering her financial security and a more assured place in society than she had any right to expect. What could she give in return? "I shall try to make you a good wife," she said.

"I don't want a good wife and the blunt means nothing; forget it."

"Then what do you want?"

She had no idea if he was serious or not. "I want Acton Mead, of course," he said.

It was late evening when they arrived at Acton Mead and the house was shadowed in the failing light. It lay in a fold of hills and the grounds ran down to the water meadows of the Thames. Part of the façade was lost in a thick growth of ivy, but the grounds appeared to have been kept up, even if not quite to the standard of King's Acton. There were sheep instead of roe deer grazing the lawn. Richard hammered at the door, and in a few moments it was opened and an elderly butler peered out.

"Master Richard! Bless my soul!"

"Are you going to let me in, Hood? Or must I stand in the dark like a beggar at my own door?"

"Well, you gave me a turn, my lord, and that's a fact," said Hood, throwing open the door. "We have most of the house in dust sheets."

"Devil take the dust sheets. All I require tonight is the preparation of two bedchambers and a simple meal. How is Mrs. Hood?"

They were ushered into the hallway and Richard began to peel off his coat.

"You will find her in the pink, my lord, as always. There's not much rattles my Mistress Hood." The butler's expression was torn between his delight at seeing the viscount and the furtive glances he was casting at Helena.

"Then go and fetch her, sir. I would like her to meet Lady Lenwood."

Hood gaped, then his wrinkled face broke into smiles. "Lady Lenwood! Then you're a married man, my lord!"

"Indeed, and I have come to claim my home."

"Master Richard! Well, bless us all!" A round-faced woman had bustled into the hallway. It was obviously Mrs. Hood, for she gave the butler a buffet in the ribs. "Now, what on earth are you thinking of, Mr. Hood, to let them stand in the hallway like this? We don't have the house open, my lord. But if you would condescend to join us in the kitchen? And is this your lady wife? God bless you, my dear! Come through now, come right through."

Richard smiled indulgently at the old housekeeper. "We should be delighted, Mrs. Hood, especially if you happen to have some of your scones."

And Helena found herself following Richard and the old couple through several shrouded rooms and into the warmth of the kitchen. The walls, painted the traditional blue to keep the flies away, were lined with row upon row of shining copper pots and pans; barrels of flour and a tall cone of sugar stood at the side of the room.

"We have a rabbit stew, my lord, and fresh bread, and I can whip up some scones on the instant. Had you thought to send warning, we'd have laid in more provisions."

"Time enough tomorrow, Mrs. Hood. Now, can you find a bedchamber for her ladyship?"

"Well, of course," she sniffed. "All the bedrooms are kept clean and aired. I should hope that I know my duty."

Helena watched with amazement as Richard, heir to an earldom, happily ate rabbit stew in the kitchen with the housekeeper and butler. A plate of fragrant scones soon appeared from the wall oven, and were served with generous helpings of cream and honey. Then Mrs. Hood disappeared when the meal was over to see to the beds. Richard seemed free of all shadows and laughed uproariously more than once at some anecdote of the old man's.

"And do you remember, my lord," wheezed Hood, "when Master Harry caught the frogs and put one in your grandmama's bed?"

"How could I possibly forget, sir? It was I who received the beating." And he threw back his yellow head and laughed again.

"Yet Master Harry caught it too when you tied together your sisters' plaits."

"It was nothing more than was richly deserved. Yet I don't know if Joanna has forgiven us yet."

"You lived here as children?" asked Helena.

His smile was as warm as the sun. "We came here every

summer, my brothers and sisters and I, and cavorted under the indulgent eye of the dowager Countess of Acton, my father's late mother. It was the only place, I think, that we ever were happy."

No wonder he had longed to own it. He must feel for Acton Mead as she felt for Trethaerin House. As if reading her thoughts, Richard leaned across to her and took her hand. "Exactly, my lady. And I hope it will become a place of happiness for you."

Helena smiled back at him. He was extraordinarily attractive in this mood. He did not let go of her fingers. After Mrs. Hood returned and all four of them began to share the jokes, he still kept her hand in his, while his thumb began to weave a delicious pattern across her palm. Suddenly, he leapt to his feet.

"Enough! Tomorrow we must hire in staff and open the house. We shall stay here for what's left of the summer. But now to bed!"

"Will her ladyship require any assistance, my lord?" asked Mrs. Hood.

Richard gave Helena a questioning glance and smiled. "None that I can't provide," he said to the housekeeper. "We'll see you in the morning. Good night!"

Helena followed him through the silent hallways and up several flights of stairs. At last, he pushed open a solid oak door and led her inside. She felt instantly welcome. The room was beautiful. A frieze of plaster leaves and flowers ran around the ceiling and down to the fireplace. Though the September night was not cold, a fire burned brightly in the grate; fresh linen sheets were already turned back on the large bed.

"This is your room," he said. "Do you like it?"

"How could I not? It's lovely!"

"Then I shall share it with you tonight."

Helena's blood turned instantly to water. She felt her voice stick solidly in her throat, and gulped. "I thought you preferred to sleep alone," she mumbled at last.

"Yes, but I don't intend that we sleep, my dear. You're my bride, remember? It's time that I ravished you, don't you think?"

She knew that there was no color left in her face at all. In fact, she felt faint. She must not give way to the vapors! Richard took her hand and sat her in a chair by the fire.

"We are married and this is what married people do. Without it there would be no babies and that would be a great shame, wouldn't it?" Helena could feel her hand tremble a little in his, and he raised her fingers to his lips and gently kissed her palm. "The great secret is that there is nothing more wonderful in the world."

"Than babies?" asked Helena, deliberately misunderstanding.

Richard laughed. "Than what you are about to discover. Don't be afraid, sweetheart. You will like it, and if you don't, I'll stop. It's no worse, I assure you, than a cavalry charge."

She forced herself to be calm, but her voice shook. "Don't tease me, Richard! I have never been in a cavalry charge."

"Yes, I know. But I have."

He went to the side table and poured her a glass of wine. The firelight made it shine like a ruby.

"Now drink this very slowly and think of nothing but the way it tastes. I'll be back in a moment."

There was a door at the side of the room, and he stepped through it. Obviously, his bedchamber lay beyond. The moment he was gone, Helena leapt to her feet and began to pace frantically back and forth. Every woman went through this, and most on their wedding night, not several days later. Surely it couldn't be so dreadful? Yet she wanted to run out of the house into the dark garden and hide. Good God! She had made him solemn vows at the little church in Exeter; she couldn't back out now! He was providing her with a home and protection and this was part of the bargain, wasn't it? But what did he expect of her? Should she undress and put on her nightgown? Take down her hair? She had no idea! Without thinking, she went back to the fireplace and gulped down some wine.

The door opened behind her and she whirled around.

"You have the look of a doe at bay, Helena, or the princess tied to a rock awaiting the dragon," said Richard softly. He was dressed in a long blue silk robe open at the neck. The lines of his throat were shadowed like a sculpture in the fire-light and his fair head shone like a halo. The faintest of smiles played at the corners of his mouth. "I thought you were made of nobler stuff."

"But I'm not of noble blood!"

"Then mine will have to count for both of us, I suppose. You might try to see me as St. George rather than the monster, you know."

"Yes, but it's the being tied to the rock as the tide comes in that's a little unnerving," replied Helena.

"There is really nothing to be afraid of," he said, and he came up to her and took her head in his hands. "Trust me, sweet."

She gazed back up at him, her gray eyes huge. "I don't know what to do!" she whispered.

"You're not supposed to know," he replied. "Just relax." And gently he touched her lips with his own. She stood as rigid as a poker in his grasp, but his kiss was as light and fleeting as the one he had given her after their wedding. She felt suddenly reassured; perhaps she could trust him. She closed her eyes as his fingers gently smoothed over her lids.

"Do you know that you are beautiful?" he said softly in her ear. "Don't think, just feel."

Helena was afraid to move or to speak, so she merely nodded her head a little. She could feel careful fingers pulling the pins out of her hair. As it fell around her shoulders, he smoothed it away from her face as if he were soothing a frightened horse.

"Your hair alone would be enticing enough to launch all the thousand ships," he whispered. "Helen of Troy would have been jealous."

His hands ran down the fall of her hair. The feeling was wonderful and she smiled tremulously at him. She dared not open her eyes, so she had no idea what his expression was. And then his fingers began a strange and delicious stroking on the back of her neck, while one hand slid down her arm, lingering on the sensitive skin inside her elbow and wrist. He lifted her hand and she felt his tongue trail lightly across her palm before gently sucking at each fingertip. Something very odd began to happen to her insides. His mouth touched her temple and the lobe of her ear before he moved to kiss the pulse at the base of her throat, and she trembled like a reed in the wind at the delicious sensation. When his lips closed once again over hers, she could not keep herself from responding.

"There, you see," he whispered when he finally lifted his lips from hers. "That wasn't so bad, was it?"

Her eyes flew open. She felt breathless and dizzy. "No," she said honestly. "It was lovely."

"Then would you mind if I did it again?"

"I think I might even like it."

"And I think, truthful Helena, that I am glad that I married you."

His eyes were pools of darkness; if she looked into them for another moment, she might be lost forever, so she dropped her head and looked away. Richard led her to the bed.

"When you were a child," he said casually, pulling her to his lap, "did you ever take off your dress and stockings and lie on the hot summer sand of Trethaerin Cove and let the sun wash over your skin like a wave?"

She smiled nervously. Richard's body felt strong and warm against her, and his silk robe caressed her arm. His fingers were slowly moving her hair until it lay in a sheer curtain across her breast. "Of course I did, though I risked a beating if I were ever found out."

"But it was worth it, wasn't it?"

He bent his head and took her lips again; it felt as sweet as honey. She barely noticed that his clever fingers had unbuttoned the row of fasteners at the back of her dress until it slithered to her waist and she was clothed in nothing but the fall of hair over her thin chemise.

"Imagine the hot sun," he whispered softly as his hand moved up the bare skin of her back, "and the sound of the waves. There has never been a more beautiful summer day."

Six

When Helena awoke in the morning, she was alone. She could not remember him leaving. She must have fallen asleep after . . . She blushed a little, then smiled to herself. How on earth was such an amazing thing kept secret? Was this what men and women did together, that people all through history had risked honor, reputation, or even life itself to find? She thought for a moment about what had happened. Richard had asked for her trust and she had given it. Then he had touched her heart in ways she had not known were possible. He had said they would make love. How could you not love the agent of such pleasure? She would never be afraid again. It seemed that marriage was a one-sided bargain after all, and every facet was a gift from him to her.

Slipping from the bed, she went to the window and looked out over the grounds of Acton Mead. A scattering of great old trees punctuated a sweep of green lawn and gave shade to a flock of black and white sheep. In the distance lay the blue ribbon of the river, divided from the park by an iron railing and the waving tufts of cattails. A brightly painted barge went slowly by, as small and neat as a toy. The tow horse seemed to be led by a tiny boy. I would bear Richard's child with gladness, she thought suddenly.

Quickly she splashed cold water over her face and body from the jug on the dresser, and slipped into her green and ivory muslin. Her hair was bundled into a knot on the top of her head, and she went down the stairs to the kitchen. Mrs. Hood looked up at her entrance.

"Well, bless me, your ladyship! Why didn't you ring for hot water?"

"Where is Viscount Lenwood, Mrs. Hood?"

"He took off early for the City, my lady. He said not to disturb you till you woke by yourself, or I'd have brought up some tea for you."

"To the City? London, you mean?" She fought hard to keep the despair from her voice.

"There's a lot of business to do, my lady, to open up a big house like Acton Mead again. Why, we've been under covers these three years, ever since the dowager countess died. It does my old heart good to see your bonny face and think of Master Richard living here with a pretty young wife, and maybe a nursery as well before too long. Bless me! I'm letting my old tongue run away with me. Forgive me if I speak out of turn, your ladyship. And here we are talking in the kitchen!"

"The kitchen seems to me to be an excellent place, Mrs. Hood. In fact, I should like breakfast. And perhaps afterwards, you might show me the house and we'll begin to see about those dust covers."

Helena appeared perfectly composed as she ate her simple meal, but her heart sank within her. She had refined too much on what had transpired last night. He had left without even saying good-bye. Of course, it didn't mean the same to him as it had to her. Men had their needs and women accommodated them. If he had been skilled enough that she had been so moved by it, that meant only that he was experienced. What had she overheard his father say? "Why not set her up in a place in London like your other mistresses?"

Men did the very same thing with their mistresses, didn't they? She must not let it disturb her. Yet it did. Very much. In fact, she couldn't bear to think that he would act that way with any other woman. Good Lord! Was she falling in love with him?

In something akin to panic, she looked up at Mrs. Hood. "I should like to see the house right away," she heard herself say calmly. "Shall we begin downstairs?"

They began in the hallway. Helena had hardly noticed the previous night, but the entrance was simple and elegant, with an ornate Jacobean ceiling. Several doors led off into the formal rooms. As they passed through, Mrs. Hood flung wide the wooden shutters and let the bright sunshine stream in. Yellow beams danced over shrouded chairs and sofas and desks, over the dining table, the sideboards, the leather backs of the books in the library.

"Everything seems to be in very good order," Helena commented eventually. "You have surely not kept up all this by yourself?"

"Oh, no, my lady. We get a gaggle of girls up from the village every week to scrub and polish. Of course, Hood does all the silver himself, and no one else is allowed to touch the books or paintings but ourselves."

"Then let us see if any of those girls are in need of a permanent place. Eventually we shall need a complete staff, but for now I shall put it in your hands to hire on a minimum complement of servants until Viscount Lenwood returns. But I would like this blue drawing room usable right away."

The room was lovely. French windows looked out over the back of the house. From what she could see, there was a mass of white roses flowing over a wicker arch that framed the entrance to a stone patio. She must have a room to use until Richard returned, and how could she guess when that might be? And the housekeeper and butler could hardly take care of the house alone now that there was family in residence. Or would it be only herself? Would Richard come back at all?

"This can be my retreat for now," she said serenely.

Mrs. Hood nodded and continued to lead her through room after room. No wonder her husband loved this house. It was neither enormously grand nor pretentious, but each chamber had classic proportions that welcomed and lifted the spirit. They left the family apartments, and Helena followed the housekeeper through the workrooms: the cool sunken buttery with its marble counters; the laundry with its huge copper cauldron; the pantry, stillroom, and wine cellar. Nothing had been allowed to gather dust. Upstairs was the same. Helena inspected bedrooms and withdrawing rooms and dressing rooms. She even took a look at the servants' quarters in the attics. By the time Mrs. Hood served her a light luncheon in the kitchen, they had inspected every room in the house, except, of course, Richard's bedroom and his study. No one but Hood himself saw to the master's rooms.

The next day the village girls arrived and made their nods and curtsies to the new mistress. Dust covers began to be folded and disappear into the labyrinth of storage rooms. Under Mrs. Hood's capable direction, the house began to reappear like a butterfly from the chrysalis. Helena left her at it and, tying on her straw bonnet, went out into the garden. In a few moments she was sitting beneath the bower of roses and castigating herself thoroughly for allowing silent tears to slip down her cheeks.

How could Richard have gone off to London without her? How long did he intend to leave her there? And why, in heaven's name, should she suddenly care so much? It had been not much more than a week since he had arrived at

Trethaerin, with his haunted eyes and his compassion for her loss of Edward. Dear Cousin Edward! She had mourned him as a childhood friend, but they had long been apart. His infrequent letters might have been dutifully written to an aged aunt. Yet had he come back, she would probably have married him; then she might never have met Richard at all. She dried her eyes on her handkerchief and laughed at herself. What on earth had she anticipated when she married a perfect stranger? The countess had warned her of what she might expect. She was fortunate if he treated her with kindness and was a tender, passionate lover. Many women were grateful for much less.

With a new determination Helena walked down through the gardens of Acton Mead. She had learned that funds had arrived regularly from a trust left by Richard's grandmother to pay for its upkeep, and certainly nothing had gone neglected. She discovered a regular army of gardeners maintaining the grounds, and there was apparently a perfectly competent estate manager who ran the home farm and oversaw the tenants. He had his own house in the village of Mead Farthing. Nevertheless, there was plenty for her to do.

Three days later Helena was busy in a stone-flagged outbuilding, her hair wrapped in a scarf and her oldest dress covered in a long white apron borrowed from the understairs maid. There was a great deal of laughing and giggling, for she was overseeing the making of ink, and the village girls had never done it before. All of them seemed to be liberally coated with soot.

"I declare, my lady," said one of the girls. "It's more messy than the making of gooseberry pie."

"At least when you make pie, you may lick the spills off

your fingers," said Helena gaily. "I don't think our ink would taste as good. Now, this mess is all yours. I leave you to it."

She stepped out of the shed and began to pull the rag from her hair, when suddenly strong hands grasped her around the waist. She whirled around to find herself gazing into a pair of merry blue eyes. Their owner smiled at her, revealing a set of perfect teeth, and tossed back a lock of black hair that had fallen over his forehead. His dress declared him a gentleman, but he did not seem inclined to act like one.

"What on earth have we here? I came looking for a fellow with hair just your color, but the devil has put a wench in my path instead! I think I would happily make it a permanent trade." And pulling her to his broad chest, he began to kiss her very thoroughly on the lips. Helena was furious; his mouth aroused no feelings in her at all except a very strong desire to slap the insolent smile off his face.

"If you were looking for me, Harry," said a cool voice, "you have a very odd way of conducting your search, for that wench you are manhandling is my wife, and I'm damned if I won't call you out."

The owner of the blue eyes instantly spun away from Helena. Richard stood watching them, tapping a riding crop in one hand. He was dressed in tall boots and his plain brown riding coat, and the dust of the road still dulled his clothes.

"God's teeth, Richard," said Harry. "How was I to know?"

"You couldn't, of course," replied Viscount Lenwood. "Let me introduce you: Helena, this is my brother, the Honorable Henry Acton, who has apparently seen fit to come down from Oxford for the express purpose of dishonorably accosting you in the garden. Harry, my wife, Lady Lenwood."

The line was drawn deep between the black eyes. But Harry laughed and gave her a bow. "A pleasure to make your acquaintance, sister-in-law. I congratulate brother Dickon on his taste. It seems every good fortune comes his way: you, Acton Mead, and at last, but of course not least, the earldom."

"I have heard of you, sir," said Helena serenely. "But I don't think I can so easily forgive you."

"Damn it all, my lady," said Harry, giving her a charming smile. "How can you blame me? I'm only human. Richard might have thought to give you a decent gown or two and hire some servants. I took you for a maid!"

Helena smiled. "Exactly, sir. And I would prefer that the maids are not targets for unwelcome advances in my house."

Helena thought suddenly she had gone too far, for Richard was looking at her in open astonishment. Oh, Lord, she thought. It's his house! And his brother! How could I? Now I have been rude!

But Harry gave her another big smile and gallantly bowed again. "I am suitably chastised, my lady. I shall be as grave and sober as a monk, if you will only forgive me and say I may stay at Acton Mead and visit solemnly with you and brother Dickon."

"It isn't for me to say, sir," she said. "Unless Viscount Lenwood agrees."

"For God's sake, come up to the house, Harry," said Richard. "And tell me how much money you need. I can't offer you much in the way of creature comfort, I'm afraid. The house has been shut up for years."

He turned on his heel and strode away up the path. Helena and Harry followed behind. Richard was home! She felt her heart lift within her.

"It looks pretty sumptuous to me, old fellow," said Harry as they walked in, and a new maid curtsied and took their gloves. "Can your table live up to the standard of your accommodations? I hope so, because I'm starving."

Helena saw the black eyes widen as Richard glanced through the open doorway at the bright room beyond. What had happened to the dust sheets? And had the furniture been rearranged? There was a sparkle to everything as if it had all just been buffed and polished. Whatever the cause, it looked extremely welcoming. "I have no idea," he said quietly. "You had better ask my wife."

Nigel Garthwood ground his teeth as he rode along the turnpike. Information about the brandy flask had not been in the least difficult to obtain, for the chambermaid at the Anchor in Blacksands had seen it in Captain Acton's room.

"Oh, yes, Mr. Garthwood"—she dimpled as she pocketed his coin—"I couldn't be mistaken. For I wondered at the time why he had ordered so many bottles to drink, when he already had his own flask. But, of course, his was empty."

"You checked to see?"

The girl blushed. "I meant no harm, sir. I was just curious. He seemed such a sad gentleman."

"And you're a smart and pretty miss. You could be a lady's maid."

"Oh, sir, I never could!"

"In Paris, a clever girl with your looks would be paid in gold coin. There's a shortage of good girls like you." He chucked her under the chin and she curtsied, flattered.

So Acton had Edward Blake's flask in his possession and he undoubtedly knew what it contained. Why else would he have come all the way down to Cornwall and married Helena Trethaerin? Devil take it! If the letter had only come into his hands a few days earlier! Well, that was water under the bridge. Captain Acton obviously did not intend to tell his new bride immediately, but eventually the contents of the brandy flask would be conveniently discovered, and then he would come back to Cornwall and make his claim.

Garthwood grimaced to himself. He should have acted long since and forced marriage with her himself. Never had he imagined that it would prove so important. To think that he had actually been glad for a moment that she had been taken off his hands! Damnation! Acton had stolen the prize from right under his nose! Garthwood kicked his horse into a canter. Captain Acton might be laughing up his sleeve at this moment, but his mirth wouldn't last long. Nigel Garthwood would make sure of it himself.

Seven

Richard looked steadily across the table at Helena. She was not aware of his gaze, since she was serenely listening to a long-winded anecdote of Harry's. She laughed in all the right places. Damn Harry! If it wasn't just like his little brother to turn up at the most inopportune moment. Richard had deliberately left early for the City, thinking he could be back the same day. There had seemed no point in waking Helena. Already dressed for the road, he had stepped quietly into her chamber and gazed down at her sleeping face. Her mouth had been relaxed in a small smile, and the golden hair lay spread on the pillow around her. The intense rush of desire had taken him entirely unaware. She was beautiful, his stranger wife. Beautiful and passionate and honest. She had responded to him like a lyre. He wanted nothing more than to make love to her again and continue to open to her all the enchanted paths of ardor. Instead, he had turned and quietly left the room.

The business in London had taken longer than he planned. Firstly to close up his grandmother's trust and sign all the necessary paperwork to transfer complete title for Acton Mead to himself and Helena. Then to change his will to reflect his new responsibility for her. Richard was used to the urgency of the battlefield. Lawyers had no interest in speeding up their interminable timetables, even for the future

Earl of Acton. Then he had checked briefly with one of his men about the progress of the Paris affair.

"It's a rum do, my lord, and that's a fact. There's someone with a keen mind behind it."

"A keen mind and a dull conscience," Richard had replied with a grimace. Was there nothing more he could do? The thought haunted him.

But mostly it had taken time to terminate his arrangement with Marie. She had proved awkward. She was a widow and they had been friends for years. Every time he had come back to England, Marie was waiting, though probably not faithfully. Why should his marriage make any difference to their little friendship? Wouldn't he still be lonely when he came to the City to do business? And then the new little Lady Lenwood would surely begin increasing soon and dear Richard would still have his needs. Marie would understand if he saw her less often, but to drop her entirely? A diamond bracelet and a discreet introduction to a future duke had finally done the trick, and she made him a tearful farewell.

"I shall miss you, Richard! Not many ladies have had such a lover."

Perhaps Marie was right and he had been crazy to give her up. To trade a skilled courtesan's charms for those of an innocent? But he would not go from her bed to Helena's. In fact, he had thought of nothing else but Helena's bed all the way from London to Acton Mead. And then he had found her kissing his brother in the garden.

"You're not saying much, brother Dickon!" laughed Harry. "How can you presume to take a seat in the House of Lords when you can't string two words together in a sentence at dinner?"

It seemed to Helena to amount almost to a challenge, but Richard merely smiled. His voice was perfectly casual. "At least when I am able to cobble together a phrase or two, Harry, I have something to say besides gossip."

"Your husband would have us believe, my lady, that still waters run deep, but we know better. Richard is struck dumb contemplating his coup."

"What coup?" asked Helena.

"Marrying you, of course. Where did he find you? Drifting to shore in a scallop shell? Or running at night through the woods with your bow, a pack of white hounds at your heels?"

To the young man's immense surprise, Helena laughed aloud. "Not white hounds with red ears, like the ones that followed the goddess? You are ridiculous, aren't you? Is that how you have such success with the maids?" Then she instantly relented as Harry's expression turned from merriment to open astonishment. "Oh, forgive me, brother Harry. I'm just a country girl and I'm not used to your gallantry! As a matter of fact, he found me in a lane with a basket. Very prosaic, I assure you."

Harry had recovered instantly. "Lady Lenwood, my brother has all the luck in this life!" He flung a hand in the air and began to declaim. "There was a poor fellow called Harry/Who long at the table did tarry . . ."

"I didn't know that limericks were a family trait," interrupted Helena.

"Poor Harry did plot . . ."

"But it all came to naught/For the lady had already married," finished Richard rapidly.

"That's an insultingly poor rhyme, brother," said Harry, pouring another glass of wine.

"Don't quibble, sir!" Richard was laughing. "It's good enough for the purpose."

Harry turned to Helena. "I hoped you and I might enter a conspiracy to hasten brother Dickon to his rest in the family plot at King's Acton, but unless I thought I might have a chance with you after his demise, what would be the point?" He clasped his hands dramatically over his heart. "Say you would have me when Dickon turns up his toes, or the earldom will mean nothing!"

"I intend to outlive you, Harry," said Richard with a grin. "I did not survive the Peninsula only to conveniently drop dead on my return. If you continue to act the fool, it will be your sudden demise that Helena will mourn. And unless you mend your sorry ways in a hurry, it will be I that hastens you to it!"

"A challenge! Noble brother, let us meet in the water meadow with pistols at dawn!"

"And get wet feet and a chill?" said Helena. "Let me leave you gentlemen to your port, and you may fight it out in the comfort of the dining room."

She rose gracefully to her feet and left the table. When she reached the safety of the hall, she leaned her head for a moment against the cool plaster wall. Richard had been gone three days and then hardly given her a glance since his return. He had walked through the rooms that she had opened without a murmur.

"I hope you aren't displeased, Richard," she had managed to whisper to him. "I thought I had best begin to uncover the furniture at least."

"How could I be displeased?" he had said. "This is your home. Do as you like."

Then Harry had reclaimed his brother's attention. Well, she must stifle this terrible longing. Richard had married her for the house and to fulfill a promise to Edward. He had not pretended otherwise. She was to be a housekeeper and, presumably, bear him an heir. Nothing more. The barbed words of the countess rang in her ears. She must not impose on his freedom.

The door to the dining room opened as a footman carried in a tray and she heard Harry's merry voice ring quite clear for a moment.

"Devil take you, Richard! I'd give my eyeteeth to be in your shoes at this moment. Three days in London to cavort with your delectable mistress! So how is Marie?"

Helena went straight to her chamber and to bed. Eventually, she was even able to go to sleep. She was wakened by the sound of the door softly closing and sat up. No one was in the room. Had Richard come to her and found her asleep, and not liked to disturb her? Or had he merely been checking on her before retiring to dreams of his mistress? Damnation! Lady Acton had made things more than clear. How could she be so foolish? She was fascinated by a man she barely knew, who already had a life from which she was totally excluded. Somehow she would have to make a meaningful existence for herself and allow him to go his own way. Yet it would be easier if Richard weren't quite so devastatingly attractive!

She awoke to a burst of birdsong. Richard sat on her bed.

"How did you sleep?" he asked.

Helena gazed up at him. He was wearing only the blue dressing gown. Sunlight danced on the planes of his face and struck golden lights in his hair. His eyes seemed fathomless.

"Is it morning?"

"I'm going to ride as far as the village with Harry, before I pack him off."

Sitting up, she glanced out of the window. "But it's barely dawn!"

"I know. That's why I'm here."

"What's why you're here?"

Richard smiled suddenly, and Helena tried to stop her heart from running away. "I have an hour I can spend with you, if you will let me."

An hour! He would fit her in between his other obligations whenever he could spare a moment. Marie had been given three days!

"Of course," she said.

His fingers reached for her cheek and lingered there for a moment. Then he shrugged out of the dressing gown and slipped in between the sheets. The glimpse of his body made her instantly breathless.

"I owe you another apology," he said, turning and stroking the hair away from her face. "It was not my intention to leave you so long without notice. Yet you don't seem to have missed me. Are you always so self-contained and competent?"

She did not want to say it! Had she no pride left at all? But it was only the truth. "I missed you," she said.

"Oh, God, sweet Helena!"

His lips seared her mouth with the intensity of his desire. She felt herself respond with abandon. Savor these moments! she told herself; nothing else matters.

Nigel Garthwood stood quietly in the woods and contemplated the house. So Richard Acton was the son of an earl! It made no difference at all. He had watched Richard ride away with a younger dark-haired man. They were laughing together. A brother, perhaps? That could be more than useful. He would pursue it. A few moments later Helena herself stepped out with a basket, and Garthwood watched her disappear into the gardens. There seemed to be a dearth of staff, so it should be no problem at all to pursue his goal. And if he were not successful? An earl's son was as vulnerable as a tinker's. The long lips curved into a smile, and Garthwood moved silently through the shrubbery and up to the side door.

Helena came back into the house with her basket full of autumn flowers. She moved steadily through the rooms, filling vases and urns with the bounty of the late dowager countess's gardens. A door banged somewhere, but she was intent on her task. When Richard came into the room, she looked up and smiled. The smile died on her lips.

"What the devil were you looking for in my room?"

"Your room?"

"I would rather you didn't parrot me like the nymph who haunted Narcissus!"

His tone was impossible to read, but Helena felt her heart contract at the reference to Echo. "I have never been in your room!"

He raised a brow. "The entire house is yours to do with as you like. I require only that my study and my own chamber be private. If you need something, you have only to ask."

"And I have respected that!"

"Helena, I have lived for years in a world of shifting sands. I thought you were honest. For God's sake, who else would dare to disturb my things?"

"I don't know. One of the maids? Harry?"

"Not even Mrs. Hood would dream of it, and I trust my

brother as I trust myself. Harry may appear a rattle-brained dandy, but his honor is absolute."

"And mine isn't?"

"Apparently not!" He wrung his hand over his face. "Oh, devil take it, I'm sorry. Forget I said that! Harry and I were talking about something that made me particularly bloody-minded. I had no right at all to take it out on you."

"You have just accused me of rifling through your possessions and then denying it! You impugn my honor, then you expect me to pretend it never happened? Like Narcissus, do you do nothing but gaze at your own reflection in a pool and think of the feelings of no one else? I thought we could live together in harmony, but if you doubt my word, my position here is untenable! As for your brother, if he has so little principle that he would seize a maidservant and kiss her as a matter of habit, then your definition of honor is different from mine!"

"Harry would not dream of kissing the maids, Helena. In spite of your apron, he knew it was you. It was getting the news from our mother of my marriage that sent him here in the first place. He wanted to see what you were like."

"By kissing me?"

Richard suddenly looked amused. "That was just because he saw I was coming, of course."

"You mean he deliberately wanted to challenge you, using me?" Helena stepped forward and laid her hand on his sleeve. "Did you mean it when you said you would call him out? What on earth is between you?"

"Whatever is between my brother and me doesn't concern you. How could it?"

His face gave away nothing. Why was she forcing a quarrel with him? Was her dignity so important? Confused, Helena stepped back. Her hand came away with a trace of red across the palm. "Oh, heavens, you're hurt!"

Richard glanced down at the tear in his sleeve and the trace of blood that was beginning to dry on the fabric.

"It's nothing, a scratch. I was winged in the woods after Harry left."

"Richard, what on earth happened?"

He smiled with an amused indifference. "A poacher appears to have mistaken me for a partridge. Luckily he was not a better shot; scattered a few feathers, that's all."

"You were shot!"

Richard laughed. "Don't look so horrified; I've survived worse. The village lads have undoubtedly been in the habit of supplementing their larders with the bounty of my grandmother's woods and haven't yet learned the difference between the master and his game. Some luckless fellow is now cowering in his mother's house in fear of the hangman. Though I regret his attempt to ventilate me, I shan't try and hunt him down."

"But you could have been killed!"

"And was not. It is a matter of no moment whatsoever. Now, if you would kindly stop looking as if you had just heard the knell of doom?"

Helena flushed. "I'm sorry. I didn't mean to refine so much on an accident. And meanwhile, there is still the matter of your room. I beg you will believe me: I did not go in there!"

"Being mistaken for St. Stephen apparently caused more holes in my thinking than in my coat. I hope they will be as easy to mend."

Helena stared up at him. His eyes were unfathomable. "Is that an apology?"

He reached out a hand, and his long fingers gently caressed her cheek. "I don't know," he said very softly. "There is no one else, you see. I have already asked Mrs. Hood. She is organizing the staff. She had all the maidservants in her room for instructions the entire morning. They are to learn to leave the books in the library alone except for the dust they can reach with a goose wing and to use tea leaves to settle the dirt on the floors before sweeping. None of the maids had the opportunity."

"You would take the word of the housekeeper over mine?"

"I have known Mrs. Hood since I was a child, Helena. I apologize for accusing you without evidence, and of course I accept your word. It's a perfectly trivial thing anyway. Yet I would like it very much if you, dear wife, did not seem to be the last person I can trust."

Richard turned on his heel and left her in the wreckage of the flowers that had dropped unnoticed around her feet.

Harry rode away from Acton Mead with a slight frown. What Richard had told him was extremely disturbing. If it wasn't just like his brother to inform him of trouble, then leave out the details and demand that he not interfere, although in this case it seemed there was nothing he could do. Harry, of course, did not tell all of his own intentions either. For instance, he was not planning to go straight back to Oxford. Nor, however, was he planning on being followed. Since he was in no hurry and hadn't given a thought to any kind of secrecy, his pursuer didn't have the least difficulty in tracing him. In fact, at the inn where Harry stopped for lunch and ordered himself a dish of oysters, the pursuer had already caught up.

"I believe we've met, sir," said a tall gentleman with an unpleasant smile.

Harry looked up in annoyance from his oysters and gave the fellow an insolent stare. "You're mistaken, sir. I never clapped eyes on you in my life."

"Then please forgive me if I have interrupted your luncheon. The inn is so full, I felt my heart lift when I thought I saw an old acquaintance who could offer me a place at his table."

Harry recognized a hint when he heard it, and he laughed at the fellow's effrontery. The place was indeed crowded; it didn't matter to him in the least if the chap wanted to share his table. "Then by all means, sit down, sir. The oysters are excellent."

Nigel Garthwood took the chair indicated and offered to share a bottle of wine in gratitude.

"You would seem to be a man of the world, sir," he began.

Within thirty minutes Garthwood and Harry were laughing together in apparent amity and Garthwood had turned the discussion to Harry's family. Though Harry was normally more reticent with strangers, by the end of the afternoon there was little that Nigel Garthwood thought he had left to learn about Richard Acton, Viscount Lenwood, the man who had so inconveniently married Helena.

Helena awoke that night to the distinct sound of a cry. Was it an owl? She sat up in bed and listened. The moonlight shone brightly across the fine carpet on the floor. Perhaps she had imagined it. Then, quite distinctly, she heard a low moan. No wild creature ever made such a soul-disturbing sound. Slipping quietly from the bed, she took up her dressing gown and wrapped it around her shoulders. There was the sound of a slight thud, which resolved itself instantly into the pace of footsteps marching back and forth in the room next to hers. Without hesitation she went to the door to Richard's room and knocked. It flew open to reveal the fair head edged with the glint of silver in the moonlight. The blue silk dressing gown appeared black in the shadows.

"I woke you?" he said. "I'm sorry."

"Richard, what is it? The wound? Is it troubling you?"

She could see the play of shadows on his face as his mouth twisted in a self-mocking smile. " 'Perhaps some dungeon hears thee groan/Maim'd, mangled by inhuman men?' Go back to bed."

"Let me see it. If there's infection, it must be taken care of."

"Generous Helena," he said, coming into her room and closing the door behind him before leaning back against it and fixing her with his midnight gaze. "Can you still express concern for a fellow who exhibited such scurrilous behavior to you? May I hope you have forgiven me?"

"For your accusations? No, I haven't, but I've no desire to see you develop a fever and be consumed before your time like the Lionheart."

"Ah, noble crusader king! No one was so solicitous of his wounds, were they?"

"If they had been, perhaps he would have lived out his natural days and not been succeeded by his intemperate brother, bad King John."

Richard walked quietly to the window and gazed out at the moonlit gardens. Helena watched his lithe movement, then sat down in the chair by the fire and folded her hands. She was unaware that her knuckles shone white with tension. It may not have been the cry of a wild creature, she thought, but he certainly moves like one! Helena, dear girl, the man has made it quite clear why he married you, and he doesn't even trust you. Be careful, for heaven's sake!

At last he turned, and crossing the silver-dappled carpet, stopped in front of her. To her surprise, he dropped on one knee beside her chair. "Helena, I'm a sorry fellow and a worse husband. The wound to my arm doesn't even hurt and I have no fever. I have darker secrets than that, my dear."

With sudden insight, Helena knew exactly what he was going to say next. Why he had cried out. Why danger lay like a shadow behind his eyes. Why he would not share his bed at the inn, and why he had left hers before she awoke.

"You have nightmares," she whispered.

"Alas, it's pretty pathetic, isn't it?"

"I don't see why. You've been in a war, after all."

He ran his hand lightly down her arm until his fingers rested over hers. "Do you think King Richard wailed in the night like a banshee?"

"If he didn't, it was only because he was hardened to destruction. Look at what happened at Acre! Blameless prisoners lined up for slaughter."

"Yet he has come down to us as the very model of chivalry! At least I don't have the slaying of innocents on my conscience."

Helena was wise enough to stay silent. Was there something else on his conscience? Or was it the remembered terrors, the things he must have witnessed?

"All I want in the world is tranquillity, Helena."

"And Acton Mead," she said with a rueful grin.

A hand had moved to her shoulder. "Which you have brought me."

"Yet I can't bring you tranquillity, can I?" Because you don't trust me, she thought, and without trust we can never make anything of this imprudent marriage.

Her answer was a low laugh. "I don't see why not," he said, and pulled her forward into his embrace.

He had taken her face in both his hands before he smoothed his fingers back over her hair. She felt herself tremble with the unexpected rush of response. His left hand went on down to her waist, leaving a trail of delicate sensation coursing through her neck and back. Meanwhile long fingers gently took her chin and lifted her face to his. His lips were smiling as they met her partly open mouth.

There was a loud crash in the hallway, as if an entire wall of iron tools had leapt from their hooks and all hit the floor together. Instantly, Richard pulled away from her.

"Damnation!" he said lightly, and in one lithe movement was on his feet. " 'Ring the alarum-bell:—murder and treason!' "

The crash was followed by muffled thuds and the sound of a voice cursing. Richard had already crossed Helena's room and entered his own. Moments later he reappeared. There was a flash of white as his teeth caught the moonlight. He was laughing! Yet he had armed himself with a pistol. With rapid movements he was priming and loading it.

"Richard, for God's sake! Do you suspect something?"

"More someone, dear heart. Inanimate objects don't usually move around by themselves or raise such an intemperate amount of noise in the night. Stay here."

Eight

Which was more than any human had the right to expect. Helena followed Richard into the hallway. The figure of a man was struggling with the remains of a suit of armor that had stood before the long window at the end for perhaps a hundred years, and before that must have graced the castle of some Acton progenitor. Greaves and cuisses clattered aside in a tumble of metal, and the man cursed again. He tossed aside a pauldron as if it were some old kitchen pot and tried to stand. The armor had fallen in pieces around him, but the intruder had put his foot through the open neck of the sallet and he fell to the floor again in a cacophony of clatter.

Richard laid down the pistol and calmly struck a spark from the tinderbox that sat on the hall table by Helena's door. In an instant there was a blaze of light as flame jumped from the candles in the sconce. The trespasser looked up and squinted into the light.

"Is that you, Dickon?" he said. The blue eyes were slack-lidded. "I seem to have founder—I seem to have found . . ." He grinned at them.

"You have both found and foundered on our ancestor, Sir Lionel, dear boy," said Richard as the intruder's eyes tried vainly to focus.

"It's Harry!" exclaimed Helena.

"Indeed," replied Richard, going to his brother and removing the steel neckpiece from his foot. "And splendidly drunk, perhaps."

"How did he get in?"

"Up the ivy, as we did as boys. Come on, old fellow."

Harry grinned again and tried to bow to Helena. The result was that he slammed his head into what remained of bold Sir Lionel's armor stand, and slumped like a rag doll to the floor. Richard picked him up bodily, like a child, and slung his brother over his shoulder.

"Go to bed, Helena," he said calmly. "I can manage."

"But he broke into the house!"

Richard's eyes were shadowed by the flickering candlelight, but silver lights danced off his hair. "So?"

"I would have thought that even you could see that someone who would get drunk and climb the ivy in the middle of the night, for God knows what purposes, might not be the person in whom one should repose such infinite confidence!"

"You know nothing about it."

"If I don't know enough to understand what is going on in this house, it might be related, don't you think, to your remarkable reluctance to confide even the most basic facts? Richard, how do you know Harry is to be trusted?"

Richard shifted Harry's weight a little and turned with his burden toward the guest bedrooms. Helena wasn't sure what enabled him to so control his emotions, but his voice was perfectly level as he delivered the parting comment.

"Helena, you were an only child. The delights of being the oldest of six are beyond your understanding. And I won't have you trying to interfere with my family. Go to bed!"

And since Helena saw that there was really nothing else she could do, she did so.

But not to sleep. Birds had begun their dawn chorus and pink light began to steal in at the windows before she eventually closed her eyes in exhaustion. Richard had armed himself with a pistol against his own brother! Did he think his life was in danger? Would Harry really try to harm him? Who had fired that shot in the woods that had slashed Richard's coat sleeve? Without question the second son stood to gain everything if his older brother died. The thought went through Helena like a knife blade. Harry was just another irresponsible sprig of a wastrel aristocracy, but Richard shone in her world like a sun. She hadn't expected it, although she remembered the intense feeling of premonition she had felt when she had first seen him riding up the drive at Trethaerin. What did she know about him? He was the son of an earl who did not get along with his father. He had mistresses in London, and one was called Marie. He had traveled the world and read almost everything ever written. He had fought in the Peninsula. To Cousin Edward he had been the ideal of manhood. He could make up limericks. Instead of smiling at the thought, Helena was horrified to find tears trailing down her cheeks. She thumped at her pillow and with determination rolled over and buried her face in its soft comfort.

Richard was not at the table for breakfast, nor was Harry. It was midmorning before Richard came into the small sitting room that Helena had set aside for herself, and where she could go over the household accounts and the menus. The goose quill she had left the day before on her desk had dried and twisted, and she was making herself a new pen. She had left the tall French windows open to the bright autumn sunshine, and without a sound he stepped through from the garden, the white roses blazing in glory behind him.

"You're very proficient with your penknife, Lady Lenwood."

Helena looked up at him. The blond hair was ruffled from the breezy day. "I should hope so. I have enough years of practice, after all."

Richard glanced over the books and papers scattered on Helena's desk.

"You're a more than practiced housekeeper, aren't you?"

"I kept house for my father for many years after my mother died. It's the least I can do."

"For me?" he said with a sudden laugh. "Dear creature. If I had wanted a housekeeper, I could have hired one."

"Yes, but Acton Mead would not have come with her, would it?"

"Touché. But I want you to enjoy life, too. I know I haven't been fair. Helena, will you allow me to try to start all over again?"

There was a slight rap at the door, and when Helena called out permission to enter, a tousled dark head appeared, to be followed as the door opened all the way by Harry. There were dark circles under the blue eyes.

"I'm not interrupting, am I?"

"Of course you are, damn you," said Richard good-naturedly. "How's your head?"

"Like a boiled turnip."

"I'll have a mixture made up for you," said Helena, but Harry made a face.

"Rather be cured by the hair of the dog."

"You will go to Mrs. Hood this instant and swallow whatever remedy she feels moved to recommend," said Richard sternly. "I intend to talk to my wife about horses and about the delights of the view from Marrow Hill, and I don't need your amiable commentary."

Harry began to laugh, then winced. As he left the room, he managed to wink at Helena. "Sorry about Sir Lionel," he said. "Dismembered more thoroughly than he ever was in the Crusades!"

Helena had already dismissed him. Her attention was entirely on Richard. "What did you want to say about horses?"

"I don't even know if you ride. Do you?"

"A little; not well, that is. Well enough to get about Trethaerin and Friarswell on a nice gentle old nag."

"Good, because I have the very old nag to suit you. We're going riding."

The old nag proved to be a rather pretty chestnut gelding called Bob. He had two white stockings and a blaze. Bob was, however, perfectly gentle, and Helena was able to take the reins with confidence once Richard had swung her up into the saddle. Bayard stood like a gentleman as his master mounted and tossed his head only once in impatience at Bob's careful gait once they started.

"I want you to see all of Acton Mead. We'll go up to the top of infamous Marrow Hill; there's a view all the way to London."

Richard seemed lighthearted and cheerful as they rode together through the home wood and past the patchwork of fields and lanes that surrounded the house. Helena did her best not to let her eyes feast on his strong back and lean thighs. Did he know quite how splendid he looked on horseback? Probably. Little that Richard did seemed to be done without an impressive awareness of all the consequences. In which case, why had he come to Cornwall and so casually married her? A debt to Edward, of course. But was that enough to make him marry a stranger? She remembered the earl's words at King's Acton. One of the Salisbury daughters would just as surely have given him possession of Acton Mead. But for better or for worse, they were wed, and he had offered her a new beginning. She was determined to take the opportunity with both hands.

Marrow Hill proved to be a rocky prominence bristling with trees. As they began to ride up the narrow trail through the dark woods and leave the green fields behind, Helena felt as if she were entering a foreign land.

"As boys, this trail was the place for grand deeds of derring-do!" said Richard suddenly. "Here we could be Charlemagne or Sir Lancelot. A suitable spot for dark intrigues and swashbuckling adventures, don't you think?"

"I think it's more a place for hanging on to one's saddle and closing one's eyes," replied Helena. The rocks were plunging away to her right into the gorge of a little stream, and the resulting chasm seemed to be entirely too close to Bob's hooves as he walked steadily up the path. To the left, a thick growth of trees began to block the sunlight. They were passing a final brave stand of ancient oaks before the woods became dense with undergrowth.

"Yes, but the view from the top is worth it," said Richard.

And with those words, Bayard exploded. Bob jumped out of the way of the charger's flailing hooves, and Helena was almost thrown from the saddle. She grasped at the reins, but the reliable chestnut had already come trembling to a halt and she was able to look back over her shoulder. Bayard was still airborne. He came down with a twist and then bucked again. Richard had stayed with him through the first leap, but as the power of half a ton of horseflesh erupted once more, Helena knew without question that it would be beyond any human power to stay astride. At the same instant, she saw that the horse's hind feet had landed almost over the edge of the trail. In the next bound, they did so. Bayard lost his footing and went staggering backward. He threw up his beautiful bold head and rolled into the gorge. There was the dreadful sound of rending branches and the harsh crash of rocks as boulders were dislodged and bushes uprooted by the animal's flailing body tumbling over and over to the streambed below.

Richard did not go with him. By some superhuman effort, as it seemed to Helena, he had sprung from the saddle and caught at the branch of an overhanging oak. In a shower of leaves he dropped back to the ground and immediately swung over the edge of the trail after his horse.

"For heaven's sake, Richard!" called Helena. "He must have been killed!"

"That brave creature saved my life many times. I damned if I'm going to let him die in a stinking little toy canyon in England."

In a tangle of skirts, Helena slithered from Bob's broad back and ran to the edge of the precipice. "But he almost killed you!" she cried.

There was no reply. Richard was climbing steadily down into the ravine. She watched his bright head as it moved in and out of the sunlight and the lithe play of shadows across his shoulders before he disappeared beneath a canopy of leaves. Somewhere below Marrow Hill, the stream that had cut down through the rock and created the chasm must empty out onto level ground. Since there was no way to bring a horse back up the cliff, if Bayard was not dead and Richard could lead him out, that would be the only way. Leading Bob by the bridle, Helena picked her way back down the path. As she suspected, she was able to work her way around the edge of the woods until she met the stream gurgling out among the trees. She tied Bob to a low branch and started into the woods. She walked straight into Harry. He grinned at her as if nothing in the world were wrong, and greeted her with a quote from Shakespeare.

" 'How now, spirit! whither wander you?' "

The black hair was encrusted with twigs and Harry's jacket looked much as if he had slept in it—or raced carelessly down from Marrow Hill? Helena wanted to take him by the lapels and scream at him, but a cool voice cut in before she could speak.

" 'Over hill, over dale/Through bush, through briar,' dear brother." Richard turned to Helena. "It's all right. Bayard is hurt, but he's not dead. With ropes and some men, I can get him out."

Leaving Helena ready to weep with relief and frustration, Richard issued rapid explanations and orders to Harry, who took Bob and stripped off the saddle.

"Having left my nag on the other side of Marrow Hill, I am obliged to borrow the noble Bob. How the devil do you ladies ride in these things?" he complained as he flung aside the sidesaddle. "If I meet anyone riding bareback, I shall be the laughingstock of the county!"

"Unless you get back in five minutes with help, you will wish for such a wholesome result," snapped Richard. "Get going, damn you!"

And Harry galloped away. Richard instantly turned and plunged back into the wood. Helena followed.

"Why did Bayard do such a thing?" she questioned breathlessly. Richard's long legs caused him to pull away from her unless she trotted like a child, and then there was really no trail. Several times they scrambled over fallen rocks and once squeezed through a narrow cut in the cliff. There was no chance that a horse could come out this way. It was hard enough for a man to get in, but not once did Richard offer to help her. "Are you mad to ride such an unpredictable horse?"

She thought for a moment that he wasn't going to answer, but then his voice came back to her as casually as if they were in the drawing room. "As for the first, I can't tell you. And the second? I don't know."

They came out into a small clearing. The bay charger stood tied to a tree, head hanging. He was liberally scraped and cut, and his once-glossy coat seemed to have been wrung in a mangle. As Richard came up, the horse lifted his head and nickered.

"It's all right, old friend," said Richard, running his fine hand down Bayard's neck. "We'll get you out of here."

"You have a remarkably generous spirit," said Helena. "He just did his damnedest to kill you!"

"Did he?" said Richard. "Then he's paying for it. He's lame in the stifle and may have pulled a tendon in front." He smiled as the horse pushed at his shoulder with its sensitive nose. "It'll be a little while before he gets the chance to try again."

For some reason, Richard's nonchalance infuriated Helena.

"For God's sake, your father was right! You are entirely too irresponsible for the duties of the eldest son!"

Richard turned to face her. "And how do you know that the noble and blueblooded Earl of Acton has such a sad lack of paternal feeling?"

"Because I overheard him say so at King's Acton, if you must know. Since his voice rang like the church bells, I could hardly help but hear it."

"I can imagine," he said dryly.

Helena knew she was scarlet. "Eavesdropping is not actually an everyday pastime, just one I wallow in on Sundays."

"And no doubt you learned much more for your edification. You may have married into my family, Helena, but I advise you not to indulge yourself in too close an acquaintance with them."

"And what about Harry?"

Richard had thrown off his coat and was washing Bayard with his handkerchief made wet in the stream. The water ran pink off the animal's flanks. He stopped for a moment and turned to face her again.

"I would particularly recommend that you don't try to interfere with Harry."

"How can I avoid it when he breaks into the house in the night? And what was he doing so conveniently on the scene today? It has not escaped my notice that he had just left you when you were shot in the arm. Is Harry always around when your life is endangered?"

"No, as a matter of fact, he is not. What are you trying to say, Helena?"

"That it seems to me that it would have been very convenient for Harry if you had gone over this cliff with Bayard today!"

"But I didn't, did I? For God's sake, Helena. I don't remember seeing any Gothic romances in the library at Trethaerin that would account for such an overactive imagination. Harry is my brother!"

"Yes, exactly," said Helena.

Nine

Several men followed Harry up from Acton Mead. The procession was led by the estate manager riding a sensible white cob, and brought up in the rear by a stout wagon drawn by two massive Suffolk draft horses. Various ropes and pulleys and bundles of canvas seemed to be piled on the wagon, and Bob was tied on behind with another great Suffolk Punch. Some of the men were walking, but most were perched among the rescue equipment like birds in a nest. Harry was mounted on a hack and was entertaining himself by cantering in circles around the cavalcade.

Helena had followed Richard back out from the wood, leaving Bayard standing quietly by the stream. Instantly the men were deployed and they leapt to obey as if Napoleon's troops lay hidden among the oak leaves and shrubs, instead of the innocent creatures of an English wood. The wagon was left at the bottom of the hill, while some of the men were sent into the gorge and others followed Richard back up the narrow trail, bringing the single Suffolk Punch with them. Helena watched in amazement as Harry was sent scrambling up the tallest oak, a large pulley in hand and a coil of rope over one shoulder. Meanwhile a sling was being fashioned out of canvas and Richard tossed it over the edge of the cliff to the men waiting below. The chestnut coat of the gargantuan cart horse gleamed and rippled over his powerful muscles as he was harnessed to the other end of the rope and Richard gave the signal for him to be led forward. The horse strained, and the rope pulled taut and groaned in the pulley. Sitting above them in the tree, Harry began to chant gently.

"An earl's son rode perfectly well/But was languishing under a spell/It was cast by his wife/And near cost him his life/When his horse tried to send him to hell."

"Are you trying to suggest, dear brother," said Richard, "that this accident was my wife's fault?"

"I've no idea how it happened," laughed Harry, dropping to the ground. "I wasn't here, worse luck! Either old age is softening your faculties or it's the disturbing presence of Helena. But I do have to admit that it seems the oddest thing for you to let your horse fall off the path on Marrow Hill!"

"Senility, obviously," said Richard calmly as Bayard was hauled up over the rim. The horse had been blindfolded and his legs were caught in an elaborate cat's cradle of rope, so he couldn't struggle against the canvas sling that had been placed under his belly yet could still gain some purchase on the surface as he was dragged over it. His body was bundled in more canvas and padding, and each leg had been wrapped in cotton and bandages. The Acton Mead grooms had no doubts as to quite how precious this horse was to their master. Richard instantly began to talk to him, and with the help of Harry and one of the men, managed to position the charger so that his hooves would land on the track. Bayard scrambled a little as he felt the solid ground once again, then stood quiet under the soothing hand of his master as the sling and the ropes were removed. With infinite care and patience, Richard gentled him down the path and the horse followed as faithfully as a puppy. At last they reached the wagon that had been backed against a shallow bank and, limping seriously, the charger was led aboard. Richard stayed by his head and directed the men to whip up the team. Bayard was to be carried home.

Helena had picked up Richard's jacket when he had dropped it beside the stream, and throughout the proceedings she had hugged it to her, as if by shielding his clothing she somehow could protect him. As she looked at the confident, carefree way he stood on the wagon, it suddenly seemed the most absurd emotion.

"You might want this garment again someday, Richard," she said casually, and with a smile she held it out to him. As she did so, something pricked her hand and brought up a bead of blood. Without thinking, she felt in the pocket, and gasped as her hand was punctured again.

"You will find something smooth and hard with a vicious point," said Richard quietly so that no one else could hear. "I pray you will not take it out and cause too much of a frisson of excitement among the tenants. There were in fact two of them, but the other must have come out and been lost on the cliff."

"It's some kind of dart!" exclaimed Helena, instantly withdrawing her hand.

"Exactly. But don't, my dear, set up the hue and cry, will you?"

She looked down, biting her lip, and without another word gave him the coat, but she could have screamed aloud. Bayard hadn't tried to kill his master at all. Someone else had. Someone who had hidden in the woods with a blowpipe or bow of some kind, or maybe just a strong throwing arm and a deadly aim, and had felt no compunction in wounding an innocent beast if it might hurt his rider. Someone had just tried to kill Richard! And Richard was going to cover it up.

The team of Suffolk Punches leaned into their harness,

and Richard soothed Bayard as the horse shifted restlessly at the movement beneath his feet. The estate manager rounded up the men and equipment, and they began to move off after the wagon. Harry turned to Helena.

"It's left to me, sister-in-law, at Richard's imperious request, to escort you back to Acton Mead, scene of all our boyhood rivalries."

Helena looked sternly at Harry as he saddled her horse and met a glance of pure astonishment in return. For a moment she wished she were a man so that she could call him out. Did Harry think it was a prank to shoot a man in the arm, or send vicious darts into his horse on the edge of a cliff? Instead, she allowed Harry to toss her into Bob's kindly saddle. But none of Harry's nonsense or teasing would make her do other than ignore him.

Richard spent the afternoon with his horse in the stable and Harry assisted him. Bayard was stitched up here and there, and his injured legs packed in precious ice. A bran mash was received with elegant condescension and the charger deigned to accept a carrot or two, but he turned up his velvet nose at his hay.

"Not surprising he's off his feed, after what he went through," said Harry.

"I imagine I would be justified if I went off mine as well," answered Richard with a dry grin. "Look at this."

He held out his hand. Lying in the palm was the thin metal dart that had pierced Helena's finger.

"What a nasty thing," said Harry quietly.

"I don't know that I mind for myself." Richard turned the weapon in his hand. Sunlight ran up and down the slender shaft and struck bright colors in the feathering at the end.

"Though I can think of ways in which I would prefer my enemies to make their point. But I mind a great deal for Bayard. Why the hell can't you either be more efficient or stay out of my affairs altogether?" He spun and threw the dart with deadly accuracy across the barn so that it pierced through the string holding up a bundle of hay nets and hung quivering in the wall.

Harry was busy packing ice into a leather boot around Bayard's damaged tendon. His face was impossible to see. Richard had lost his temper for only a moment, but it was sufficient to prevent Harry from telling him something that he very much needed to hear.

It was not enough to prevent Harry from resuming his irrepressible good humor at dinner. Helena had spent the afternoon in considerable distress. So she was not to be allowed to interfere between the brothers even when Richard's life was at stake? Yet surely her position in the house as Richard's wife brought her some rights? Acton Mead, for better or for worse, was her home, and Richard had made it clear that he was giving her full rein over the running of the household. In which case, if people broke in during the night and scattered suits of armor about the hallway, it was her business. And if her husband was wounded by a bullet and then almost thrown to his death by his horse? She would not mention the dart that had caused Bayard to panic even if it had created a painful puncture in her own palm, but she was damned if she wasn't going to let Harry know what she thought of him.

So as the soup plates were removed and the rack of lamb with mint sauce was set on the table, Helena primed her guns and delivered the first broadside.

"I have been in an agony of indecision, Harry, over whether you were trying to convince me of your venality by breaking up Sir Lionel in such a rude way last night, or if you just don't know any better?"

Richard's black eyes darkened into velvet. "We shared the same upbringing, Helena," he said instantly. "So if you find Harry's manners wanting, you had better watch out for mine."

He should not protect his brother! "In that case, since, as everybody knows your manners are a model of perfection, Harry must just have been intent on turpitude."

"Baseness, vileness, or an excess of wickedness?" laughed Harry. "Dear sister, I seem to have been basely, vilely, and excessively drunk. I plead guilty!"

"Do you?" said Helena, calmly watching as the maid served them with cauliflower. "In which case, I suppose you had no nefarious purpose in entering the house at midnight through a window instead of presenting yourself at the front door like a normal human being."

Richard had leaned back in his chair and was casually studying his wineglass. There was the faintest quirk at the corner of his mouth.

"Well, I don't suppose I am a normal human being," said Harry thoughtfully. "I'm an Acton, after all; we're an odd breed, you know. And anyway, the front door is locked at night."

"So your attack on poor Sir Lionel was innocent?"

"Oh, no! Of course I had a nefarious purpose!"

"Which was?"

"This!" said Harry dramatically, producing from his pocket a sheet of paper and waving it across the table. Richard laughed aloud.

"For God's sake, Harry!" he said. "Helena will think you belong in Bedlam!"

"Well, if you would allow me to see that object," said Helena quickly. "Perhaps I could judge for myself?"

"I brought it for that very purpose!" announced Harry, and the sheet fell into Helena's hand.

"It's an announcement," she said, surprised, as the garish colors and swirling print stared up at her from the paper.

"Indeed, sister! For a grand fair!"

"With jugglers, and acrobats, and—elephants?"

"I had to inform you both right away. The darn thing will be in Reading tomorrow! Elephants, indeed!"

"What on earth makes you think that I care to see elephants, Harry?" said Richard.

"Oh, you're so damn jaded, even if Leviathan were to raise his ugly snout from the deep or the Chimera to fly at this moment across the dining room, you would only raise an eyebrow and possibly sneeze in an elegant way."

"I'm not sure a sneeze can be elegant," objected Helena. She was entirely out of her depth. If Harry had tried to murder his brother only this morning and Richard knew it, how on earth could they sit together at table and talk arrant nonsense to each other?

"Then you don't know your own husband, sweet Helena," said Harry instantly, which since it was true, left Helena with no possible response. "Nothing he does is without elegance."

"There is also to be a lion." Richard had picked up the bill where Helena had dropped it on the table. " 'Most Magnificent King of Beasts from Barbary,' " he read aloud. " 'Trained to Leap through Hoops. Amazing Feats of Acrobatic Prowess'—I'm not sure if that's referring to the lion or the jugglers—"

"Or the elephants?" interrupted Harry. "Helena, I am sure, has never seen an elephant!"

"Have you?" asked Richard turning to her.

"I grew up in Cornwall," said Helena. "Where even though we have unicorns behind each sand dune and the giants Corineus and Goemot are reliably reported to have fought on Plymouth Hoe, we don't grow elephants."

"Then we shall go to Reading tomorrow and admire the menagerie," said Richard.

"And the jugglers and the acrobats," added Harry. "And the Learned Pig, and the dairymaids all in a row."

"We don't need to hire any dairymaids," said Richard. "But no doubt there will be any number of stalls bearing entrancing merchandise. Helena, you must be waiting with wild impatience."

"So that I may pursue the female pastime of spending money?" asked Helena.

"So that you may be entertained with the absurdity of human ingenuity, my dear." Richard's long fingers took up the wine and he refilled his brother's glass. "And no doubt Harry will take part in the shooting competition?"

"I'll do my best to bring away all the prizes for the sake of family honor, Dickon, never fear."

"Fear is something I don't waste my time with," said Richard firmly. "I thought you would know that about me by now."

Helena knew exactly the opposite feeling. She was very afraid and she picked instantly on the piece of the conversation that mattered.

"Don't tell me you're a good shot, Harry?" she asked innocently. "Can you do better than wing your bird and ruffle its feathers?"

Harry's blue eyes narrowed in indignation and Richard

threw back his bright head and laughed. "Wherever did you get that idea, Helena?" he said. "My little brother is a crack shot. I'm sure he will be only too pleased to demonstrate his precision and his excellent eye for a target tomorrow."

Which was the very thing that Helena was afraid of. The other thing she was afraid of happened that night.

Ten

Richard did not come to her bed. Was it only last night that she had awoken to the sound of his moan and he had let down the impenetrability of his defenses for a moment? She could still feel the sensation of his long fingers brushing through her hair and the caress of his lips on hers. She buried her face in her hands. It was too short a time to have moved from the fear of a man's desire to a longing for it, but she hungered for the feel of his strength and warmth beside her, and the rush of answering heat in her own limbs. Helena looked up and caught sight of herself in the mirror.

"For heaven's sake, dear girl," she said aloud, and laughed at herself. "You are pining like a ninny!"

The footman had come in after dinner and said that Richard's presence was desired in the stable. Bayard had taken a turn for the worse and the gentlemen's opinion was wanted. He and Harry had immediately taken their coats and gone out. Helena knew nothing about horses other than that they were a convenient way to get about, but she knew what the charger meant to Richard. She could hardly resent it if he was going to spend the night in the stable and not in her bed. Bayard was surely a much better rival than the beautiful Marie in London!

Nevertheless, she was aware of dismay, because it meant that the moment of understanding they had achieved had been lost, and who could say if it would ever happen again? She was cut out of his life and his concerns. Richard didn't need her. And that was what she was afraid of.

They rode to the fair in the curricle. Bayard was declared out of immediate danger, but he would be laid up for ten weeks. So the matched grays Richard had purchased in Exeter trotted through the dust and the first falling leaves of October in the lanes, pulling the curricle with its three passengers and two servants. The fair was laid out in a large field between Reading and Henley. The sound hit their ears long before their eyes were assailed by the brilliant variety of color and shape. The noise came not only from several thousand animal and human throats—the latter laughing and screeching and touting and singing—but from organ grinders and trumpets and Gypsy violins, and underlying the whole disharmony, the counterpoint of a brass band, manfully pumping out the popular tunes of the day.

The first sight to greet them as they jostled along the road with a cavalcade of other carriages and horsemen and sturdy walkers was an impromptu horse race. Several young bloods, considerably the worse for drink, were matching their steeds against one another to the accompaniment of serious wagers and even more serious boasting.

"If Bayard were not nursing the headache, he'd leave all those sorry jades in the dust," said Harry.

"Very likely," replied Richard dryly. "But he is sorely hung over, like a lord. There is the elephant."

They had turned off the road with the procession of equipages, and the fair was laid out before them like a feast. Booths of colored canvas, bravely sporting flags and bunting, were laid out in staggered rows in the sun. Beyond them seemed to be acres of pens where sheep and cattle waited to be judged or sold. A gaggle of boys ran by after a hoop, followed by a ragged assortment of dogs. The entire pack instantly became entangled with a furious farmwife, who had brought her cow to the edge of the field and was selling fresh milk. The hoop bowled right between the cow and her stool and upset the pail over her skirts. The cow let out a kick and caught one of the boys in the knee to the accompaniment of much screeching. The dogs began to bark.

At the end of the first row of tents stood a Punch and Judy show, where the ancient characters forever reenacted the standard domestic drama, to the appreciative roar of a crowd. After that it seemed that anything and everything was for sale, as long as it was either colorful or savory. Peddlers went up and down the ranks of booths, hawking ribbons and pins and hot mutton pies. Some booths seemed to be offering mysterious sights, or a chance to shy at an apple for a farthing, and one held nothing but gingerbread.

Helena saw it all in a blur. Her attention was riveted on the dusty gray back that rose like a mountain in the center of the confusion. As she watched, a long, supple trunk rose like the neck of a swan and the elephant blew hay all over its back.

Richard handed the reins of the curricle to his tigers and handed Helena down onto the grass. "We shall have to run the gauntlet of the entire affair in order to visit Behemoth," he laughed. "Stay between Harry and me."

With a natural, unconscious courtesy, Richard tucked her hand into his arm, and they set off. The crowd instantly swallowed them. Merchant and laborer, beggar and gentleman, even the occasional lord, were welcomed into the noise and clutter and confusion without discrimination. Helena clung to Richard's arm as if it were a lifeline.

"Relax, dear heart," he whispered in her ear. "Harry is right with us. He can hardly take a potshot at me when I have him in plain sight, can he?"

Helena looked up at his face. He was laughing.

"Then you concede everything?" she hissed back, astonished.

"I will tell you anything that will make you relax and enjoy yourself," he replied. "Now, I beg you to do so."

Helena looked away in confusion. If Harry were indeed yesterday's assailant, then it was true he was unlikely to harm his brother when walking beside them in the crowd. If not, how could any enemy possibly reach them when they were buried in such a milling throng? Besides, the very nature of the occasion seemed to preclude the very possibility of any dastardly act. She glanced back at Richard and smiled.

"To be honest, I am vastly more interested at this moment in the elephant," she said.

It was not necessary in the end to elbow their way to the menagerie, for the country people courteously made way for the gentry, yet the density of the crowd made it inevitable that they should be jostled.

"Anyone who deliberately bumps us is a pickpocket," said Richard in an aside to Helena. "Hold on to your purse."

The Magnificent Menagerie turned out to consist of one mangy lion who lay slumped in a horse-drawn cage, and a trio of monkeys that leapt and rattled at their bars in the next cart and screeched at the crowd.

"He may be Trained to Jump through Hoops," said Harry, putting their coins in the cup, "but it's the monkeys doing all the jumping. Ah, Behemoth at last."

They were face-to-face with the elephant. Helena gazed with awe at the huge monster. Its very skin seemed to her to be as ancient as the hills. She couldn't take her eyes from the great sail-like ears and the tiny, wise eyes that stared back into hers. The elephant lifted its trunk and carefully picked up a single wisp of hay which it carried into its delicate pointed mouth.

"It's wonderful," she breathed.

A tiny brown-faced man in a turban stepped bowing before them. "The lady would wish to survey the world like an Indian princess?"

Before she could reply, Richard said something in the oddest language she had ever heard. His face wreathed in smiles, the elephant keeper replied in the same tongue.

"Good God," said Harry with a grin. "Are we witnessing secret messages or about to be carried off into sacred Hindu rites?"

"Neither," said Richard. "We merely exchange courtesies—and at four, Behemoth gives rides for a guinea. Are you game?"

"You could never keep me from it!" said Harry instantly. "Lady Lenwood, may we prevail upon you to ride with us upon this mighty beast?"

"I am not even much of a horsewoman, sir," laughed Helena. "Does the elephant have a saddle?"

"She will have a little basket attached to her back. You would be quite safe," said Richard.

"Then I won't quail either. At four I also intend to ride the elephant."

Richard suddenly lifted her hand to his lips and kissed her fingers. "Until then, we have the rest of the fair!"

At one end of the field there had earlier been a hiring fair, where dairymaids and shepherds, laborers and housemaids, had put themselves out for hire for another year, each wearing the badge or carrying the tools of their trade. Those who had been hired were now disporting themselves and spending the shilling they had received as a token from their new masters. The young men were also taking part in uproarious games: leaping, running, climbing a greased pole, a blindfolded wheelbarrow race in which the participants seemed in serious danger of deadly injury. The prizes might be a shift or a pair of breeches, but the fame and glory attached to winning and impressing the girls provided equal motivation. To her amazement, Helena found that many of the gentry were laying wagers on the outcome of the competitions, and a few sprigs of the aristocracy had even laid by their jackets to take part.

They left the games and wandered down between the stalls. Soon Helena found herself buying things after all. Amid the tawdry and the glitter were also examples of the highest craftsmanship and good taste, and then they came across the exotic imports at the apothecary's stand.

"Oh, look!" said Helena, pulling out her purse. "Galls of Aleppo!"

"And what, in heaven's name, is that?" queried Harry.

"A growth in the bark of the Mediterranean gall oak," said Richard. "A short, thickset cousin of our English oak."

"But the best blue ones come from Aleppo!" said Helena. "I used to get them from a traveling peddler in Cornwall. Nothing makes better black ink. One and a half pounds to six quarts of rainwater with eight ounces of green copperas, eight ounces of gum arabic, and two ounces of roche alum. The addition of a little salt and brandy will prevent the ink from either molding or freezing. To think I wasted time making ink with lampblack!"

Harry looked completely astonished. "But what do the galls do?" he asked.

"Make a superior black dye," said Richard with a laugh. "Come, wife, how many pounds do we need?"

Helena was soon laden with packages, and they went back to their carriage for lunch. Mrs. Hood had packed a picnic which was supplemented with fresh gingerbread and a hot mutton pie purchased by Harry. It was the merriest possible meal. Helena could hardly believe that she had ever been concerned either for Richard or about his brother. Perhaps both of the frightening incidents had just been accidents, after all? A stray shot from a poacher, a malicious trick from a child with a dart who didn't understand how dangerous the consequences might have been. Murder and mayhem seemed very far away from this bright English field.

"We haven't seen the Learned Pig yet," said Harry at last.

"Nor have we demonstrated our prowess in the shooting gallery. Come along!" replied Richard, getting up. "Helena will think the Actons are a sorry pair."

The Learned Pig turned out to be a perfectly ordinary little sow who followed her trainer like a dog—until she was presented with problems of arithmetic and with stamps of her little cloven hooves was able to rap out the correct answers. The crowd roared with appreciation.

"I declare," said someone behind them, "it's a miracle!"

"Surely," whispered Helena to Richard, "the pig can't really count?"

"Watch the trainer instead of the animal."

As the next problem was posed to the pig, Helena kept her eye on the man. Sure enough, she could see that he was making small nods of his head as the pig counted. She laughed. "It's still very clever," she said.

"No doubt," said Richard with a wink, and they moved on.

The shooting gallery was not set up like Manton's in London, where gentlemen could practice their aim and try out fine weapons before purchase. Instead, with a backdrop of a hayrick and a target of a row of coconuts, the prize of a bunch of blue ribbons and a guinea was being offered to anyone who could shoot six nuts in a row without missing. Several gentlemen had already tried and a few had succeeded, but it was a long shot with an unfamiliar pistol. The guinea received as a prize was dwarfed by the amounts being laid amid much jocularity in wagers.

"I wager you six——" began Harry.

"No, you don't," interrupted Richard instantly. "I know better. Win the ribbons and be content. You shan't get the contents of my purse as well."

With a laugh, Harry paid his fee and took up the pistol. Helena didn't really doubt the outcome. Her brother-in-law gave her a wink, then carelessly raised the weapon. The six coconuts fell in a row, spilling their milk one after another.

"Your turn," said Harry, pocketing the guinea and presenting the blue ribbons to Helena with a bow.

Richard picked up the pistol and took careful aim. Helena held her breath. She very much wanted him to do as well as his brother, and then she castigated herself for such an unworthy thought. What did it matter? To her delight, the first four coconuts joined their fellows in the grass, but the fifth shot went over the target and thudded into the hay. Harry had gaily jolted his brother's arm from behind.

"I should reserve this last bullet for your skull!" said Richard, but he was laughing.

Harry bowed, a picture of contrition, and Richard fired again. But his concentration was broken and the sixth shot grazed by the target.

"You have failed, sir!" said Harry. "Had you taken my wager, I should never have been able to interfere in honor with your aim, but now Helena will never know if you can shoot better than a poacher."

"I can shoot well enough, brother," said Richard. "But I shall never be as good as you. Besides, poachers are quite often good shots."

Helena said nothing. If it was a poacher who had wounded Richard, thank God he wasn't better.

"And now it's time for the elephant."

They left the young bloods still laying bets on the death of the coconuts, and walked back to the menagerie. The elephant had been saddled with a bright red and gold contraption and, freed from her chain, was being led out of the crowd to a rickety-looking platform with steps, where anyone brave enough to mount her could climb to their perch. There was a thick stand of trees behind the open space in which she could ponderously parade up and down with her expected burden of squealing maids and shouting men.

As they appeared through the crowd, the man in the turban saw Richard and waved to him before calling out something in the language they had used before.

"I am summoned," said Richard, "by our Indian friend. He wants my opinion of his magnificent harness. I shan't be a moment."

And with that, he bowed and left Helena with Harry as he slipped through the rope that kept back the spectators, and walked up to the elephant.

"Good God," said Harry. "Stay here!" And leaving Helena alone, he ran for the trees.

The elephant suddenly threw up its trunk and bellowed, the little eyes no longer kindly and wise, and tearing away from the grasp of its handler, lumbered into a canter and began to bear down on Richard, defenseless in the open. The mahout called out and took up a hooked iron staff and vainly tried to grab at his pet as it thundered away. Now he was running after the huge lumbering feet and shouting. Helena, against her nature and her training, screamed.

Yet surely Richard could duck out of the way? The maddened elephant, trunk in the air and ears wide, seemed to be oblivious of the slight figure of the man who stood in her path. Meanwhile the crowd had begun to panic and a mass of people surged back away from the rope. If Richard didn't move immediately, then he would be trampled and the elephant would plunge into the spectators. Using all her strength, Helena hung on to the rope and watched, eyes wide. Richard changed his grip on his cane, and as the elephant was almost upon him, he leapt not away from the creature's feet, but as it seemed to Helena, right under them. Yet in the next instant he had caught a trailing rope on the animal's harness and then swung himself up behind its great ears and was straddling the humped gray neck. Using both cane and booted heel, he began to flail at the elephant's hide and speak sternly to it in Urdu. At the last possible moment, the giant turned aside from the crowd and stopped. The mahout rushed up and caught Richard as he slipped down from his perch, and, with tears running down his brown face, kissed him repeatedly. Then he ran his hands over his elephant and produced something which he showed to Richard.

"Some boy plays tricks, sir! It is not my little lady's fault! She is as gentle as a palfrey!"

Helena had slipped under the rope and joined them. Richard turned to her.

"Where's Harry?" he said.

"For heaven's sake!" cried Helena, her heart in her mouth. "Is that another of those darts?"

"Unfortunately so, my lady. Where's Harry?"

"In the trees," said Helena, pointing. And then she had to

run to keep up as Richard made straight for the place she had indicated.

Harry was kneeling under a spreading beech with a handful of darts in his hand. He looked up at them as they approached.

"Damnation!" he said. "Survived again, my lord?"

Eleven

They rode back to Acton Mead in silence. Richard would
not discuss in front of the tigers what had happened. Harry
seemed to be deep in a reverie of his own, and Helena felt
lost in confusion and fear. Who had lain hidden in the trees
to take the chance to attack Richard again? Did Harry have
an accomplice? Who else would want to murder her husband? There seemed to be no answer that made sense. But
she could no longer pretend to herself that these events were
accidents. Someone was trying to harm her husband and
didn't care who got in the way. The welcoming façade of
Acton Mead at last put a stop to her whirling thoughts. Mrs.
Hood appeared smiling on the steps. They stepped down out
of the carriage and Helena went up to her room to change
her dress for dinner, leaving the men alone together in the
study.

"We should be grateful," said Harry as he flung himself
into a chair and took a brandy from his brother, "that you
know so much about elephants. Though I have to admit I
had no idea I would ever get to witness your training as a
mahout! It was really rather splendid, you know."

Richard stood frowning down into the fireplace. "I
thought the attack on Bayard unconscionable, but this!" He
turned and fixed his careless brother with his black eyes.
"For God's sake! If I had failed, the elephant might have

plowed into the crowd. There were women and children at risk!"

"And Lady Helena Lenwood."

"Why didn't you stay with her as I asked?"

Harry sat up and met his brother's gaze. "I thought I saw someone moving in the trees. After what happened yesterday, I went to investigate. Unfortunately, I was too late. The man had gone."

"Scared off by your crashing through the underbrush, no doubt. For crying out loud, Harry, your place was with my wife!"

"I think you might for once express some gratitude, sir. Had I not disturbed the fellow, he might have fired another dart, then not even you could have tamed the indignant Behemoth!"

"I was in absolutely no peril, as you know very well. Yet you left my wife alone and in danger in the rabble. Will you do as you're asked next time, sir?"

Harry stood up and deliberately set down his glass. "You aren't Earl of Acton yet, brother," he said. "I am not under your orders. I have failed twice, I admit, but it was not for want of trying."

"There were three of these absurd attempts. Someone took a potshot at me when you left the first time. Luckily he was not as good of a shot as you, or the earldom would fall into your hands after all."

"As a matter of fact," said Harry, "I don't want the earldom! Perhaps it would be better if I did not stay for dinner?"

Richard leaned his head on his hands for a moment. "For God's sake, Harry!" he said. Then he straightened and walked to the sideboard where he poured himself a second brandy. "At least no one is trying to harm Helena, but my presence here has twice put her in danger. I'm going to go back to London. Perhaps you could on occasion look in and see that she's all right?"

"I'm not sure, Dickon," replied Harry with a rueful grin, "that she'll let me. Won't you tell me more about this sordid business you have involved yourself in? I would help you if you'd let me."

"No," said Richard slowly. "I won't. If these attacks are connected with the Paris affair, as I suspect, there is nothing you can do about that. Go back to Oxford and forget it."

When Helena came down, it was to find that Harry had gone. She allowed Richard to lead her into dinner and they made nothing but polite conversation as long as the servants were in the room. At last the viscount and his lady retired to the drawing room for coffee and were private.

"Where's Harry?" she asked immediately.

"The question of the day? I sent him off to Oxford," said Richard. "This time I believe he has gone there."

Helena locked her hands together and forced herself to go on. "Richard, in the last couple of days, three attempts have been made on your life. In each case, your brother seems to have been involved. He was certainly in the vicinity. Why on earth do you shield him?"

"I am not shielding him, Helena."

"For heaven's sake, my lord! Who else has had either the opportunity or the motivation?"

"Helena, don't go on with this. I have traveled the world, no doubt offending people as I went. Any one of a hundred could wish me harm. I assure you that Harry is innocent. Take my word for it!"

"How can I take your word? He supposedly rides away, but five minutes later you are shot and wounded in the arm!

That night, instead of having returned to Oxford, he breaks into the house. The next morning, a dart pierces your horse on Marrow Hill, almost casting you into the gorge, and he appears out of the wood! He disappears for a moment at the fair, then the elephant is stabbed and you are almost crushed and we find Harry in the trees with a handful of darts. What else am I to believe?"

"You could try believing me," said Richard gently.

"I can't," replied Helena.

"Then, my outspoken Helena, believe your own common sense! You saw for yourself my brother is an outstanding shot. If he had tried to take my life with a pistol, I would be dead."

"Unless he mistimed it and was too far away when you rode by. Perhaps next time the bullet will find its mark."

To her amazement, Richard laughed. "I don't believe there will be another bullet. These ventures are meant to look like accidents, and it would arouse a great deal of suspicion if I were to be shot at on a daily basis. As for Harry, he would never hurt a horse or any other beast, and he is far more efficient than the perpetrator of these bumbling attempts. Besides, no one who knew me would try to kill me using an elephant!"

"Why not?"

"Because, as Harry knows very well, I have lived in India."

"Then perhaps it is some kind of a game with him, Richard."

"Helena, I won't stand here and listen to this! Can't you trust me to tell you the truth about my own brother?"

"As you trusted me?" she said. "When someone went through your room? Who else but Harry would try to harm you?"

"I don't know. And I shan't stay here to find out. I am going to London in the morning." He smiled regretfully at her, but he seemed already preoccupied with other thoughts.

"I thought you had wanted Acton Mead," she said. Did he flee her because of these attacks, or was he missing his mistress?

"Then I suppose I was mistaken." He bowed formally. "Good night, my lady."

And leaving Helena standing alone before the fireplace, he walked out of the room. She had no idea when or if she would see him again.

Richard hired a four-horse chaise and armed his driver and tigers with pistols. He had no desire to die just yet. As an additional precaution, he kept a servant with him whenever he went outside his London lodgings. Assassination is easy enough. Richard had no romantic notions that his own athletic prowess could save him from a bullet or a knife in the dark. So far the attempts against him had been amateurish and insignificant. That would probably change. Four days passed entirely without incident as he quietly put back into motion his network to gather information about the Paris affair. The fog was thick for October, and London was empty of society when Richard walked quietly to his club one night, his man at his heels and every sense alert.

For some reason, he had not expected that it would come with such crude, overwhelming force. There seemed to be at least half a dozen dark shadows lurching at him out of the swirling mist. His servant went down right away under a heavy blow from behind, but instantly Richard's sword hissed from its cane and met the onslaught of attack. There was no room for pistols.

"Do your worst, gentlemen," he said, and slipped aside so that the first blow hit hard into the wall where he had just been standing. The fog might have allowed the attackers to take him by surprise, but he could use it too.

Then he found himself stabbing blindly at an unknown number of assailants who came at him with knives and cudgels. Keeping his back to the wall, he knew he had wounded at least two of them before a blow caught him from the left that almost broke his arm. He gasped aloud and his blade fell to the ground. The iron pipe swung again. In the next instant, he went down. With feet and hands and head, using every trick that his travels around the world had taught him, he dealt a series of disabling blows. In the next moment he had rearmed himself with a small dagger that he pulled from his boot and someone cried out as the knife found its mark. He was proving a more difficult adversary than these thugs had expected. The number of attackers still alive or able to fight was rapidly diminishing. At one point, above the grunts and curses of the brawl, he heard footsteps limping away— someone was hurt badly enough to give up. Perhaps he would make it, once again, by the skin of his teeth.

The next blow that struck him knocked the breath from his body, and as he felt his arm go limp, the dagger was lost among the cobbles. He saw the glint of light on steel, but was too winded to fulfill his sudden irresponsible desire to laugh. He felt blood well up on his shoulder as the metal was withdrawn for a second thrust. The bastard had found his sword in the dark. Then strong hands found and held him mercilessly spread-eagled as the attacker positioned himself for the final blow. Richard Arthur Lysander Acton, Viscount Lenwood and heir to an earldom, was going to die in an alley on his own blade and leave Helena Trethaerin a widow.

As he took a breath at last, it was only to allow the laughter full rein.

Helena awoke to the quiet sounds of the country. She dressed with her normal care and went calmly down to face the household. Richard was gone. He could not confide in her and he did not trust her, and not only because they were strangers. How long, she wondered dully, had he known Marie? Several years, perhaps? Did gentlemen talk with their mistresses, or only go to bed with them? Perhaps he really loved Marie and would have married her had she been eligible. She knew nothing of the life of a man like Richard. Her father and his neighbors had been simple country squires, content with the daily round and the local customs. They were none of them members of great families.

What kind of resources did Richard's family control? Enough to allow them to do as they liked, without regard to convention. Enough for Richard to have traveled to India and entertained himself learning Urdu and how to ride an elephant. She thought of that extraordinary journey up from Cornwall, where the treasures of his intelligence had been revealed little by little, like glimpses of some far bright country seen in a dream. He was too far above her in maturity and knowledge, in reading, in experience. What on earth could an ordinary mortal like herself offer in return? He had married her because she was poor and unconnected, so that she would not interfere with his life. One of Lord Salisbury's daughters would complain to her family if she felt neglected, but Helena had no one in the world beside Richard himself. She buried her head in her hands.

When Mrs. Hood found her, however, she was calmly sitting at her desk, writing an ordinary and amusing letter to her friend Catherine Hunter.

"There's post for you, my lady," said Mrs. Hood.

Helena took the letter and glanced at the wax seal. It was the Acton crest. She had seen it on the backs of all those ranks of chairs at King's Acton. Unfolding the paper, she glanced at the signature, then rapidly perused the writing.

"It would seem, Mrs. Hood," she said with a smile, "that we are to be honored with a visit from the countess."

"Master Richard's mother, my lady? Lady Acton? Well, bless my soul!"

"Bless all of us," said Helena wryly. "We had better start seeing to the best bedroom."

"'It is a beauteous evening, calm and free,'" quoted a man's voice quietly.

"Damn you, sir!" It hurt him a little to speak; he must have a cut lip in addition to the other injuries. "So far it has been anything but!"

"By Jove, he's coming around!" said another voice, both less cultured and more recently familiar. "I thought you was dead as a doornail, my lord."

The first voice continued to quote gently, but this time from another poem: "'Young Blount his armor did unlace/And gazing on his ghastly face/Said, "By Saint George, he's gone!/That spear wound has our master sped/And see the deep cut on his head!/Good-night to Marmion."'"

"'"Unnurtured Blount!"'" continued Richard softly, ignoring the pain. "'"Thy brawling cease:/He opes his eyes," said Eustace; "peace!"' Am I to assume that I am somehow in the presence of Charles de Dagonet, or do they quote Walter Scott in heaven?"

"If you would match the words of the poem and open your eyes, you could see for yourself," said Dagonet. "Of course, you have a splendid black eye, so it will probably hurt like the blazes. I have moved the candle aside, however, so don't fear instant blinding."

Richard slowly opened his eyes and in spite of his lip, grinned. "I never thought, sir, that your face would prove more welcome than that of angels, but it is, remarkably, the case." He tried to sit up and fell instantly back against the pillows. "Damnation!" he said.

"Yes," said Dagonet. "You are regrettably fenestrated. 'The breastplate pierced!—Ay, much I fear/Weak fence wert though 'gainst foeman's spear.' "

"It was my own bloody sword," said Richard with considerable irony, "that made the punctures. How did I get here? And where the hell am I?"

"You are in the spare room at my lodgings in Jermyn Street, sir," said Dagonet. "I beg you will accept my humble hospitality, at least until you are able to walk."

"How much damage is there?" asked Richard grimly.

"Surprisingly little, considering the amount of blood your man and I have been obliged to wash away. Of course, I don't suppose it was all yours. I refrained from calling a quack, knowing you share my distrust of the breed. He would have wanted to take yet more blood, and I believe you have lost enough, so we have patched you up ourselves. You seem to have no broken bones, though your face and arms sport a large number of unsightly bruises. Your shoulder is stabbed and there's another window closer to your chest. Had you not twisted that fellow's hamstring to break his grip as he tried to hold you down, and then managed to roll mostly out of the way, I believe the swordsman would have pierced your heart."

" 'And then made fatal entrance here/As these dark blood-gouts say.' If you witnessed that, then you must have appeared on the scene in time to prevent him from trying again. Thank you, sir."

"Unfortunately one of his friends managed to thump you on the head instead, as a parting blow, as it were. They didn't seem to be very well-bred."

Richard couldn't help himself, though it hurt abominably to laugh. "But you also had your sword cane, no doubt, and the rascals fled at your approach. Otherwise there would be a terrible pile of bodies for the watch to dispose of. I can only regret that I didn't stay conscious long enough to enjoy seeing you use your weapon. I assume you then carried me back here with the aid of my man, who by this time had regained his senses. Were you able to recover my blade?"

"The ruffian dropped it in his terror at my fearsome appearance. Your sword is now innocent of stain and returned to its case." Dagonet smiled and stood. "It would appear, dear Captain Acton, that someone doesn't like you very much," he said softly as he put on his coat. "But I think you must rest. No one knows you are here. I had planned on using this room for a manservant as soon as I can afford to hire one. In the meantime, it's yours. I, regrettably, am about to go out and gamble. I have just arrived in London myself, and it's time I savored her less wholesome delights."

" 'And all the ways of men, so vain and melancholy'?"

"I certainly can't put it better than Wordsworth, dear Acton. Farewell until tomorrow!"

Dagonet made his elegant bow before leaving the room. Richard closed his eyes, but sleep eluded him. His manservant, who had a sore head of his own, was soon nodding off in a chair beside the bed and the snores began to echo about the small chamber. There was no doubt of it this time. Someone wanted him dead, and if Charles de Dagonet had not happened along, this time they would have succeeded. Richard smiled a little ironically to himself. There had been times when it really wouldn't have mattered very much. Now, however, he wanted rather badly to live and he couldn't be quite sure why.

Lady Acton, Richard's beautiful mother, arrived at Acton Mead with three carriages, outriders, and her own servants, and announced that she would not be staying more than one night. She had more fashionable friends to visit, no doubt.

"And where is Richard?" she said as soon as she had removed her gloves.

"He is in London, my lady," replied Helena.

The perfect eyebrows rose a little above the lovely black eyes that her eldest son had inherited. "Then I am sorry to miss him. When do you expect him back?"

Helena knew to her chagrin that she had blushed. "I can't say, Lady Acton."

But Richard's mother did not, as Helena had expected, make any cruel comment. Instead, she smiled and led the way to the drawing room, where Helena had tea and cakes served immediately. The beautiful eyes surveyed the room.

"You would seem," she said archly, "to know how to run a house at least."

"I may come from the remoter corners of the realm, your ladyship, but we are not all savages there."

"I mean no such thing, I assure you. Does my son intend to take you to town?"

"I don't know," said Helena.

"Because if he does, you will need clothes. I recommend Madame Trouet. I use her for my own daughters when necessary. Of course, schoolgirls don't need much, but they must look a credit to their name when they visit friends in the holidays."

"They don't come home in the holidays?"

"Of course not! Acton and I will be with friends for Christmas and we can't have three girls who aren't 'out' trailing at our heels, nor can they rattle about alone at King's Acton. If they do not receive invitations, they can stay at school."

"For Christmas?" asked Helena, horrified. To be left at school when all the other girls went away to be welcomed home by loving families! "What about John? How old is he? Surely he can't be left at school?"

"John is a frightful handful," said Lady Acton with the slightest of elegant shudders. "At fourteen he has hardly acquired enough polish to grace a drawing room!"

"Then they can all come here!" said Helena instantly.

"My dear child," said Richard's mother with a little laugh. "You don't know what you're saying! I can hardly imagine that Viscount Lenwood would want his siblings under his feet at Christmas."

"I don't expect him to be home," said Helena, and as she said it, she knew with a sinking heart that it was true. Richard would be in London, sharing the holiday with his mistress. She had no idea if he would still be in any danger from his brother, but he seemed to treat the attacks very lightly. He must know that he really could handle Harry after all. Either way, there was nothing to bring him back to Acton Mead.

"No, of course, he will hardly rusticate here. Richard was the most difficult of my children, you know. He has always done as he liked." She sighed. "If you want to entertain his siblings, of course you are welcome to try. They all used to come here in the summer when the dowager was alive, as did Richard. It was convenient enough."

"Yes, he told me," said Helena. His words came back to her as clearly as if he were in the room: *It was the only place, I think, that we ever were happy,* he had said.

Richard's mother smiled. It seemed more sad than sarcastic. "You are doing a brave job of holding up your head by yourself, aren't you?" she said. And to Helena's amazement, she leaned forward and laid her hand over Helena's fingers. "He will never love you as want to be loved," she said. "Don't break your heart over him, my dear. Men aren't worth it."

Twelve

Richard was out of bed by the time Dagonet returned, a little the worse for lack of sleep, in the early morning. He had roused his servant and had the man bandage his wounds, then sent the fellow to fetch him new clothes. It was too risky to have him go back to their lodging, so the man had to go to Richard's tailor in Bond Street and purchase anew everything that the viscount would need. Then he would send the fellow back home. There was no use in endangering him also.

"Good God!" said Dagonet as he entered. "Apart from the interesting colors of your skin, you would seem to be arisen from the dead unscathed, like Lazarus."

"And hungry." Richard gave the other man a lazy smile. "I have taken the liberty of having my fellow fix us breakfast."

"And then?"

"And then I think I must discover who so urgently wishes my untimely demise."

The men sat down at the table, where Richard's servant served them with coffee, fresh bread, and a selection of meat and egg dishes.

"Then last night's little brawl was not an isolated incident?"

"It was the fourth attempt in the last ten days."

"Good God! Have you any idea why?"

Richard had been looking in a rather abstracted way at his plate of eggs, but he leaned back and laughed. "None at all! I thought my manners so impeccable that I had managed to scrape my way around the world without once giving offense. I swear I am innocent of enemies, Dagonet. I admit I have collected a rather motley crew of friends over the years, but . . ."

"Il est plus honteux de se défier de ses amis, que d'en être trompé?"

"Disgrace is more in suspecting a friend than being deceived by him—exactly."

Dagonet sat back in his chair and surveyed his companion. "What about that business in Paris?"

"A handful of girls were rescued and brought back to England, only to be immediately replaced. My man there finds no pattern to their procurement, and I have no idea who is behind it, but the villain can have no reason to kill me! Even if he knows that I have interfered, it has hardly put any serious dent in the operation."

"No, it seems extremely farfetched that he would find your existence intolerable. You can't have done more than mildly inconvenience him, and why wait until now?"

"Yet I can't think of any other reason for the attacks against me."

"If only what we found in Paris weren't so blindly tolerated by the law! Did you talk with your father as you planned?"

Richard's expression seemed closed to all emotion. "The Earl of Acton has no interest in changing the situation, though he admits his influence would go a long way toward so doing. He believes strenuously that government has no business interfering in the private affairs of gentlemen or regulating the working conditions of the less fortunate classes."

"Even when those private affairs are with children?" Dagonet's face also did not change, but his voice betrayed his disgust.

Richard stood and helped himself to more coffee. His movements were still noticeably careful and stiff. "We quarreled seriously about it, I'm afraid. It made my last visit to King's Acton even more frosty than I expected."

"And since then?"

"I have been otherwise employed. I have come into possession of Acton Mead, you see. I married Edward Blake's cousin Helena."

Dagonet raised a brow. "My felicitations, dear friend."

"It is a marriage of convenience for us both, of course; yet Helena is rather a remarkable woman. I really owe her more than to abandon her there." As he said it, he was surprised by the depth of his longing to see her again. "It's damnable that all this should begin so soon after our wedding. Two of the attacks put her in some danger as well. I can't in honor stay with her and watch the bullet take her life next time! It seems like an odd thing: I married to try to win some domestic peace, and instead find my very existence imperiled!"

"Then it would seem you must stay here until some kind of sense can be made out it. What will you tell your wife?"

"What can I tell her?" asked Richard. "That some of her countrymen are selling young girls into Paris brothels and her father-in-law sees nothing wrong with it? That her husband went to one of those establishments . . ."

"Yes, but not for that reason, sir. I was with you, so you malign us both to suggest otherwise!"

"But what difference can that make? No gently reared

female can be told any part of such a thing! Anyway, as I told you, it's a marriage of convenience. Helena is very self-sufficient. I don't suppose she'll miss me."

"Yet if you stay in London, sir, and display your rather unique coloring in public, there will surely be another attempt. *C'est guerre à outrance, n'est-ce pas?* It is possible that a reward is out for your death among the less-principled inhabitants of our noble capital."

"I have thought of that, Dagonet." Richard had eased himself back into his chair. Infuriatingly he was aware that at least one of his wounds was bleeding again. "But I fortunately have the solution. It is one that I used in North Africa."

He stood painfully once more and went into the bedroom, where his clothes from the previous night were still lying draped over a chair, and felt in the pockets. In a moment he was back and displaying some small round objects in the palm of his hand.

"What are those interesting members of the vegetable kingdom?" asked Charles de Dagonet.

"Something I stole from my wife," answered Richard with a grin. "Galls of Aleppo. But if you will excuse me for an hour or so, dear fellow, I think I must retire yet again to your spare chamber."

And with that he slipped gracefully to the floor. Dagonet bent over him and felt for his pulse. Viscount Lenwood was quite unconscious.

Helena now had the household running like clockwork and she began to take an interest in the estates. Acton Mead possessed a home farm that supplied the house with all of its meat, milk, cheese, fruit, and vegetables. There were also several properties leased to tenants, and she spent several

days in Mead Farthing with the agent, going over the books
and records. She then had the man take her out on a tour of
inspection. Everything seemed to be in excellent repair. Even
the farm laborers' cottages had snug roofs and pretty gardens. She wondered briefly whether Richard had played any
part in the good ordering of the estate, only to have the agent
tell her that Viscount Lenwood had seen personally to it that
he was the man hired and had been in constant communica-
tion with him, even though Acton Mead was not then legally
his. It confirmed everything she already believed about her
husband. He was an excellent judge of men and he cared
deeply for justice and fair treatment. Why, then, was he so
blind about his own brother?

"Dare I think, dear sister, that you are dreaming of me?"
said an amused voice.

Helena was sitting in the little courtyard enjoying the
sweet October sunshine. Leaves had begun to turn brown in
the home woods, but there was still a scattering of white
roses on the trellis where the warmth of the house had pro-
tected them from the early frost. She jumped and turned
around. Harry was leaning nonchalantly in the doorway.

"Mrs. Hood said I would find you here," he said.

"Good heavens, are you in the habit of creeping up on
people in their own homes, Harry?"

He came over and dropped onto the bench beside her. "I
am sorry, my lady. I should have had the footman announce
me. But I used to play in this house as a boy, you know. I
rather hoped I would be welcome."

Helena had no idea how to reply. Of all people, Harry
was the least welcome right now. She had bravely struggled
with her loneliness and her longing for Richard and tried
to fill her days so that she wouldn't actively miss him. No
doubt her husband was enjoying all the pleasures of Lon-

don with his mistress. Somehow for Harry to find her here alone and neglected made the humiliation that much worse.

"I can hardly deny family, of course," she said.

"But you would if Richard had not disallowed it, wouldn't you?"

"What do you mean, sir?"

Harry grinned. "Well, you aren't in the least happy to see me, are you? You are anyway reputed to have very little family feeling, my lady. I have met your cousin Nigel Garthwood, you see."

"Garthwood!"

"The same. I can hardly blame you if you don't want to see him: not the pleasantest of fellows. But he told me that you cared very little for your other cousin Edward Blake, who was killed. You don't even treasure a keepsake for his memory, I understand, even though you were to be married."

"I can hardly credit that you have discussed me with Mr. Garthwood! I have nothing of Edward's, but not because I didn't care for him! How dare you talk about me in such a way?"

"Because you have married Dickon, of course," said Harry. So she had nothing of Sir Edward Blake's after all. Why did Garthwood think that she had, and why was it so important to him?

"It would seem to me," said Helena, rising to her feet and with a sudden blush of color rushing to her cheeks, "that you are the last person to express concern for Richard! As for Mr. Garthwood, he is as welcome here as you are, sir!"

"Rats," said Harry. "I was rather afraid of that. But I will stop in from time to time nevertheless."

"You really don't need to trouble yourself, sir."

Harry stood and made her an elegant bow, but his expression was irrepressibly merry. "Don't you think I should come and stay for some shooting?"

"I would prefer it, sir, if you did not even stay to take tea."

"But I'm under orders, my lady. I must. Though tea isn't necessary."

"Under orders?" said Helena, thoroughly confused. "Whose orders?"

And this time Harry laughed out loud before bowing again and striding away to the stable. "Richard's, of course," he said, and winked.

Helena plunged into the organization of the house. She had every room turned out and cleaned, and supervised the laying in of supplies for the winter. Then she found solace in the library. Among the ranks of leather-bound books, she discovered several titles that Richard had mentioned, and she devoured them. There were also geographic guides and travelers' tales. From the books about India she learned the history of that far-flung continent. He was there, she thought; he has seen all this. Did he go hunting tigers on elephants? No wonder he doesn't want to settle down at home. But then, why marry in order to gain Acton Mead if he didn't actually intend to live there?

It was almost November. The nights were now noticeably dominating the days, and most of the leaves were stripped from the trees to dance in the cold wind. The last petals from the white roses went skipping off to join them. Helena came up through the home wood from the village, where she had been visiting a sick family, and walked into the drawing room. A bright fire was burning in the grate and before it in a cut-off jacket and Eton collar was a boy. There was no mistaking those black eyes and the shock of yellow hair, but the hands were rather grubby and he looked as if he could use a good wash behind the ears.

"Hello," said Helena. "You must be John."

"Who are you? How did you know?"

"I am Lady Lenwood, your brother Richard's wife, and it was easy to guess who you are. Richard told me about you and you look just like him."

"Is he here?" said John hopefully.

"Well," said Helena, sitting down and waving the boy to a chair. "I'm afraid not, so I'll have to do at present. How can I help you, sir?"

"I wouldn't mind some tea, actually," said John. "I'm awfully hungry. I came all the way here in a wagon, you know. The blunt Pater sends wouldn't stretch to a seat in the post chaise. Then I walked up from Mead Farthing and came in through the blue-room windows. I say, it looks awfully pretty in there now."

"Thank you," said Helena with a wry smile. He had the family charm, obviously, as well as the good looks. "I'll ring for some tea—and cakes and scones, perhaps? First things first. Then I think you had better tell me why you have decided to visit."

Half an hour later, after the tray of tea and cakes had been reduced to a couple of cold cups and a scattering of crumbs, and John had manfully endured the hugs and exclamations of Mrs. Hood, Helena invited him to sit opposite her at the fireplace once again and begin.

"Well, I ran away, if you must know. Harris Major is an awful bully and he's been picking dreadfully on some of the little chaps, so some of the fellows and I thought we'd pay him back."

"What did you do?"

"We dumped all his clothes in the ditch in a pouring rainstorm. He's a horrid dandy too. You should have seen his face when he discovered all his collars and things all limp with mud."

"Yes, I can imagine."

"Well, Harris Major put up a frightful stink and we had to 'fess up. Three weeks detention and a whipping from old Mason for me—as ringleader, you know. I didn't see that it was fair at all, so I ran away."

"I see. And why did you come here?"

"I got a letter from Mater saying I was to come here for Christmas and I wanted to see Richard! He does live here now, doesn't he?"

Helena looked away from the pleading black eyes and busied herself with the tea things. "He's in London at the moment."

"Then can't I stay here till he comes back? I'll be on my best behavior, promise. Cross my heart and all that. I can help you with stuff and I'm awfully good at shooting sparrows. Richard will be pleased to see me when he comes home. He stopped by at school a few times and the other fellows weren't half jealous that he was my brother, I can tell you. One time he was in uniform, it was splendid! I do want to hear some more of his stories too. Richard really has the very best stories, you know!"

"Yes, I know," said Helena.

"Then I can stay! That's terribly decent of you, Lady Lenwood. You won't regret letting me visit here with you for a minute. Would you like to play a game of whist? I'm pretty good at whist."

And so Helena found to her amazement that she was laughing and enjoying herself for the first time since the fateful day of the fair, by entertaining Richard's little brother

John across the card table. He was good at whist. By the time she packed him off to bed, John had supplemented his pocket money with several shillings won from her purse.

The next day they went together to the village and John carried her basket. Helena could tell that he was really trying hard to act the gentleman, but on the way back she let him loose with his slingshot after sparrows and carried the empty basket herself. A few sparrows met an untimely shock, but less mayhem resulted than she had feared and a great deal of youthful energy was expended in the exercise. They came in together in the greatest good humor, and the weary youth who was finally chased into bed by Mrs. Hood had more than earned the additional five shillings extracted from his hostess across the whist table.

With a smile, Helena combed out her hair that night, thinking about some of the things John had said. He had all the family wit; he had even made up an impromptu limerick. Richard never had told her the end to those verses he had begun that day in the inn at Exeter. Then she shook her head and looked at herself in the mirror. She had one candle burning in front of the glass and was wearing only her silk night rail, since the dancing light from the flames in the fireplace cast a warm glow over the room. The daily walks in the brisk air had brought color to her face, but she was paying for it in the inevitable entanglements that resulted in spite of the bonnet that she wore. She was proud of her hair, but otherwise she really was quite ordinary looking. Was Marie a beauty? She ran the comb carefully through the last of the tangles. Then something moved in the shadows near the window and she felt the breath freeze in her chest.

The dark shape solidified into the tall figure of a man. He seemed to be clad from head to toe in black and gray: a midnight coat over gray breeches, plain black riding boots.

His face was carved by shadows and the hair lay like sooty thatch on his brow. As she recognized him, she felt a constriction in her throat that threatened to suffocate her.

"Don't stop," he said. "Your hair is irresistible. It's like a sheet of golden silk. I have never seen you comb it before."

"What are you doing here?" she said as the breath came back. "How did you get in?"

He smiled gaily and sent shadows running up the creases beside his mouth. She had almost forgotten quite the way that happened. "The traditional method, of course: up the ivy. I didn't particularly want to be seen."

Helena sat down suddenly at her dressing table. Her heart was bounding like a landed fish. Her limbs felt paralyzed. How did he expect her to react? "So the house is to be broken into once again?" she said shakily. "At least Sir Lionel didn't go rattling to the floor and shake the rafters this time. But suppose I had cried out and roused the household?"

"But you didn't. Thank you for your forbearance, my lady."

She watched him in the mirror as he bowed. The comb was taken from her hand and he bent to kiss her fingers as he did so. His hair was as black as ink.

"I have been wanting to do this for a very long time," he said. "It's so beautiful. I can't decide if your hair reminds me more of gold or of celandines."

And without a murmur of protest she let him comb her long hair over and over again, back away from her forehead, until it fell like a waterfall to her waist. The feeling was delicious. I have been so longing for this, she thought. I can't make any protest now!

The comb fell unnoticed to the ground as, still standing behind her, he gently slipped the silk from her shoulders and began to smooth her hair over her bare skin with his hands.

Helena gasped and bit her lip to stop herself from moaning aloud as the stroking reached lower and he brushed repeatedly over the soft flesh of her breasts. Heat began to run in rivers through her blood when he at last took the tips in his long fingers. She watched, fascinated, in the mirror as he bent his head and the sooty hair entangled with her own blond tresses, while he kissed the back of her neck and the pulse where it shook under his lips at her throat. And then he bent her head back to his and kissed her full on the mouth.

"May I take you to bed, my lady?" he said at last.

Vibrating in his hands like a violin, Helena could only nod and bury her face in his strong neck as he lifted her from the stool and carried her across the chamber.

He laid her on the sheets and smoothed her hair out over the pillow. " 'And all the faith,' " he quoted softly from "A Midsummer Night's Dream," " 'the virtue of my heart/The object and the pleasure of mine eye/Is only Helena.' "

Thirteen

"And what," she said lazily some time later, "have you done to your hair?"

"I have dyed it black, sweet wife," said Richard, sitting up in the disordered bed and swinging his legs to the ground. "Thanks to your foresight, the materials were to hand."

"You mean you took some of my galls of Aleppo? I thought I had been shorted by the man at the fair!"

"I plead guilty. I thought it might be better not to have such an obvious and garish yellow flag on my head for a while. As it happens, I was right."

"You didn't dye your hair black for a whim! Richard, what's going on?"

"I don't know, to be honest. But there's no danger anymore. You must trust that I can take care of myself. I've been doing it for a very long time."

"There is more that you could tell me. Richard, for heaven's sake, there is some huge mystery here, isn't there? And there is obviously terrible danger! Don't you think I have a right to know?"

"Don't, Helena. I can never tell you."

Helena closed her eyes for a moment. How could he make love to her as he had just done and then close her back out of his life? What lay between him and Harry?

"But you stay in London?" she asked at last.

"Helena, you must understand. There are some things that in all honor a gentleman cannot tell his wife."

"Of course," she said. "I didn't mean to pry."

How could she have been so clumsy? Whatever else was going on in his life, no man ever told his wife about his mistress. And maybe there really was no danger any longer. Perhaps if he stayed in London and lived quietly in disguise with Marie, Harry would leave him alone. It might be that it was Acton Mead of which Harry was jealous and there would be no more attacks as long as Richard didn't live there. None of it made any sense at all. Only one fact remained clear: He would rather live in London with a courtesan than at home with a wife.

"You must believe, Helena," said Richard at last, as if inexorably reaching the same conclusion, "that I would never deliberately hurt or deceive you. You are my wife and I owe you all the honor that the title implies. If I were free to do so, I would be here with you at Acton Mead. It was my original intent, but there is something that binds me to London just now. Be patient, I beg."

If he would not tell her, there was nothing more she could do. To continue to press him would only drive him further away. So instead she said, "Did you hunt tigers from the backs of elephants in India?"

He turned to her, surprised. "What?"

"I have been reading your books. In the library. The maharajahs go on great elephant hunts after tigers. Is that how you learned about elephants?"

He laughed. "Let me get a dressing gown and I'll tell you."

With that he strode to his own chamber, his body as lithe as a panther's in the flickering firelight. While he was gone, Helena slipped from beneath the sheets and recovered her night rail where it lay abandoned by the dressing table and her own silk gown from its hook on the door. Richard came back and led her to the chairs by the fireside. He had brought wine from his room and he poured two glasses.

"I learned to ride elephants from an old rascal in Bengal. They are remarkable beasts. And yes, I'm afraid I was obliged on later occasions to ride with a certain maharajah after tigers. Though it seems a sin against nature to try to bring about the death of such a terribly beautiful creature, for a tiger hunt they go to great and fascinating lengths of pomp and circumstance. Nothing could have kept me away. It was like being fed on a diet of syllabub for days at a time."

And with that he began to tell her about India. A place where the quality of light itself is different. The colors, the smells, the hubbub; towering mountains, dusty deserts, strange beasts, flowering plants; the life of a people with entirely different beliefs and culture and a unique view of the universe—nothing had escaped his notice. A picture of the exotic subcontinent began to weave itself at Helena's hearth like a rich silk tapestry.

"We have gone into their country with the greatest arrogance," he said at last. "With the view that England can teach everything to the world. But India is a great and ancient civilization, and I believe she will outlast us in the end."

He knelt and put more wood on the fire, then turned and looked at Helena. She seemed spellbound, her lips slightly apart.

"We have made the most dreadful mess of your hair," he said, and reached up to brush it back from her face.

She laughed, surprised. "It doesn't matter."

"Good, because I think we might do it again."

With that he pulled her from the chair to join him on the rug in front of the flames. Helena was not sure later how they had finally moved again to the bed. She knew only that she was being peeled like a withy, layer after layer, until her innermost soul lay stripped in his care. *With my body I thee worship,* she thought abstractedly. I never understood that before.

They awoke to the sound of rain trickling and gurgling in the gutters. A dull light seeped into the room and, taking his dressing gown, Richard strode to the windows and threw back the shutters. Then he rebuilt the dying fire before he came and sat on the bed beside her.

"I think I understand at last something that I heard in Exmoor," he said, twining a strand of blond hair around his fingers.

Helena gave him a puzzled look. Then she remembered. He had visited David Morris at Fernbridge and met the Hunter sisters there. Catherine had written to her about it and Richard had mentioned it himself when they first met at Trethaerin.

"What was that?" she asked.

"When Captain Morris introduced me to his future wife, he said: 'She is my peace.' Of course you know her, don't you? Amelia Hunter."

"Amy Hunter isn't a terribly peaceful person, though. She's as giddy as a top."

Richard smiled. "That's not what he meant. Are you ready for breakfast?" His grin told her that he was not thinking immediately of food.

Helena reached up her arms and touched the warm strength of his chest. "I'm starving," she replied. He began to shrug out of his dressing gown. At the sight of his body in the clear daylight, she gasped. "Good heavens, Richard! This is a new scar! And this! What happened to your shoulder?"

"Nothing very much, luckily. I was a little clumsy, that's all, and was unfortunate enough to be punctured."

He did not tell her that he had then been very ill. Charles de Dagonet had nursed him solidly through a dangerous fever. His sword had picked up some unwelcome filth on the streets of London before his attacker had sunk its blade in his flesh.

"You were attacked again! You said there was no danger!"

"Whoever dislikes me so intensely is looking for a yellow-headed gentleman, not a black-visaged vagabond. I am quite safe. I am staying where no one will find me."

Helena was instantly silenced. No doubt Marie had a very discreet house. Instantly her mood changed and she dropped her hands from him.

"What are your plans now?" she said at last.

"I am going to France."

He, too, seemed distracted. His illness had delayed him in his search for the unknown enemy. But it was time to move now. There was nothing more that England could tell him; the answer could lie only in the French capital. Dagonet had contacts with London's underground and would pass on any information he could find. He had already discovered that the ruffians who attacked Richard had indeed been paid by a gentleman to seek him out. It was not a random attack motivated by robbery, but then Richard had never thought for a moment that it was. No meaningful identity of the paymaster could be gained—the description could fit any of a hundred men. No, it was time to return to the lion's den: Madame Relet's nasty little brothel in Paris. "I couldn't leave without saying goodbye."

"Is that why you came here last night?"

"Among other reasons. And unfortunately, however insistent those reasons may be, I must leave again. I hadn't meant to stay with you so long."

And Helena grasped at the one thread of happiness offered. Even if he felt he must leave again, he had stayed with her the entire night and slept until morning in her bed. No nightmares had come to disturb their sleep; he hadn't thought it necessary to protect himself from her when he was at his most vulnerable. He might not be able to share with her the fact that he kept a mistress, or the perfidy of his brother, but he had broken his own rule. He had shared his sleep. She sat up in the bed.

"Then you might as well have some coffee and eggs before you go."

Richard laughed and, leaning forward, kissed her on the lips. "It wasn't coffee and eggs that I had in mind," he said.

They went down together to the breakfast parlor at last. John was already sitting at the table with his mouth stuffed with toast. As they came in, he leapt to his feet and hurled himself at his brother.

"Richard! Helena said you weren't here! What have you done to your hair? Are you in disguise? Oh, this is capital!"

"And what in heaven's name are you doing here, young man? Why aren't you at school?"

John shuffled his feet and refused to meet the eyes that were so like his own. Then he sat back down at the table and tried to look nonchalant. "I ran away, if you must know."

"Then you are about to return. Today."

"Richard, you won't make him! They're going to beat him!"

"All the more reason! I can hardly believe that a brother

of mine would be too much of a coward to face just punishment!"

"But it's not fair at all, sir!" wailed John, and the story he had told Helena poured out. To her surprise, Richard didn't seem in the least amused or sympathetic.

"Your reasons make no difference at all," he said sternly. "You took an action of your own free will and that action had consequences. A gentleman does not run away from what he has done because the results are unpleasant."

"But it was for a noble cause," said Helena. "John wanted to teach a bully a lesson."

"And did so, perhaps. But the virtue of his intent isn't relevant, nor is the efficacy, or otherwise, of his revenge on Master Harris. There is a price to be paid for well-meaning actions as often as for wrong ones. A man of honor is prepared to pay it, not bewail the fact that the world isn't fair, and he would certainly not hide behind the skirts of a lady."

"I'll get another drubbing for having run away," said John sulkily.

"And I trust you can face it like an Acton, sir."

Helena laid her hand on his arm. "Richard, this is intolerable! A note from you explaining John's side of the story would surely be all that's necessary. And he has stayed here at my invitation! If I had known he would be punished for being here, I would never have let him."

"You should have sent him back right away, Helena. By shielding him you have only made it worse! John, go and get ready, we leave in half an hour."

"Yes, sir!" said the boy, and with one apologetic look at Helena, he left the room.

"Richard, for heaven's sake! Why are you so hard on him? John is not even to be commended for trying to stand up against bullying? He's barely more than a child and he worships you!"

"Then I have a responsibility to see that he develops into a gentleman of honor!"

"Yet you will allow Harry anything, any license—even to attack you and wound your horse! Was Harry at the end of the knife blade in London? Is he the cause of the scars on your shoulder? Does his honorable development not count?"

"Stop! Helena, I have told you before that Harry is as trustworthy as I am myself. If you will not believe it, there is nothing more to be said."

"Then perhaps neither of you is to be trusted! Why did you send Harry here to spy on me?"

Richard looked truly astonished for a moment, but then his expression closed like a door. "I asked Harry to make sure you were all right, that is all."

"Then why is he so friendly with Nigel Garthwood?"

"What?" said Richard.

"He has been asking Mr. Garthwood about me and Edward! Was that also at your request? It's unconscionable!"

If she could only make him see that Harry was a threat to his life! He must be put on guard against his brother. But instead, she was only destroying whatever understanding they had reached the night before.

John reappeared in the doorway. "I am sorry if I caused you any trouble, Lady Lenwood," he said formally, and gave her a contrite little bow. She noticed with some satisfaction that his neck was considerably cleaner than it had been when he arrived. "Is it still all right if I come at Christmas?"

"I shall be devastated if you don't," she replied. "I must win back my money."

"Christmas?" Richard looked from one to the other.

"I have arranged it with your mother," said Helena with

a defiant dignity. "Unless you object, Eleanor, Joanna, and Matilda are all coming here, and John, too."

"Good God!" said Richard faintly.

"You'll be here as well, won't you, sir?" asked John.

"Very probably not," said Richard, and taking John by the shoulder, he steered him from the room. His brain was working furiously. He would indeed like to know very much why Harry had met Garthwood, but it could hardly be relevant to the matter at hand, and his passage to France was already booked. An interview with his brother would have to wait.

Helena went to the door to see them off. Bayard had been visited, but although he was well on the way to recovery, he remained in his stall. Richard was riding a nondescript nag that the groom had brought around from the stable. He would never be recognized by anyone who didn't know him well as either the Captain Acton who had ridden up the drive at Trethaerin, or as the Viscount Lenwood who had taken possession of Acton Mead. John was to be dropped at the gates of Eton by Coachman, who had turned out the curricle in preparation. The boy was loaded and the carriage took off. Richard stood holding the reins of his horse for a moment, then he glanced up at Helena, where she stood in the porch.

"Don't let us quarrel, Helena," he said suddenly. "I can't help what's going on now. It's something I have to do. But it doesn't involve you, and I beg of you to believe that it doesn't involve Harry. If it is making me into a monster, I rely on your infinite generosity to find it in your heart to forgive me." Then he smiled and winked at her. It was enough to make her want to forgive him anything, even Marie. "Good luck with the medieval princesses!"

He swung onto his horse and was gone. Helena puzzled for a moment over the reference to royalty, then she realized. He and his brothers were christened, although in the wrong order, for three of the sons of King Henry II. The Acton girls carried the names of his daughters. Had she bitten off more than she could handle by inviting them all to Acton Mead for Christmas? Fools rush in, she thought to herself. But she had done well enough with John, hadn't she, even if Richard didn't agree. Would Richard's sisters be that much more difficult?

Fourteen

December had arrived with a vengeance. Snow coated the roads and lay like a muffling blanket on the bare branches of trees as Richard rode his hired horse back to London. As he entered the slush-filled streets of the city, servants were sweeping the steps of the houses and some of the footmen had been assigned to climb onto the roofs and chisel away the ice from the corbels to the imminent danger of passersby. Richard's own lodgings had lain empty since the attack on him in October. He knew they were watched and he had no intention of further imposing on Charles de Dagonet. So he found a room in a cheap boardinghouse and gave his name as Mr. Lysander. The next morning, however, he walked swiftly to Jermyn Street. A manservant opened the door.

"Mr. de Dagonet is from home, sir," the fellow said stiffly. He was looking at Richard as if he thought he must have come to dun his master for debts.

"But has, like Merlin, magically reappeared when wanted. How do you do, dear fellow? By all means come in."

Richard turned. Dagonet, dressed in a many-caped greatcoat, stood behind him in the hall, brushing snow from his shoulders. There was a faint sheen of exhaustion lying over his features. The men went into the austere sitting room together, and the manservant disappeared to prepare a hot drink.

"So you have returned to grace our great nation once again with your presence, my lord viscount?" said Dagonet. "How was France? 'I traveled among unknown men/In lands beyond the sea;/Nor, England! did I know till then/What love I bore to thee.' I have also been away from London, but no farther than Marlborough, alas, where I made a bloody fool of myself. Don't ask me! Wild horses wouldn't make me reveal what I've done, and it's nothing germane to the Paris affair. Welcome home."

Richard dropped into a chair and waited until his friend was also comfortable. "France is unfortunately in an orgy of confusion, Dagonet. King Louis overflows his throne, but doesn't seem to realize that it shakes beneath him. Wellington is finding his post there as ambassador more and more difficult, and if it weren't that the great man refuses to leave whatever the danger, he would be safer in Vienna. There is a lot of discontent in France. If Napoleon were to reappear just now, I believe they would welcome him as a savior. Meanwhile the once-dispossessed aristocracy have descended on Paris like vultures. No excess is exciting enough: wine, women, corruption. It's as if they had learned nothing at all from Madame Guillotine."

Dagonet digested all this without surprise. "And Madame Relet?" he said quietly.

"Plies her trade, essentially unmolested. She finds me an amusement, to be brushed aside."

"I have come across nothing in London, Richard," said Dagonet. "The girls aren't coming from here."

"No, they're country wenches. From Somerset and Devon and Cornwall, mostly. Girls who believe they're about to better their lot, become ladies' maids or learn French millinery. If I could find the man behind this, I would strangle him."

"And are you any closer to revealing his identity?"

Richard stood up and crossed to the fire. His back was to his friend as he warmed his hands. "I have one clue," he said.

"Which is?"

Richard turned and faced the handsome features that were watching him so narrowly. "The word *Trethaerin*—not too common, is it?"

"Cela viendra," said Dagonet. His emerald eyes had not moved from Richard's black ones. "It should be easy enough to trace."

"There's no need, as it happens," replied Richard, his voice bleak. "It's already known to me: Helena Trethaerin is the name of my wife."

Dagonet was wise enough to say nothing as the other man returned to his chair and the servant came in with hot wine. As soon as he retired, Richard leaned back and closed his eyes.

"Have you ever been in love, Charles?"

"My dear friend, I'm a rake! But yes." He did not say that he was deeply in love at that moment. It was not the time for his own troubles to be aired; Richard needed his ear and his counsel.

"Edward Blake was her cousin. As he was dying, he spoke her name and it seemed he was pleading with me, although he couldn't articulate what he wanted. I thought he was begging me to protect her, and I swore to do so. As I told you before, I married her."

There was silence for a moment. A log fell in the fireplace and Dagonet rearranged it with the tongs.

"Suppose," Richard went on, "that I misunderstood him. What if Edward were trying to tell me what she might be involved in? Or that she was a person to be guarded against?

Supposing he was not trying to enlist my protection, but was warning me against her?"

"If that's true, dear friend, then you are in rather a damnable situation."

Richard leapt to his feet and began to stride back and forth. "There is no reason, you see, for whoever is masterminding this Paris affair to try to harm me. This visit to France has made that clear. All I can do is buy freedom for some of the girls, which only gives him the blunt to beguile more. With the law as it stands, the operation can't be touched. There's no difference in a thirteen-year-old girl gracing a Paris brothel or one in London, except that the children are being enticed there under false pretenses and are then alone and helpless in a foreign country."

"And you think your wife has been involved in this?" asked Dagonet incredulously.

"Whether she has or not, the attacks on me didn't begin until after we were married. I found her living at her old home, Trethaerin House, under the protection of her cousin Nigel Garthwood, an extremely unpleasant fellow. He may well be involved also. In fact, he's probably our mastermind. But if I die, Helena will come into possession of Acton Mead and a great deal of money. That's a comfortable prize for someone who has no scruples, wouldn't you say?"

"Richard, I can hardly believe . . ."

"Someone has been after my life, Charles! What other reason could there be?"

"Then alter your will and let her know you have done so. Divorce isn't easy, but you should be able to arrange it."

Richard dropped back into his chair and buried his head for a moment in his hands. Then he looked up at his friend and laughed. "The trouble is, you see, that I'm not sure that I want to."

Dagonet rose and poured him more wine, which he held out in silence. Richard took it and swallowed the entire glass in one draft. "I'm afraid that I have been damn fool enough to fall in love with her," he said. "And my oath to Edward, however wrongheaded, still stands. I have sworn to provide for her. I would just rather it did not take my death to do so."

"Then what do you intend to do?" asked Dagonet.

"Now that I know that you have discovered there is nothing more for me in London, I think I must go and see my brother Harry."

"And your wife?"

"I can do nothing better than stay away from her for now, don't you think? Because if I go to Acton Mead, I shall take her to bed. And it would offend every tenet I have ever tried to live by if I were to make love to a lady while entertaining suspicions that she has been hiring people to kill me."

The snow lay over the parks and trees of Acton Mead like sugar as Coachman tooled the carriage up the drive. Helena and Mrs. Hood ran to the door and waited impatiently for Mr. Hood to open it as they heard the horses stop and blow through their nostrils into the frosty air. The sound was instantly followed by some squealing and giggling. The medieval princesses had arrived.

It was Mr. and Mrs. Hood, however, who threw their arms around the three girls as they entered. Helena allowed the reunion to take place without interference and took a good look at Richard's sisters. Eleanor, the oldest, wasn't much younger than she was herself, and Helena was surprised that she was still languishing at school. Her face was flushed with the frosty air, enhancing a perfect complexion, except that the tip of her nose was a bright pink. But otherwise Eleanor seemed to have been bypassed when the family's good looks were handed out. Her hair was neither golden like Richard's nor black like Harry's; instead, it was a very ordinary shade of chestnut. Nor had she managed to inherit her mother's splendid eyes. The glance she gave Helena was candid and open, but it was a simple, friendly brown one. It was Joanna, at fifteen, who was the beauty, with Richard's eyes and Harry's hair. And little Matilda, whose coloring was entirely fair was going to become, in a few years, a serious rival to her sister.

"I can hardly formally welcome you to Acton Mead," said Helena as she shook hands with Eleanor and smiled at the other two, "for you must feel that it is more your home than mine. Richard told me you spent much of your childhood here with your grandmother."

"Which was entirely different," said Joanna. "We were little girls then. Why on earth did Mother insist we come here for Christmas? We never came here in the winter! I could have gone to Fenton Stacey with Lucinda Sail instead."

"Yes, but Milly had nowhere to go," said Eleanor quickly, "and neither did I. Don't you think it will be nice to all be together for the holidays?" She sneezed and had to apologize.

"Will Richard and Harry be here, too?" asked Matilda, known to her family as Milly.

"No," replied Helena. "But John arrives in a few days."

"Oh, no!" wailed Milly. "John's horrid! I'd rather have stayed at school with Eleanor."

"Well, we're here now," said Joanna. "I for one expect an absolutely boring time. But it's very kind of you to invite us, Lady Lenwood. I know how Mama can get her own way. We shan't be any trouble. Eleanor will keep John under control, I expect, and I'll just read in my room. If you let Milly go out and hang around the stables, that'll keep her occupied until we can get back to the academy. Mama must think it'll be good for our characters, I suppose, to be forced to rusticate for two and a half weeks and attempt to put up with each other."

"Well, you are welcome all the same, and perhaps we can have a good time. And since you are here, I would much rather you call me Helena." She didn't dare to tell Joanna that Christmas at Acton Mead had been her own idea. With a sinking heart, she wondered if it might turn out to be a complete disaster.

The next morning her worst fears were realized. Eleanor seemed to have caught a cold from the journey and was forced to stay in bed. Helena allowed Mrs. Hood to minister to her and tried to cope by herself with Joanna and Milly. All her suggestions for things they might do together met with a polite indifference. As she had promised, Joanna selected a book from the library and buried her beautiful head in its pages. It was snowing again and bitterly cold. When Helena was forced to forbid Milly a visit to the stables, the blue eyes filled with angry tears and the child stamped her foot.

"You're not the boss of me! I can do as I like!"

"I'm sorry, Milly, it's far too cold to go out. Maybe tomorrow, if it warms up."

"And only the family calls me Milly. My name to you is Matilda!"

And Milly ran off. All Helena's attempts to find her hiding place were in vain. Of course, the girls would know the house better than she did herself. Had it been terribly arrogant of her to think she could make them a home here and a refuge from the neglect of their mother? At least John liked her. Perhaps it would be better when he arrived?

The sun came out the next day and sparkled on a white landscape from a fairy tale. Helena visited Eleanor in her room, but her poor sister-in-law could do very little except smile wanly and blow her already reddened nose into a large lawn handkerchief. Milly had finally reappeared, but she was sulking and refused to respond to Helena's overtures, and Joanna did not come down to breakfast but insisted on drinking hot chocolate alone in her room.

"Since we have the breakfast table to ourselves," said Helena to Milly at last, "I think we might speak to each other. You may visit the horses today if you like, you know. The sun is quite warm and there's no wind."

"I shan't go out with you!" said Milly.

"Did you know that Richard's charger is here? Your brother rode him in the Peninsula with Wellington. His name is Bayard."

"I bet Richard doesn't let you near him, then."

"Well, I'm not very good with horses and I'm not a very good rider. You are much better, I expect. But Bayard was hurt at the beginning of October and he has been very gracious about accepting apple slices and carrots from me. Coachman has nursed him and he is quite better now, but I know he's very lonely for his master. Perhaps he would like to see you?"

"Can I have some sugar from the kitchen?"

"Of course you can. Why don't we go and ask Mrs. Hood now?"

Bayard nickered as he saw Helena and Matilda approach. His injuries had long healed and he was now allowed some well-blanketed turn-out time, but he had spent long hours cooped up in his box stall over the past ten weeks. Milly held out her sugar and the noble horse snuffled at her hand

and gently took it. The little girl turned very seriously to Helena.

"He likes me, you see."

"So he does. I knew he would. It took me a much longer time to make friends with him, but I found when I was lonely that he was a great comfort."

"Are you lonely?" asked Matilda, squinting into the winter sunshine.

"Pretty often," said Helena.

"Well, perhaps it mightn't be so bad while we're here. I'm not lonely—ever."

"How can you be when you have a companion like Bayard?"

Helena did not feel that they were friends when they came in together after inspecting the carriage horses and farm nags, but relations were considerably less frosty. Then Joanna met them in the hall.

"Where on earth are all the maids?" she said indignantly. "I can't find anyone and no one answers the bells!"

"Oh, I'm sorry," said Helena. "Did you need something? I'm afraid I gave the maids the day off to go out and gather greenery. Don't you think we should decorate for Christmas?"

"Are they going to bring holly and stuff?" asked Milly.

"How boring! Why would anyone ever fill the house with all that pagan nonsense? Mama never does at King's Acton."

"Because she's not there, I expect," said Helena firmly. "But I always honor the season in my house, and I'm going to go out and help the girls. Won't you come? You will, won't you, Milly? Would you go and see if Mrs. Hood has some big scissors we can borrow?"

For a moment she thought she had pushed it too far, but suddenly Milly ran off toward the kitchens.

"It's too childish!" exclaimed Joanna.

"Well, of course! But the maids love it and a good mistress must keep a happy staff. I rather hoped you would come, too, because I don't have any other lady to walk with."

"Oh, very well," said the beautiful Joanna. "I'll get my pelisse."

It was not possible to go out into the brilliant countryside and remain unmoved. The sunshine streamed out of a pale blue sky and leapt and sparkled from branch to branch and across frosted field and hedgerow. As Helena and the girls walked up into the woods, they were immediately surrounded by the gaggle of laughing maids who had been released from their household duties to pursue the age-old custom.

"Oh, my lady," said the understairs maid with an infectious giggle. "The holly is so full of berries and Peter from the stable has found some mistletoe. May we make a kissing bough?"

"Of course," said Helena. "But Mrs. Hood must oversee where it's to be hung."

"Thank you, my lady." The girl curtsied and ran off laughing to join her friends.

"What's a kissing bough?" asked Joanna. In spite of herself, she had become interested. The walk in the brilliant air had made the blood race in her veins, and it would take a marionette not to be caught up in the gaiety of the scene in the woods.

"We'll make one for the drawing room and you can find out. It's the greatest fun!" Helena was laughing, too, but her heart went out to these medieval princesses who had never even celebrated a traditional English Christmas at home.

They came home flushed with the exercise and the beauty of the estate. Mrs. Hood had hot scones and tea waiting by the fire, and Joanna so forgot her dignity as to squat beside the flames and hold out a scone to toast it. They then sorted through the boughs and branches they had brought in and Helena proceeded to teach the girls how to make a kissing bough. After a couple of hours with wire and scissors, and the provision by the kitchen of red and green apples, the creation was complete.

"It looks like umbrella ribs made from branches!" said Milly.

They had woven holly and ivy over a wire frame that the footman had bent into the correct hoop shape, then hung it with the apples and little stars and snowflakes cut from white paper. Joanna had taken charge of the stars and snowflakes, and hardly noticed that her dress was sprinkled with the clippings. In the center, in pride of place, Helena attached a generous sprig of mistletoe complete with white berries that Peter the stable boy had gathered at great risk to life and limb, to the mixed delight and consternation of the maids.

"Now we must hang it," said Helena.

"Oh, can I?" begged Milly. "Please?"

"If you will let us hold you, that's an excellent notion!"

And so with much giggling and a blessed good-fellowship, the kissing bough was hoisted to the ceiling and suspended from the chandelier. That evening over dinner, Helena found herself describing to her two sisters-in-law the merry way Christmas had been celebrated at Friarswell and Trethaerin. To her delight, they were full of questions and determined immediately to share with Eleanor everything that they had learned. Milly stopped in the doorway as they left to go upstairs.

"Can you teach us to play all those games? Hot Cockles and Hunt the Slipper?"

"Of course," laughed Helena. "Now Eleanor is waiting to hear all about your kissing bough."

She went into the drawing room alone, carrying her tea-cup. She would let the sisters have some time together without her. The curtains had long been drawn against the evening dark and a fire burned merrily in the grate beneath the swags of holly and green ivy. What arrested her was the unexpected sound of music. There was a dark-haired man sitting at the pianoforte, idly picking out a tune. He turned as she entered, and smiled. It was a smile of considerable charm.

"I hope I haven't startled you, Lady Lenwood," he said. "Your household seems to be in an uproar of hilarity, and I could get no one to show me in, thus I have disgracefully made free with your drawing room." He finished the piece with what Helena instantly recognized to be an uncommon skill, then stood and made her his bow. "I do hope you won't call the footmen to throw me out. I knew your husband in the Peninsula. My name is Charles de Dagonet."

Fifteen

Richard began to think as he passed through High Wycombe and went up onto the rise of the Chilterns that he was heartily sick of riding about the countryside in winter. He missed the comfort of a decent bed and a warm chair beside the fire; he missed the feel of a good horse under him instead of a hired nag; he missed—God help him—Helena. It was also tiresome to keep mixing up the black dye, and he had stopped bothering with it before he left France. His hat anyway covered his hair when he was traveling and the attacks on him had ceased, so he was allowing the gold to shine through at the roots. If there had been more hired assassins looking for a yellow-headed gentleman in London or in Paris, they had been foiled. He was no closer to discovering why the assaults had happened, in spite of extremely competent undercover work in both cities, which left him nothing but his marriage to Helena. Surely there was some other explanation, something he had missed?

It took a long day of hard riding to get from London to Oxford, and it was well after dark when Richard arrived. He was wet to the skin. Harry was not at his lodgings. In a dark mood, Richard left him a message, found a room at an inn, and turned in for the night.

"Good God!" said a voice in his ear. "You would seem to be piebald!" Richard opened one eye. A brace of candles had been lit and Harry sat on a chair beside the bed. "Land-lord let me in. Not without some misgivings, mind you. I threatened him with your dire displeasure if he didn't oblige, and you know that my charm is irresistible. Besides, he knows me. I hope it's truly urgent, because it's morning and I haven't been to bed yet."

"Harry, when will you ever learn manners? It may be morning, but I rode some sixty miles yesterday and I'm damned if I want to be woken to the sight of your cheerful face at some time in the wee hours."

"You needed wakening, old fellow. You've been moaning like a banshee."

Richard slipped from the bed and splashed cold water over his face. One glance at his watch told him that by most defi-nitions, morning was still some way off. "A regrettable habit of mine. Why are you here so early?"

"Good Lord! You summoned and I came!"

"Like the genie? Very well. Why don't you fetch us some hot liquid refreshment while I get dressed? Then I want to talk with you."

"What about?"

"About my wife, as it happens."

"Oh," said Harry with a grin from the doorway. "I thought you were going to explain the delightful thing you have done to your hair."

The teacup crashed to the ground. Dagonet knelt imme-diately to pick up the pieces.

"My humble apologies, my lady. I didn't mean to alarm you."

"No! Oh, no, please tell me right away: Has something happened to Richard?"

"I left him in the best of health. Here, sit down. Can I fetch you some more tea?"

"No, nothing. Where is he, sir? Is he all right?"

Dagonet led her to a chair by the fire and watched the color slowly come back to her face. He had not expected to discover so quickly what he had come to find out, but the answer was very obvious. Helena Trethaerin, now Lady Lenwood, could not be behind the attacks on her husband. She was very desperately in love with him.

"Lady Lenwood, I came only because Richard is a friend. He didn't send me."

Helena covered up her feelings instantly. "Let me offer you some wine, Mr. de Dagonet. Has my husband returned from France?"

"He is safe in England."

"You must think me a complete fool." She smiled and calmly handed him a glass. The return of her self-control seemed effortless. "It was more than kind of you to drop in. I certainly didn't mean to greet a stranger with hysterical theatrics and broken crockery."

"No, *les crises de nerfs* isn't your usual style at all, is it? But I know about the attempts on Richard's life. Yet to my knowledge he hasn't been attacked since October."

"What is behind it, Mr. de Dagonet? You were with my husband in Spain, you said. Did he make enemies there?"

"No more than any of us."

"But something haunts him!"

Charles de Dagonet looked at her and made a decision. Richard would never tell her, but he could in general terms give her some clues to understanding her husband. "We are all haunted, I suppose," he said gently. "In one way or another. Richard and I and several others were part of a group that Wellington pleased to call his *jeunesse dorée*. We col-

lected intelligence on enemy movements and ran liaison with
the local partisans."

"Golden youth?" asked Helena.

Dagonet gave her a wry smile. "Yes, a minor conceit of
our great general. Not all of us were either gilded or rich!
I'm afraid our work led us into other things besides battle-
fields, terrible though they are." The remarkable sea-green
eyes still held her gray ones, and his expression did not
change. His cultured voice remained matter-of-fact, as if to
somehow soften the import of what he was saying. "More
than once we came across the results of French reprisals
against the Spanish peasants. Napoleon's men were often
starving and desperate toward the end. Unfortunately they
didn't hesitate to take it out on women and children."

"I see," said Helena.

Dagonet knew that she couldn't possibly really understand,
but perhaps he had said enough. "We all have nightmares,"
he said.

Helena looked away into the dancing flames in the hearth.
This didn't account, of course, for whatever Richard was
involved in now, and it said nothing as to why someone was
trying to kill him, but still she was grateful.

Dagonet stood up and set down his glass. "And we also
learned to trust no one except each other. Be patient with
him, my lady. As the fool said: 'To say the truth, reason and
love keep little company together now-a-days; the more the
pity—' I know just how it feels."

"You do look quite haggard, Dickon," said Harry. "I wish
you would tell me all about it."

"In due course. It's your turn to spill the beans. When did

you first meet Helena's cousin, Nigel Garthwood? And why the hell didn't you tell me about it at the time?"

Harry had the grace to color just a little. "Because you were being so damned superior and bloody-minded, if you must know. I was going to tell you the day we were in the stable with Bayard after he was shot with the darts, but you seemed to be so certain that you had everything under control. It was the reason, actually, that I came back to the house that night instead of going on to London as I had planned."

"I thought you were going to Oxford when you left?"

"I do have a life of my own, you know. I had promised some of the fellows to fetch some particular wine."

"Which you consumed and with which you put yourself into a drunken stupor?"

"Witness the encounter with Sir Lionel? Actually, no. I can't quite figure that one out. I hadn't drunk any more than normal, but I admit I was crapulous. And I never made it to London. I spent the afternoon with Mr. Garthwood at an inn. He doesn't like you."

"Did he say so?"

"Oh, no, not at all. But he wanted with great subtlety to engage my help to discover your interests and habits, which I hope I refrained from giving him."

"Thank you," said Richard dryly.

"All his concern is for Helena, of course. He implied that he was her greatest friend and confidant, her only blood relative left alive and all that. Yet I had the feeling that he wanted to enlist me in some nefarious scheme if I would just once give him an opening. He also seemed rather more interested than was seemly in whether I would inherit if you met with some accident."

"And what did you tell him?" Would it be obvious that he had left everything to Helena if he died? Harry instead would become Earl of Acton in due course, but Acton Mead was Richard's own to dispose of and so was his considerable private fortune. Did Garthwood think to profit if Viscount Lenwood died? Only surely if Helena were in league with him, otherwise her sudden independent wealth wouldn't benefit Nigel Garthwood at all.

Harry took a swallow of wine. "I think I managed to leave him guessing about my real feelings and I'm sure I told him nothing of your private dispositions. It's not exactly his business, is it? But I still had a rather insistent premonition of danger at the time."

"So you returned to Acton Mead and followed us to the wood on Marrow Hill the next day. But you saw nothing?"

"Not a thing. But my premonition was right. Someone was dogging your footsteps with evil intent, weren't they? It was my intention to keep an eye on you and effect the heroic rescue. Woeful failure, I'm afraid. That day and at the fair."

"I did understand your motives, dear fellow," said Richard gently. "I'm sorry if I seemed ungrateful."

"It was only later that I wondered if Garthwood had followed me back and tried to take out his spleen on poor Bayard and the defenseless Behemoth. I did see him again, you see, on my way to Oxford. He was staying conveniently in the area."

"Have you seen him recently?"

"When you disappeared from the face of the realm, he turned up here to see if I knew where you'd gone. Since I couldn't help him, he went off to Cornwall, I believe. The man seemed in a oddly desperate case. He must want you dead very badly, and when you didn't oblige, he was like a mad dog."

"It's rather obvious, isn't it?" Richard leaned back in his chair, his face bleak. "I had no idea until now he had ever left Trethaerin, but from what you tell me, Garthwood has had the fortunate opportunity to be in the vicinity for each of the attacks on my precious existence. When his own amateur attempts met with such dismal failure, I suppose he decided to call in some professional help, thus the attack in London. And the description of the man who hired that unwelcome little company would fit him very well."

"In London?"

Richard gave his brother a brief description of the attack that had very nearly succeeded. "Look, Harry," he went on. "When you were leaving Acton Mead that first time, you remember you asked me the cause of my latest falling-out with Father. I told you that I had discovered something foul in Paris, and I'm afraid just to think of it put me in the filthiest temper. Well, I should have told you the whole or nothing. For that I apologize. I thought there was nothing you could do, and I was right. There is nothing that I can do either." Harry listened in silence as Richard described what he had found at Madame Relet's *maison* in Paris. "My interference has been so ineffective as to be grounds for laughter rather than murder," Richard continued. "There is no possible reason, I am quite certain, for this affair to be behind the attacks against me. I really have no proof except a confused note left by a poor girl who decided to take her own life, but I now believe Nigel Garthwood is involved in it. Even if he is, there is no reason he should try to harm me; I believe he does nothing except for money. No, my life is forfeit for some other reason that I cannot fathom."

Then Harry asked the critical question that had been haunting Richard like a barghest. "But if Nigel Garthwood is trying to kill you, and if it's not because of Paris, what possible motivation could he have? Why should your death bring him riches?"

"I don't know," said Richard. "There is no other connection between us, except that he's Helena's cousin."

"Surely you don't think that she's involved, sir!"

"What else am I supposed to think? Oh, damn it all, Harry. Go home to your bed before I forget that I am supposed to be a model gentleman and I too get drunk in earnest."

Charles de Dagonet would not accept the offer of a bed for the night and rode away in the dark. "I have to get to a ball at Lady Easthaven's before too many more days elapse, my lady, so if I am to fit in Richard's affairs among my own, it behooves me to waste no more time." He kissed her fingers. *"Au revoir,* Lady Lenwood. *Les plus sages ne le sont pas toujours."*

Even the wisest aren't always so. It was small comfort.

John arrived the next day. Helena had achieved something close to a peace treaty with Joanna and Milly, and she had high hopes of moving toward truly amicable relations. It was painfully obvious that the girls had built up layers of defenses against giving their affections too casually, yet she had effected a small breach, perhaps. She smiled wryly to herself. The same could be said for their oldest brother, but she was not sure that her siege had touched him at all.

John marched into the hallway and gave her a little bow.

"Where are Richard and Harry?" he said right away.

"As you already know very well, they can't be here, sir," replied Helena with a smile. "But your sisters are in the drawing room, except for Eleanor, who is unhappily abed with a cold."

"A chap was never so put upon!" John threw his top hat

onto a chair. "What am I expected to do for two weeks in a house full of women?"

"I would hope," replied Helena softly, "that you would be a gracious and chivalrous gentleman, as Richard would anticipate."

"Well, don't expect me to put up with Milly! Eleanor's all right; she's a real brick when a fellow's in trouble, but Joanna never could stand the sight of me!"

"I doubt seriously the veracity of that, sir, but I for one am very happy at the sight of you. I intend to win back some of my shillings."

Suddenly the sulky pout was replaced with an open grin. "Do you? Say, I did have fun that time staying with you here. It was worth the drubbing I got when I got back, and you should have seen the fellows' faces when I just sauntered into the hall as if nothing were wrong. Harris Major's face was red as a flag; he'd wagered with some of the other lads that I'd run off for good."

"So you did get your beating?"

"Rather! But it didn't bother me any! Is tea ready?"

Helena led him into the drawing room, where Joanna looked up and made a little face, and Milly instantly jumped up and ran behind her sister.

"What's this?" said John with a grin. "Two frogs out of the pond? What on earth are those frizzes around your face, Joanna? It looks like a border of fixed bayonets!"

Joanna had been the victim of a small accident with her curling irons that morning and her ebony ringlets had a slightly fried look which Helena had tactfully ignored. "At least I don't have a face like the back end of a cart horse!" she replied instantly.

"I don't know who's calling who a horse's tail!" yelled John instantly, and launched himself at his sisters.

At the same moment, the footman came in with the tea tray. John hit the liveried elbow with the force of a cannonball and the tray shot out of the poor man's grasp. Hot water, teapot, spoons, scones, cakes, and teacups slid in a splendid cavalcade to the carpet to form a magnificent muddle of broken crockery and wet crumbs amid a soaking pool of tea and raspberry jam. The carpets at Acton Mead seem to be getting some rough handling recently, thought Helena. It was almost the same place where she had dropped her own teacup.

There was an appalled silence, and Milly began to cry.

"I beg your pardon, my lady," began the footman.

"It was not your fault, Williams," said Helena instantly. "Just send a maid in to clean up and ask Mrs. Hood for some more tea."

The footman bowed his head and left.

"Now, see!" said Joanna instantly. "Look what you've done, John! I declare, it's like having barbarians in the drawing room. You are a hateful little boy!"

"All right," said Helena. "John, you had better go to your room. I shall talk with you later."

There was something in her tone that made him obey instantly. She also suspected that he too was very close to tears. It would be a terrible humiliation to him to break down in front of his sisters.

"I told you he was horrid!" wailed Milly. "He spoiled all the tea!"

Helena sat down and pulled Milly to her. To her delight, the child allowed herself to be hugged. "And we shall have a whole new tea in a minute. In the meantime, don't you think we had better decide what to do about John?"

"You could lock him in his room the whole time," suggested Joanna.

"No, I mean more than that. John feels very overwhelmed, you know, being here with all us females. I think we are going to have to go to great lengths to make him feel comfortable."

"Why on earth should we?" said Joanna. "He's a brat!"

"Because it's good practice for us, of course. We can polish our society manners. Imagine, how would a great lady have handled such an odd remark as John made about your hair?"

"You mean a lady like a princess?" asked Milly.

"If you like. You all bear the names of great queens, you know."

"She'd have ignored it and frozen him out, I suppose," said Joanna after a moment.

"Very likely," answered Helena, smiling. "I doubt very seriously if she'd have told him he resembled an unmentionable part of a horse's anatomy—even if she believed it to be true."

And suddenly Joanna began to giggle. "I would like to see his face if I were to ignore him altogether!"

"Or, if she loved as a brother the fellow who so forgot himself, she could have made a joke out of it of her own," said Helena. "Laughter is a far better way to win over one's opponents than insults, you know. You could have said something that would have made him laugh with you and then he'd have been totally at your mercy. In fact, it might have been so successful that you'd find he was on your side after all. We all of us need all the allies we can get, I think. In the meantime, if you would like, I can help you with your hair. Would you like to practice putting it up— just for dinner?"

Joanna almost bridled. But she had been longing to put up her hair. "Oh, very well. I'll try and be better to John."

"Let it be our secret," said Helena. "We shall all try and be as gracious and clever as queens and see if we can win John to our side. It'll be great fun."

John might have shed a few tears, but they had been defiantly dried by the time Helena came up to his room.

"That's it for my tea, then," he said with a pout.

"Well, what do you think is fair?" asked Helena.

"To go hungry until dinner, I suppose. But a fellow never had such dreadful sisters. Joanna looked like a singed pig."

"I suppose she hadn't noticed it herself," said Helena absently.

"Oh, I'll bet she had. She's as vain as a peacock. I'll bet she was in a dreadful funk over it!"

"Then how do you suppose it made her feel to find out that you had noticed too?"

"Pretty rotten, I guess." John looked at his feet. "But she's always so superior!"

"Do you think that Richard would let that influence his behavior to a lady?" John didn't answer, but he had flushed a bright scarlet. "I think you are often very provoked, sir," said Helena kindly. "And that it must be a terrible challenge to have so many sisters to be nice to—rather a labor of Hercules, in fact. But while Richard's away, you are the only gentleman in the house and we females have no one else to look to for protection and courtesy, you know. Especially Milly, since she's younger than you. I think that a young man who has the courage to face up to a double whipping would also have the courage to apologize to his sisters and try to treat them as a gentleman should."

"Will you tell Richard?"

"About the accident with the tea tray? I rather hope that if Richard comes home suddenly, he'll find his young brother acting so well that he would never believe it."

"I am sorry, Helena, truly. Will you still play whist with me?"

"You can't keep me from the card table, sir."

"Then I will apologize to Joanna."

"If you feel yourself tempted to do otherwise, I'll give you a wink and you must think of the noble Hercules in the Aegean stables. I know you can do it, sir!"

And at dinner John made a very passable apology, though it took two winks to get him through it. Joanna, her head held as proudly as her medieval namesake's, made a gracious and funny acceptance. Matilda then dared to tell John about Bayard, and it didn't need any more winks for John to express genuine interest and enthusiasm. In fact the two youngest members of the Acton family seemed to have found grounds for a truce. Helena had won peace for at least the first evening.

Nigel Garthwood smiled when he received the messages from Oxford. Henry Acton was interested in procuring some more very fine wine and requested a meeting soon to that end. And Viscount Lenwood was back. It seemed that he had managed to disappear by dying his hair and going back to waste his time again in Paris. Now he seemed to have shed the disguise and to be openly flaunting his presence. The viscount's apparent confidence was misplaced. God knows how he had escaped from the ruffians in London, but he would not survive the next attempt. This time Garthwood would make sure of it himself, and he wouldn't trust to the results of an accident. He had some specialized knowledge that he could put to use. He would bide his time and wait for the perfect opportunity.

Sixteen

Dagonet arrived at Oxford and went from inn to inn until he discovered where Richard was staying. That night he and the viscount had dinner together. Richard had managed to visit a barber, and his hair, though now shorter than his usual habit, was once again the color of celandines.

"I can only say, my lord," said Dagonet as he helped himself to a serving of jugged hare, "that in my humble opinion, your wits have gone begging. *Il est plus aisé d'être sage pour les autres que pour soi-même, naturellement.* But I have been to see your wife."

The viscount raised a brow. "And what wisdom for others has resulted, sir?"

"She is not trying to kill you, dear Richard."

"No, I don't imagine that she is capable of being in two places at once, nor that she has the ability to shoot either bullets or darts."

"Nor, believe me, does she wish you dead!"

"You are an impeccable judge of character, aren't you, Dagonet?"

"Good enough, as are you. Neither of us would have survived this long if we hadn't learned to see through to a man's real intentions."

"Yes, but that invaluable experience didn't encompass the gentler sex, did it?"

Dagonet fixed his friend with his brilliant gaze. "You don't seriously believe that Helena Trethaerin is guilty of nefarious plots, do you? For heaven's sake, sir, you told me yourself you had fallen in love with her!"

Richard leaned back and smiled. His face seemed carved like a sculpture in the candlelight. "And I am of such splendid character that I couldn't have done so if she were not worthy? But love is blind, they say."

"Like justice, I suppose. It's interesting, isn't it, how many noble personifications are without sight? But it seems to be only the female ones. Male gods always fix us with their stony gaze and thus perhaps judge only by appearances."

"For God's sake, Charles! You don't think that I want to believe that my wife is involved in all this, do you? I don't accept for a moment that Helena knows anything about Madame Relet—she is a complete innocent about such things, thank God. But meanwhile, Harry has made it clear that her cousin Garthwood is likely to be the actual perpetrator of the attempts against me. And who else could be responsible for the villainy with the girls? But the man has no motivation whatsoever for the former that makes any sense. You must agree!"

"Of course. It's what makes it all so damnable, I do see that."

"When I met them in Cornwall, it was obvious that Helena was afraid of him. If she is still somehow in his power, who knows to what that fear may lead her to agree? Ours was a marriage of convenience only. We don't pretend any abiding affection. If I die, she will be a rich woman and her cousin Garthwood would be there to step into the breach. Helena could have kept in touch with him, informed him of my movements. How can I know what to think? Except that I have spent all these years in one adventure after another and no one ever tried to personally assassinate me until I was wed."

Dagonet poured him some wine and watched as the viscount absently sipped at the glass. Richard's food had congealed untouched on the plate in front of him.

"I realize that only you can judge what lies between you, Richard. But I want you to put an objective opinion on her side of the scales, for what it's worth. I have spoken with her and I don't think it's possible for her to be involved in any attempts against you."

"Because she's a lady?" said Richard with a wry grin.

"If you like." That Dagonet thought he knew the true state of Helena's feelings didn't tempt him for a moment to tell Richard his opinion of them. He would very probably be disbelieved and anyway, in honor it was not for him but for Helena to reveal when and if she would.

"I do hope you are right, sir," said Richard quietly.

"In the meantime, if there's a price offered on your telltale head, someone may still be waiting to collect it."

The viscount grinned, but not from amusement. "I have thought of that."

"Is it wise to discard your disguise?"

"Very probably not. But if it's true that Helena connives with her cousin and would be so indifferent to my instant demise, I'm not very sure that I care."

"Devil take it, Acton! For God's sake, be careful! Nothing I say will change your mind about Helena?"

"How can it when the facts argue so cogently against both our desires? Damnation! Let's get rid of this food!" Richard signaled to the waiter, who hurried to clear the plates. Then he leaned back and closed his eyes for a moment. "Charles, I know you have problems of your own and that London calls insistently for your return. I wish I could do as much for you as you've tried to do for me. But this is one demon, dear fellow, that I must face down for myself. In the meantime, put your mind at rest. I'm going from here to see my father at King's Acton and he has a great many burly footmen and a gamekeeper with a fearsome blunderbuss, all of whom love me like a son and would guard every last hair on my shameless head with their lives. Before I turn my attention to the problem of Helena and Garthwood, I should like to try one more time to make the earl see reason. It will haunt me for the rest of my life, however short, if that little girl who died in Paris hanged herself in vain."

"And then you return to Acton Mead? Be on your guard, Richard."

"King's Acton will buy me a few days of safety before I meet a gruesome death in some lonely field or in my own garden." Richard smiled at the other man. "I do admit it would make me feel a great deal better about it, however, if I knew for a fact that Helena would care."

It wasn't easy, since Richard's sisters and John hadn't known before what it was to have someone who cared enough to try to make a warm home for them. But little by little their hostility disappeared. With Helena, they invented games and played uproarious charades and helped in the kitchen with the stirring of the plum pudding and the chopping of fruit for the mince pies. Helena had a footman supply them all with old pewter trays and they went out tobogganing to return rosy-cheeked to the fireside. Even Joanna joined in, and John began to take a new pride in helping and protecting Milly instead of tormenting her. Helena also had them help with the packing of baskets for the poor of the parish and let them take the responsibility of delivery, while she sent stable hands out with wagons of firewood. The snow and cold was fun for the children, but there was some real hardship and suffering beyond the gates.

When Eleanor came downstairs at last, she found herself surrounded by unexpected laughter and gaiety and no one remembered to tease her about her mousy brown hair or her still-chapped nostrils. Instead, she was instantly pressed into service to help with the multitude of on-going projects, which she did with a will. Helena realized right away that her struggle to win some happiness for the children would have been a great deal easier if she had only had Eleanor's help from the beginning. The oldest sister of the Acton family was both sensible and merry, and her love for her siblings was palpable.

On Christmas Eve they all gathered in the drawing room to play the traditional games. After the chaos of Hunt the Slipper, Hoodman Blind caused as much noise as a riot in the hen house. Helena had to agree to be the first victim to be blindfolded and to allow herself to be spun until she was dizzy. The others with much hilarity dodged behind chairs and sofas as she stumbled about trying to find them.

"Surely this is Milly!" she cried as her fingers closed on some soft fabric.

"It's only the curtains!" squealed Matilda, and Helena heard her racing to hide somewhere else.

Breathless with laughter, Helena felt her way back to the center of the room. She managed to collide with the sofa and the corner of the piano before she knew herself back in the open space on the carpet. There was a sudden excited silence punctuated only with suppressed giggles. She could hear the soft sound of breathing. Someone stood directly in front of her.

"Helena's under the kissing bough!" John cried suddenly with a whoop of delight.

She put out her hands. Other hands firmly caught them and she felt herself pulled into the solid warmth of a man's chest, then her palms were turned up and a kiss planted on each one. In the next instant she felt her face being taken in gentle fingers and someone was kissing her on the mouth. Desire leapt pounding through her blood, leaving her faint and breathless as he ran his hands down her back and held her with no possibility of escape. The girls clapped their hands and John cheered.

"It's the best of all possible Christmas presents!" said Milly. "Can't we tell now, sir?"

"What, and leave Helena without the fun of the surprise? I have signaled you all to silence, young lady. Don't break it!"

The hands had moved up to her hair and the blindfold was untied. But his voice had already given him away. Helena found herself gazing into the dark, secret depths of her husband's black eyes. Then the children came racing to fling themselves at him, and Eleanor and Joanna clasped at his hands.

"Merry Christmas, everyone," said Viscount Lenwood before bestowing individual greetings all around. Only Helena hung back. She had already had her acknowledgment, she supposed. And Richard might be prepared to kiss her, but he did not otherwise seem to want to meet her eyes.

"Now you must be Hoodman!" cried John.

"Richard has only just arrived, young man," said Eleanor instantly. "Aren't you going to let him rest for a moment?"

"Oh, Richard's never tired, are you, sir? And that's the rules—the person who gets caught is the next Hoodman."

"And the rules must be obeyed?" said Richard. "Where is the blindfold? I am ready!"

Helena watched as Joanna secured the strip of black cloth over his eyes and he was spun with the greatest enthusiasm by John, who then ran off gasping with delight. Richard turned and grinned in her direction before he took two steps to the sofa, vaulted over the innocent piece of furniture, and caught Milly firmly around the waist. Only the slightest hesitation as he reached for the carved back with his hand would have betrayed to an observer that he was totally blind. For some reason, his easy confidence made Helena's breath catch in her throat. It was then Milly's turn to catch John.

"Enough!" said Helena at last. "I am sorely winded and we must have enough breath left to sing tonight!"

Dinner was passed in a state close to uproar, and then after they had gathered at the piano and sung carols together, Helena had promised to tuck Milly in bed. As soon as she had gone, John and Joanna settled into a moderately quiet game of cards. Richard went to Eleanor, where she still sat at the piano, softly playing old songs.

"What on earth is going on?" he asked seriously.

Eleanor raised a brown brow and smiled. "Going on? What makes you suppose anything is going on?"

"You know perfectly well what I mean, Eleanor, and I shall strangle you with my bare hands if you don't explain. I don't imagine a double whipping at Eton has so reformed John, nor that Joanna's putting up her beautiful hair has given her so much forbearance. I can't ever remember Milly not displaying either panics or sulks, and instead of looking frazzled, you, my beloved child, are blooming."

"You must ask Helena, dear brother. I'm afraid I arrived here with a horrid cold and spent far too many days in bed than was fair. By the time I came down, all was as you see:

peace in the family and goodwill to all Actons." She grinned at him, stopped playing, and hugged his arm. "Perhaps you married an angel by mistake?"

Richard smiled and returned the hug. "I wish I could think so, sister mine." And Eleanor was left to wonder why his voice carried so much pain beneath the surface of banter.

Two hours later Richard sat alone by the fire and stared into the flames. The others, including Helena, had gone off to bed. He sipped absently at a very fine brandy and thought carefully through everything he knew. However he cudgeled at the facts, they still left one inescapable conclusion: Garthwood had no reason to harm him, unless he expected to benefit through Helena. Yet why should he, unless Helena were a willing partner? How could he have been so foolish as to lose his heart to her, when she was still little more than a stranger? He was not even sure how it had happened, but like a thief in the night, she had robbed him of his freedom. He felt obsessed with her. And that was dangerous. How easy to have one's judgment clouded when the object of suspicion pulled at his heart like the Lorelei. How on earth could he discover the truth? At last he stood and tossed the dregs of his glass into the flames. The brandy flared up in a blaze of blue light. There was one simple solution. He would ask her.

Helena had gone to bed, but she was not asleep. She lay and stared at the ceiling and chased thoughts about in her head like a flock of confused sheep. Richard had gone off to France when?—six, no, more than seven weeks ago. He had not come to see her when he came back to England, had not even sent her a message. Charles de Dagonet had stopped by to see her, but not at Richard's request. Were even his friends concerned for him? Did they know that Harry was a threat to his brother? Then Dagonet had told her nothing of where Richard had been or what he was doing. Was Marie French? Had Richard taken her to the new Bourbon court with him? And why had he come back now? Only, surely, because the children were there for Christmas. They had married with no pretensions to love. All he owed to her was courtesy and financial security, and he had more than given her that. She had no right whatsoever to make further demands on his time or his energy. If Marie had his heart, she could neither interfere, nor, in honor, allow him to be confronted with her anguish over it. And with that thought, Richard walked into the room.

Helena sat up on her knees and tried to school her features so that he wouldn't guess that her heart was pounding like a steam engine. Her hair in a long braid, golden in the firelight, lay on the soft silken folds of her nightgown; her bare arms were white on the coverlet. Richard came and sat beside her on the bed. His silk dressing gown lay open at the neck, and she watched in fascination the steady beat of the pulse at his throat.

"Helena, I must talk with you," he said seriously. "There is something that lies between us. It has kept me away from you, and God knows, I didn't intend it to be this way."

With sudden dread she felt certain that he was going to tell her about Marie at last. That he was in love with his mistress and would never be coming back to Acton Mead. Once it was out in the open, she could no longer pretend to ignore it. He would no longer feel that he owed her even these brief visits. It was more than she could bear.

"It doesn't matter," she said lightly. "Don't tell me anything. We don't owe each other our secrets. I have never expected more from you than what you have already given me. You're here now, and that's all that counts."

And Helena, gathering her courage, leant forward and

kissed him. She meant to offer comfort, perhaps, for the indefinable pain that seemed to haunt his black eyes, and a defiant gesture of understanding about Marie. But in the next moment Richard had buried his hands in her hair and was ravishing the warm sweetness of her mouth. The braid fell apart under his hands. He pulled her with him into the cocoon of the sheets. The dark print of his dressing gown enfolded the white sheen of her discarded night rail when it slipped silent and unheeded to the floor. Richard barely noticed, lost in the scent and feel and taste of her. If she wanted him dead, he would die. Nothing mattered now except her open lips and sensitive skin, and the welcome and peace he could find in her bed.

Helena awoke in the morning to only a memory of his strength and passion. He was gone. At the breakfast table when she came down, he was already occupied with Milly on one side and John on the other, being given a detailed account of the state of Bayard's health and spirits. Eleanor and Joanna were laughing together on the other side of the table. Joanna had so forgotten herself as to tie back her lustrous black hair in a simple ribbon. She looked very much like a little girl again.

"Oh, Dickon," she said suddenly, "can't we do some limericks like we used to when Grandmama was alive?"

"I want one about me!" squealed Milly.

"Very well, who'll start?"

"I shall!" said John. He stood and bowed, then began to intone, flinging out his arm in a melodramatic gesture. "There once was a creature called Milly . . ."

"Who went out whene'er it was chilly . . ." said Eleanor right away. "You took the easy line, John."

"But although we had snow," added Richard solemnly, giving Milly a wink, "the sled wouldn't go . . ."

"Since she couldn't tell flat land from hilly. Hello everyone!"

"Harry!" Joanna had leapt up and run around the table to embrace the brother whose dark head looked so like hers.

"The same, dear children. Let me get a breath, Jo, for heaven's sake. Hello, Eleanor, you look beautiful, dear child, as does our Milly. Has Helena been feeding you all on ambrosia and syllabub? And John would seem to have joined our ranks, Dickon, and become, to no one's surprise but his own, a gentleman after all. I have brought a few bottles of that exquisite port I mentioned, dear brother. You will toast the season with me, I trust? Your humble servant, sweet sister-in-law, and Merry Christmas. Am I in time for the roast goose and sausages?"

Seventeen

That afternoon Helena watched Richard as he took his seat at the head of the table. No one would ever know that he had last come here in secret and in disguise because his very life was forfeit. Laughing and joking with his brothers and sisters, he seemed suffused with a golden glow. Did he feel no fear at all? After the roast goose, the mince pies, the frumenty and ginger, Mrs. Hood herself carried in the round plum pudding that had been steamed tied up in a cloth and which the children had helped stir. The curtains in the dining room had already been drawn against the failing dim winter light, for fresh snow had begun to fall from leaden skies outside and coat the countryside. Blue flames danced around a holly twig on the brandy-soaked pudding. Helena laughed and applauded with the rest. She was determined that no one should discover that her heart was heavy with dread. Harry was back. Would Richard be attacked again?

Christmas dinner was over and the cloth had just been cleared when Williams came in and bowed stiffly. "There is a gentleman come to the door, my lord. I have shown him into the study. He claims to be a relation."

Richard looked up. He was sucking at slightly singed fingers where he had been playing at Snapdragon with Milly and John. John seemed to have been able to snatch the most raisins from the flames, but Milly had made no objection since Richard was sharing his booty with them both. "Did the fellow give a name?"

"A Mr. Nigel Garthwood, my lord."

Instantly, Richard was on his feet. "The devil!" he said softly.

Helena hesitated only a moment before following him from the room. She hadn't seen her cousin since leaving Trethaerin. What on earth was he doing here? As she came up to the study door, she was in time to hear Richard's voice. It was tight with anger.

"You honor us with your presence, sir, at Christmastide, but you will see that with the house full of children, it would be more than tiresome for you to stay. Perhaps I may send a man with you and arrange a room in the nearest town?"

Helena opened the door and went in. "How do you do, Mr. Garthwood? May we offer you the felicitations of the season?" she said calmly.

"Dear Lady Lenwood." Garthwood bowed low over her hand. "I am called to London on business and from the sensibility of family feeling and duty wanted to stop and see how you go on. I had no idea how secluded you are here! Now I find myself benighted on Christmas Day! I hope you will allow me to offer you some small gifts in appreciation for your hospitality?" His arms were laden with packages.

Richard's voice was colder than the weather outside. "That won't be necessary, sir. As I was saying . . ."

"No, of course, you must stay the night! Welcome to Acton Mead, cousin." Helena rang the bell. "Williams, would you show Mr. Garthwood to the green room? He will be our guest for tonight."

With much bowing and scraping Nigel Garthwood set down his gifts and left the room in the wake of the servant.

Richard waited until he had gone, then he turned to Helena

with a force that she could feel across the room. "How dare you!" Helena realized that she had never seen him really angry before. "I will not have that man under my roof!"

Helena took a deep breath, but she stood her ground. Richard should not bully her out of doing what was right. "For heaven's sake, my lord, he's my cousin! I do not pretend to be happy to see him, but it's Christmas Day!"

"You don't know what he is! How dare you countermand my wishes?"

"When I was left destitute by my father's will, Mr. Garthwood allowed me to stay on unmolested at Trethaerin for months. Now that Edward is dead, he's my only living relative. It is now snowing hard and it's dark outside. Surely there is enough charity in this house that we can give him a bed, however grudgingly, for one night! I will not stand here and see anyone turned out into the weather, even Nigel Garthwood. What possible harm can he do? Why don't you forget about him and concentrate on Harry instead?"

Richard had gone to the fireplace and leaned back against the mantel. The ivy leaves behind his head made his hair shine bright gold in contrast, but the lines of his face were rigid with fury above the snowy folds of his cravat.

"For God's sake, my lady," he said at last, his voice barely under control. "You welcome Garthwood to this house, then dare to express concern about my brother. Harry kissed you once in the garden and you are so vindictive that you can't forgive him? I thought you disliked your cousin as much as I, but it seems I was wrong. Were you acting at Trethaerin? Because if so, you're a damned good actress. Both of us are going to have to show our thespian talents, aren't we, if we're to get through the rest of the day without disgracing ourselves in front of my brothers and sisters and spoiling their holiday after all. I thought— Oh, damn it all to hell!"

And he turned on his heel and walked from the room.

But the rest of the family were too sated with food and excitement to notice if Helena was a little more quiet and distracted than before. She wasn't required to do much more than bury her fear, as she had long been in the habit of doing. Richard had gone to the stable ostensibly to wish the best of the season to his beloved charger, and when he came in, his good humor seemed unchanged, even though Nigel Garthwood had now joined the family in the drawing room. There was no hint in Richard's courteous good manners that he was anything but delighted to welcome him.

Amid much secret hilarity they opened Garthwood's packages. Helena's unctuous cousin who had suddenly turned up from nowhere had brought gifts for them all. The Actons received his generosity with polite thanks, even though some of the gifts were a little odd in the children's eyes—particularly the china doll for Joanna, who had outgrown such things years before. Helena had taught them all that one must be gracious in public even if it was more than human nature could stand not to laugh to oneself in private afterward. There was a gold chain for Helena and an enameled snuffbox for Richard. As her husband made icy acknowledgments, she wondered briefly why her cousin should have gone to so much trouble for a family he had never met. He seemed particularly eager to please and flatter her. Such humble solicitude was completely out of character, but Helena received it as graciously as she could. Nigel Garthwood then had the sense to retire early to bed and Helena escorted him to his room herself.

"It was very clever of you, sir, to know just what to bring

for everyone. How did you find out about all my husband's brothers and sisters?"

"Henry told me, my dear. He and I are fast friends—on the most intimate terms, I am pleased to say. May I express how very contented I am to see you so happily situated? I shall always have an interest for you, as I trust you would find unexceptionable in a near relation. The chain I gave you is just a token of my still-abiding affection. Should you ever be in need, you would find me instantly at your side, to do whatever small service I could. You will never forget that, I trust?"

But Helena heard nothing of her cousin's protestations of family concern. His casual comment struck her like a blow. Harry had once mentioned meeting her cousin, but she had quite forgotten it. Why had he told Garthwood intimate details about the family? What other confidences did they share? Was Garthwood Harry's accomplice in a plan to harm her husband? Yet how could she possibly warn Richard, when he wouldn't hear a word against his brother?

"There is something, dear cousin," Garthwood went on, "that you could give me in return."

"Of course," said Helena. She was hardly listening.

"I have nothing personal of dear Edward's, you know. If there was some small item of his? Some memento?"

Helena turned toward him and smiled. "Don't be ridiculous, sir. You have his entire estate!"

She stepped back into the drawing room, only to be cornered by Eleanor and Joanna for piquet. Harry and Richard were deep in some conversation of their own. She stole glances at the two brothers, the dark head leaning close to the blond one. Please, my love, she wished silently, be careful! Your brother is in league with my unpleasant cousin, for heaven knows what nefarious purposes, yet it is your wife you cannot trust, isn't it? And so, I can't even tell you.

"Are you listening, Helena?" asked Joanna. "It's your turn!"

Helena laughed and apologized, then gave her attention to the game. After supper the men lingered for a long time over the port that Harry had brought down from London. She was not surprised when Richard did not come to her room that night.

Nigel Garthwood left first thing the next morning, before the family was down to breakfast. Helena had slept badly and risen early. She stood alone on the front step and watched him ride away with considerable relief. In spite of her new suspicions and her old dislike, how could she have turned him from the door on Christmas Day? Richard might not have forgiven her yet, but she felt the lonely satisfaction of having done the right thing. As Helena lost sight of her cousin at last, Eleanor appeared at her side and hugged her arm.

"You're a noble soul, Helena. How did you turn out to be so kind, when you had relatives like that?"

Helena laughed. "Eleanor, I assure you that all the rest of my family were quite unexceptionable. My cousin Edward Blake, who was killed, you know, was the warmest and kindest of boys. You would have liked him. In some ways, John makes me think of him. And now it's time to face our next problem, isn't it?"

"With John?" said Eleanor.

"He will still be smarting about the wren, I'm afraid. We shall have to come up with some other entertainment for today."

St. Stephen's Day, the day after Christmas, was supposed by tradition to be devoted to the hunting and shooting of a wren, a bird normally safe from any harassment, which would then be paraded around the grounds on a little bier. When John had first suggested the idea, Helena had vetoed it and Eleanor had of course backed her up. John had not been prepared to take this female interference in male pastimes lightly. When Eleanor and Helena went in together to breakfast, the rest of the family was already sitting at the table and John had obviously just finished pitching his appeal to Richard.

"No, I'm sorry, John, I'm afraid I do not agree," Richard was saying. "I see no need for an innocent bird to lose its life for our amusement. If the custom once had any deeper significance, it's lost now. I think we should allow the wren killing to subside into history and pursue a less deadly entertainment."

Helena was amazed. She had been prepared to have to argue with him over this. But perhaps Richard also hated to see the useless destruction of any creature. Or perhaps he didn't want to be out in the woods with his brothers, when that meant that Harry would be there with a weapon?

"John wouldn't hit it anyhow," said Milly, who was heartily relieved.

"No, but Harry would!" said John. "Harry's always been a crack shot!"

"Alas, dear John, I must leave right after breakfast. Since Richard will not allow the murder of our poor feathered friends, my skill lies unneeded. In the face of such indifference, I go to bury my sorrows in town."

"We can't persuade you to stay, Harry?" asked Richard.

"Nothing would keep me a moment longer. This is far too wholesome a household for someone of my dissolute tastes."

He winked at Helena. "Enjoy your holidays, dear children. And forget the wren, brother John; you are entirely outnumbered."

"Let's go and build a snowman instead," suggested Helena. "Come on, John, we can't do it without you, you know."

"In a minute," said John.

The others left the room and Richard went to the stables with Harry. He had promised to accompany his brother as far as Mead Farthing. With her heart in her mouth, Helena saw them go. The last time Richard had gone to see his brother off, he had returned with a bullet through his sleeve. Then bravely she herded the girls together as if nothing were wrong and sent them after their hats and pelisses.

John was left sitting alone at the dining table. He really didn't want to sulk, but the rest of the fellows at school would shoot down their wren and consider it a noble venture. He would be made to look the fool if he had to tell them he'd helped his sisters build a snowman instead. It was only his longing to please Helena and Richard that forced him to agree and not make a fuss. He had never had such a fun Christmas, and Helena was a pretty good sort, but a chap deserved some recognition of how nobly he'd been staying out of mischief, didn't he? It seemed he was to be expected to behave like a gentleman without enjoying any of the privileges of that state. It was really more than a fellow could stand.

His eye lit upon the port still standing on the sideboard from last night's supper. The servants had been allowed considerable laxity in honor of the holiday, and the bottles and glasses had not yet been cleared away. It was the stuff that Harry had brought for Richard and one bottle was half empty. The brothers had sat up late over the precious liquor. John had been denied even a sip and sent from the room as if he were a girl. How was a chap supposed to learn about port and stuff if he wasn't to be allowed to try any? Without thinking any more about it, John jumped up and poured himself a glass. The forbidden liquid shone like a ruby. With a sense of intense excitement, the boy took a sip. It was queer stuff, but he could see how the taste could grow on a fellow. He took another.

"Aren't you coming, John?" It was Milly's voice. "Williams is coming to clear away the things."

Instantly, John set down the glass and thrust it back behind the bottles. With the tingle of the port and the accompanying guilty excitement running in his veins, he went out to help build a snowman.

"Are you all right, sir?" asked Helena suddenly.

John looked up at her. They had rolled together several large balls of snow, and the girls were laughing and red-cheeked in the frosty air. John, in contrast, seemed to be the color of the snow. Helena went over to him and felt his forehead. It was clammy.

"Good heavens, John, you are chilled! Are you ill? Won't you come in?"

"I'm all right, truly," said John stoutly. He had never expected that the port would be so powerful. His head felt as if it were in the teeth of a threshing machine, and there was a horrible grinding sensation inside his guts. He grinned at Helena, then, as she slipped her arm around his shoulders, he began to retch.

Two footmen carried him inside and laid him on the couch while a maid hovered nearby, her face ashen.

"Have Williams fetch some blankets from Mrs. Hood,"

said Helena, holding tight to the boy's hand. "And warm water."

What on earth was the matter? John was sweating and his face was now the color of putty. He had already emptied the contents of his stomach, but the retching went on.

"Williams is also taken ill, my lady," said Mrs. Hood herself, rushing into the room. "Here now, John, try and take a sip of this, there's a good chap."

The kindly housekeeper held out a glass.

"I can't," whispered the boy, shaking in Helena's arms.

"Where is the viscount?" asked Mrs. Hood grimly. "He must know about this right away."

"I am here," said Richard from the doorway. Helena looked up and felt the headache she had been warding off disappear. He was still safe! And Harry was gone. "What's going on?"

"Williams brought back the tray from the breakfast table, my lord, and was taken as sick as a dog in the kitchen. And now I find my poor lad here with the same thing!"

Richard stripped off his coat and came into the room. His midnight eyes met Helena's briefly before he calmly took charge. She could not tell what he was looking for there, for he addressed his questions to Mrs. Hood, not to her.

"Did either of them eat or drink anything different from the rest of us?"

"I couldn't say, my lord. Williams is beyond speech!"

"Then you must tell me, young man," said Richard, dropping on one knee beside his brother. "You heard Mrs. Hood. There is a footman very ill. Did you help yourself to anything in the kitchen after we had all gone to bed last night?"

In an agony of misery, John shook his head.

"Then this morning? It's all right, sir; you won't get a whipping merely for having a good appetite, you know."

"I drank some of your wine," said John. "The stuff that Harry brought. I know I wasn't supposed to have any, but I took only a sip. Then I left the rest of the glass on the sideboard because I heard Milly calling. I'm terribly sorry, sir. Will you punish me?"

"I think you're getting punishment enough, don't you?" said Richard gently, smoothing the lad's hair back from his forehead. "It turned out to be rather more powerful port than you had imagined."

Mrs. Hood sat beside the boy and helped him drink some of the warm water. John was violently sick again. "There now," she said. "It'll make it worse for now, but you're to get all that poison out."

"Poison?" breathed Helena. Why hadn't it occurred to her right away?

"Mrs. Hood merely refers to the demon alcohol," said Richard quietly so that only Helena could hear him. "But it would appear so, wouldn't it?"

He had already stood, and with a last wink at John he walked swiftly through to the dining room. Helena followed. Richard took up the bottle that had been opened and carried it into the kitchen. The maids were hovering around the prostrate figure of Williams, who had been laid on a bench in front of the fire. The footman was shaking and his face had the consistency of dough.

"He's right poorly, my lord," said Mr. Hood. "He's past talking."

"Where are the glasses from the dining room?"

"Here, my lord," said one of the kitchen girls, curtsying. "We've not washed up anything yet, what with Williams having such a turn and all."

"John said he left a half-full glass," said Helena. "All of these are empty!"

Richard ignored her and squatted on his heels beside the ill footman. He took the limp hand in his own. "Now, sir," he said. "You've worked for this family for a long time and I'll not begrudge you a little port at Christmas, particularly when it's otherwise going to waste. Did you drink down half a glass that you found on the sideboard? If so, squeeze my hand as hard as you can."

The man groaned, but his fingers clenched feebly on Richard's palm.

"Take the rest of that bottle and give it to one of the pigs," said Richard.

A footman was sent hurrying to obey. He came back a moment later, his face a strange shade of green. "The pig drank it like a lord, begging your pardon, my lord, but he's dead now. Rolled over and convulsed, like, and died."

"The port that Harry gave you for Christmas?" asked Helena. Her heart had not stopped its wild dance since she had realized that someone must have deliberately adulterated the wine—and that no one else in the house but Richard might have been expected to drink it now that Harry was gone off to London. Had John and Williams not shared a glass between them, Richard might have taken two that night after dinner and not been discovered until morning. The probable consequences were only too obvious. And it was Harry's gift to his brother.

"Yes," said Richard. He gave a grim laugh. "The work of a particularly unpleasant mind, don't you think? Will someone please send to the village to fetch the doctor?"

Helena knew she could say nothing more in front of the servants, so instead she stayed silent as Richard himself saw as much as he could to the footman's comfort. Williams seemed to gather courage just from his master's presence.

"You'll be all right, young man. I guarantee you did not take as much wine as that pig! And are far better looking into the bargain." Williams grinned feebly. "You must have a purge, that's all. Hood will see to it and I must escort my wife out of your sick room, don't you think?"

The footman nodded and released Richard's hand, and so allowed his master and mistress to go back together into the corridor.

"Richard!" Helena put her hand on his arm. He turned to her.

"Yes, my lady?" Richard's face was shadowed in the cold light seeping into the hallway from the snow-clad garden outside. He seemed now only unutterably tired, as if he had not slept for days.

"You cannot ignore this!"

He took her by the elbows and the black eyes searched her face.

"I don't intend to," he said.

"Then what are you going to do?"

"As soon as John and, I hope, poor Williams are out of danger, I am going to go to Cornwall, sweet Helena."

"Cornwall? But Harry gave you the port!"

"And drank some with me last night. No, the poison was added this morning, before my brother or Garthwood left, I imagine. Anyone in the household could have done it. Yet none of the attempts against me have been made with any thought as to who else might get hurt in the process. Do you think that Harry would have risked what just happened to John?"

"But my cousin and Harry are friends, didn't you know that? Garthwood told me himself. What makes you choose between them?"

Richard gave her a smile of great sweetness. "It was exquisite port and Harry knew it. What on earth is the point of developing an educated palate if you can't tell when your wine has been tampered with? Don't you think I would have noticed a change in the taste? John and poor Williams probably thought it was how port wine is supposed to be, but if Harry were trying to poison me, he would choose something else."

She could never make him see reason. If he died, Harry would have everything. There was nothing to be gained by Richard's death for Garthwood. "But both my cousin and your brother have gone to London, Richard. For God's sake, what would take you to Cornwall?"

"Trethaerin, my dear. Your old home. I think it's time we paid it a visit."

"We?" Helena felt her pulse shaking under his grip. Did he want her with him after all? "Why should we go to Trethaerin?"

Richard released her arms and, raising one hand, kissed her fingers. "You had better come with me," he said. "Otherwise how will you know if our conspirators succeed? And besides, I will need you to show me around."

"But Garthwood has no earthly reason to harm you, Richard. What on earth do you expect to find there?"

"I don't know, which is why I am going. But it's not Harry who's my enemy, Helena, it's your cousin. If John or Williams suffers any permanent harm, I shall come back and take Nigel Garthwood's life." He did not express the obvious thought that hung between them, that if Helena had not insisted that Garthwood stay the night, it would have been much harder for him to get to the wine—unless, of course, it had been Harry after all. Instead, Richard moved away, and his last comment was made over his shoulder. "And what a damnable waste of an innocent pig."

* * *

It was the coldest January in living memory. The result was fast traveling on the deserted roads, since everywhere the surface was frozen harder than stone. John had made a remarkable recovery. The combination of a youthful constitution and the limited amount of wine he had consumed had let him get out of bed the next day, but the remainder of the holiday was subdued and Richard's siblings showed all the concern Helena could wish toward the ill footman. The day after New Year's, they were sent back to school. It took several days of dedicated nursing before Williams could be declared out of danger. The doctor had cupped him and made the poor footman swallow several evil concoctions, but the man was finally able to sit up and apologize to Richard for so forgetting himself as to drink up an abandoned glass of best port.

"I thought as how it had a flat taste, my lord," he said. "But then I remembered it had sat out in the air all night. It was only that it seemed to be going to waste. I never would have took any from the bottle."

"You may have a bottle, dear Williams. Just get well."

"If it's all the same to you, my lord," said Williams with a grimace, "I think I'm off port wine for now."

They stopped nowhere for a room. Horses were changed and meals taken in the best posting houses, but the chaise went on through the night by moonlight or the flame of their torches, warmed only by the hot bricks provided at each inn. Richard slept sitting upright in his corner, while Helena tried to curl up on the opposite seat, wrapped in a fur rug. During the day he talked courteously of nothing but commonplaces, and she followed his lead. If Richard was at last coming to terms with the fact that his brother was trying to kill him, she would try to have the grace to allow him to do it in his own way. Yet the price for her forbearance was very high. Helena felt that she might as well be traveling with a stranger. It was excessively foolish of you, my girl, she said to herself, to start caring about him to begin with! For heaven's sake, allow him his freedom now.

At least no one knew they had left for Trethaerin. Perhaps as long as they sped farther and farther from Acton Mead, Richard was safe—and it was worth almost anything for that. She would much rather he despise her and return forever to Marie than die at the hands of his brother. Helena would have lost all her hard-won equanimity if she had known that the very day of their departure, Harry had returned to his grandmother's house and once again climbed the ivy. Without compunction he had gone into Richard's room. In two minutes he had what he had come for and, mounted on a swift horse, was following his brother and his sister-in-law into Cornwall.

Eighteen

They took a room at the Anchor in Blacksands.

"You were here last autumn, weren't you, Captain?" said the landlord.

"You have a good memory for a face," smiled Richard. "I'm sure you remember my wife?"

"As was Miss Trethaerin! Well, bless my soul."

"And have you the same chamber, sir? And the same kind-hearted little girl to make up the fire?"

"Why, our Penny's gone to Paris to be a lady's maid. It's a step up in the world for her, all right."

Richard turned on the landlord as if he would strike him to the ground. "And when was this?"

The man had visibly flinched. "It's been these two months, Captain. We've had no word. She's too busy, most like."

Helena had no idea why her husband should seem so concerned about the good fortune of a chambermaid at the inn. His momentary anger disappeared beneath an instant self-control, and she wondered if she had imagined it. "No doubt she is very fine now," he said kindly, and they were shown to a bedchamber.

Helena looked at the narrow bed in silence. Richard looked drawn and tense, the vertical line deep between his brows. Were they to share a bed tonight? Was it always to be at his choice and his bidding? She would trade a great deal for the right to touch him without permission, and know she would be welcome. He threw his case on the dresser and began to unpack it.

"Don't look so full of dismay, Helena. I can't bear it," he said suddenly. "Will this room be satisfactory for tonight? There's no better inn close enough to Trethaerin."

She sat down in the one hard chair and schooled her features. "Of course. I know the Anchor quite well, after all. It's a clean and honorable hostel, even if the first quality don't usually stay here."

Richard was pulling out the gray and black clothes she remembered from the night he had climbed the ivy to her room, when his hair had also been like pitch.

"I shan't be here to find out for myself," he continued. "Your cousin's servants are unlikely to allow me entrance in his absence, so I must use baser means of entry. I want you to describe to me the entire layout of the house."

"I can do better, Richard," she said, her heart in her mouth. "I can show you."

He looked up in surprise. "Helena, God knows what I shall find there!"

"If you go stumbling about in the dark, probably a bullet in the back. What do you expect to find? You think my cousin has been engaging in criminal activity?"

"I hope he has," he said with sudden passion.

"Then take me with you. There's a secret way in from the beach by way of the old smugglers' tunnels. I doubt if Garthwood even knows of its existence."

"Helena, I can't possibly take you."

"You can't possibly leave me behind. I shall follow you. If you think to lock me in this room, the landlord will let me out. I have known the man since I was a child; he'll not gainsay me, whatever you promise him."

Richard came and took her hands. "Helena, what do you take me for? I'm not a monster."

"I never thought for a moment that you were. But although you are hiding it very well, something quite desperate is going on, isn't it? You have shrugged off attempts on your own life, but you can't ignore what happened to John. I don't know what lies between you and Harry, but I know that my cousin is involved. God knows why he should wish to harm you, but you have an idea, don't you?"

"Actually, dear wife, I do not."

"Yet you believe you will find something here that may tell you?"

"Perhaps."

"Then I have a right to be involved, don't you see? I am your wife, Richard, and Garthwood is my cousin. What can be so dreadful that I must be kept in the dark?"

Richard turned and walked away from her. He had no idea what the connection could be between Garthwood, the Paris affair, and the attempts on his life. But Trethaerin might hold the key. And only Helena could tell him what he needed to know if he was to successfully search Trethaerin House; it was as familiar to her as her own voice: every hallway, every entrance, and every hiding place. If Helena was innocent of involvement in the plots against him, there could be no harm, surely. They were far away from Garthwood in London, and even if death waited here in his absence, never had any attempt been made against Helena. If she was guilty, then he had thought to keep her under his eye, where she could do no harm. Or had he? With a painful honesty he faced the fact that he had wanted her with him because he couldn't bear to be parted from her. If she would betray him, then failure or even death didn't matter much, did it? He had nothing to lose by letting Helena come with him to her old home. And if his planning went right, there should be no danger.

"You will have to ride a horse in the dark and the cold. I am going late tonight. Can you keep up?"

"If you will show just a modicum of self-restraint, I shall. I'll be left behind instantly if you're going to ride as if you carried a message for Wellington."

He laughed. "No, indeed, we shall travel most discreetly. You must dress as warmly as you can, in something dark."

"I have my indigo cloak, and if you like, I'll black my face with soot."

"I don't think that'll be required, my lady." Suddenly his face was lit with merriment. "I plan a perfectly quiet evening's entertainment. And if I'm wrong, I only hope I live to tell Charles de Dagonet about this!"

The hedgerows and stone walls were brittle with frost as they trotted along the familiar path to Trethaerin. Helena led the way by a tiny footpath up onto the headland where she had once shown Friarswell to Captain Acton, friend of her lost fiancé, Sir Edward Blake. They turned down between the gorse bushes and tied their hired horses in the trees. Then Helena took a small track that began to drop down to the beach. The air was a deep velvety black. There was no moon, only the faint glimmer of the whitecaps on the sea and a dim gleam near the horizon. When she heard Richard stumble into the sharp spines of some gorse behind her, Helena held out her hand and he took it. She had spent her entire childhood on these headlands and beaches. If necessary, she could have found her way about blindfolded.

"This is the place," she whispered at last.

They had walked across the shifting sand and climbed

back up onto a shelf of rock. There was an old boathouse built like a bird's nest up against the cliff. Helena pushed at the rotten door and went in.

"When we were children, Edward and I would hide down here sometimes. My father thought he had closed off the smugglers' route, but this was our own shortcut."

She pulled aside some piles of old nets and half-rotten sails, then went down on her hands and knees on the floor. Moments later she had tugged at a section of old boards and revealed the hidden trapdoor that lay underneath.

"Trethaerin Cove is far too treacherous to land a boat in any weather, especially one laden with French silk or brandy, so the revenue men never came to this beach. Instead, they would swarm over the sands at Friarswell and wait in vain. Meanwhile, there's actually a narrow seaway in beneath the cliffs of the headland that leads straight to a cave beneath the house. This is just an emergency exit. Another passage leads out beyond the home wood, and that's where the goods were usually taken. Should the king's officers raid the house, they would find nothing. If they discovered the pack train on its way to the other passage, the contraband could be left hidden in the cave and never be found, and the men escape up this way and disappear over the headland."

"We shall have to risk a light," said Richard as they climbed down a set of rickety steps that soon turned into a natural narrow passage in the solid rock, long ago abandoned by the sea.

"But no one can be about. Not even a smuggler would venture out this time of year."

"It may be cold but it's calm enough," said Richard, who had been on boats. "I only hope you are right."

He stopped and knelt over a small lantern that he had carried from the Anchor. For a moment a flame flared up and sent the planes of his face into a sharp relief, then he closed the shutter until only a finger of light lit their way. For several minutes they walked over the uneven sandy floor until the passage opened up and they were looking down into a large cave. The sound of the small waves slapping against the rock was like a constant reverberating echo, and it seemed to carry with it the strong smell of brine and fish. A channel of seawater bisected the rocky floor beneath them.

"The boats could be brought right up here," said Helena. "Good Lord! Is that brandy? Richard! Is this what you expected to find? Garthwood has been smuggling!"

With a certain grim satisfaction Richard helped Helena climb down into the cave and went over to the piled casks that lay against the far wall. He turned to her with a grin. "Thank God!" he said. "This is very much against the law."

They left the cave and Helena led the way into a maze of passages. At last they had climbed several hundred feet and she whispered that they were right under the house.

"This door leads into the study, believe it or not. The opening that we passed a few minutes ago would have put us in the cellars. That's how the brandy could be brought into the house if necessary. The other one gave onto the tracks that the ponies could handle, up beyond the home wood on the other side from where we came in. Father locked those entrances with iron grilles years ago. I wonder why there is any brandy left in the cave now?"

"Perhaps your cousin left home in a hurry?" replied Richard, and he doused the lantern.

Helena listened for some minutes at the door. It was well past midnight. If there was no one in the house but servants, they should be long asleep and well out of earshot. With the sound of her own heart pounding like the sea in her ears, she pushed at the catch and opened the door. Her father's old study lay dark, silent, and deserted before them. Richard carefully relit the lantern.

"What are we looking for?" asked Helena softly.

"I have no idea. Records, perhaps; letters. Where would he hide such things?"

Helena led Richard to the desk and she tried the top drawer. It was locked.

"No," he said. "It's too obvious."

Leaving her to sit in her father's old chair, he began quickly and with a frightening thoroughness to search the room. Books were removed from their shelves and replaced, paintings lifted and examined. Nothing was overlooked, yet nothing seemed to be disturbed as he finished. Helena fought back the tide of emotion that had assailed her since they had first entered the study. She had never expected to sit in this room again. Her father had taught her to read at this very desk. They had made a game out of unlocking the drawers and finding her reader. Each time it would lie in a different spot. Part of the delight had been to go to the chimney and bring out the spare key, which Papa declared was hidden there by the fairies just for his little girl. She buried her face in her hands for a moment.

"I'm damned," said Richard's voice quietly, just behind her, "if I want to break the lock. It would be far more discreet if they didn't know we'd been here."

Helena looked up. "Try the chimney piece," she said faintly. "There's a little shelf close behind the rosettes. It's entirely hidden unless you know where to look. My father had a spare key, you see."

Richard did as she suggested. "Clever creature!" he said as he produced the little brass key. "I doubt if Garthwood knew it was there."

By the dim light of the half-shuttered lantern they began

to go through the papers stacked inside the desk. They seemed mostly to consist of household accounts.

"Look, it's a receipt for my gold chain," said Helena.

"Which I notice you never wear."

"I gave it to the parson for charity."

Richard raised a brow. "Did you? It was quite valuable, it seems. But the snuffbox I received as my token of the winter solstice is French and came in with the brandy, no doubt. See?"

Richard held out a sheaf of papers that seemed to consist of lists of goods received and sent out. He ran over the first page, then handed it to Helena. She followed the crabbed writing for several pages. There was nothing terribly incriminating there, but perhaps Richard was right. The snuffbox was listed, and the other items classed simply as merchandise would very likely be the casks of brandy that they had seen stacked below.

"The man has been making a fortune," said Richard grimly as he went over more books and papers.

Helena watched him for a while, then, when the last drawer had been emptied and they had found nothing more, Richard stood up and cursed quietly.

"As I thought, too obvious," he said.

"You give up too soon, my lord," she said lightly. "There are secret compartments." Reaching into the back of the second drawer, she pressed at a panel and brought out another handful of papers. "Here, you look at this half."

"Your cousin is a greedy man, Helena," Richard said after a moment. "What a scheme!"

"You have found something?"

"Not enough."

"What's this?" asked Helena. "It seems to be lists of girls' names and there are quite large sums listed against them, and another list of figures. Not even Friarswell and Tre-thaerin need that many housemaids."

Richard took the paper from her and silently read over the lists.

"There's a Penny there," said Helena helpfully, "and a date in October. Could that be the chambermaid from the Anchor? There's a fourteen written by her name. What does it mean?"

"Nothing," said Richard sharply. "Forget it! Ah, this is what I need! He has kept clear records of his purchases of contraband after all."

Helena was already reading another sheet. The handwriting was a beautiful copperplate, and the paper scented. A woman's hand—and the superscription was an address in Paris. She looked up at her husband's face and the golden hair glinting in the shaft of light from the lantern. "Is this what you have been hiding from me?" she said at last. "When did you meet Madame Relet?"

Nineteen

The midnight eyes met hers and widened.

"She's not very flattering about you, you know," said Helena.

Richard dropped into another chair and leaned back. "I can imagine," he said dryly. "What does she say?"

"It's in French, but I think I can translate: 'We have had some minor interference directed by a man whom I discover to be Viscount Lenwood. Why he should take an interest, I can't imagine. But dismiss him, my friend. He is no more trouble than a fly on the wall and can do us no harm. I do not waste my time thinking about him.' It doesn't sound like a conspiracy to murder you. They don't even consider you dangerous. What's this word here? My French vocabulary isn't up to it."

Richard leaned forward and took the letter from her hand. "I did not mean for you to know," he said at last. "But I suppose there's no way out now, is there? I'm sorry if I offend you, my dear. It means brothel."

Helena went white. "You mean all those girls? Penny from the Anchor?"

"I'm afraid so."

"But the landlord thought she had gone to be a lady's maid."

"So did she, no doubt."

Helena took up the list of names and went over it. "Then what are these figures here?" she asked.

"Their ages, I'm afraid."

Helena looked up into the shadowed gaze. There was nothing there now but a great sadness and compassion.

"Then some of them were just girls," she said. "As young as twelve! Oh, Richard! No wonder you have tried to stop it. Why on earth didn't you tell me before? Is this why you went to Paris?"

"Of course it is. And why I stayed there after the war. Dagonet and I heard about the English girls by accident and went to investigate. I hired men to watch the place, and some victims were saved when I purchased their freedom outright. A few are now otherwise employed in London, thank God, and a couple restored to their families. But Madame Relet is right. She could take my money and buy more, and she laughed at me for my pains. I have been essentially ineffective in stopping the trade. There is nothing unlawful about it, you see. A girl of twelve can legally consent to employment."

Helena had leapt up and was silently pacing up and down. "Without knowing, of course, to what she was consenting. And then to be trapped in a foreign country. It's monstrous! Why on earth did you keep this from me?"

"It's not an area of human endeavor that gentlemen usually discuss with their wives."

"You thought I would have the vapors or refuse to allow you back into the drawing room?"

"I don't know," said Richard slowly. "Perhaps I did. I should have known better. My fearless, sensible Helena!"

"For heaven's sake, Richard, they are children! I suppose there are such places in London too?"

Richard nodded. "But at least when desperate, the girls

have a chance if they run away. In Paris, with no money and no knowledge of the language, they are helpless, and Garthwood has been enticing them there with false promises."

"Like little Penny. If it's not illegal, it should be! The law must be changed."

"I have been endeavoring to bring my father to that view. But as you may have surmised for yourself, the earl is of the old school. 'Laissez-faire' is his motto. He sees no role for government in righting social ills. And I shan't have enough influence myself until I inherit the title, which could be thirty years or more."

"No wonder there is bad blood between you. Then what can we do?"

And suddenly Richard grinned. "Mr. Garthwood wasn't content with the profit to be made from Madame Relet in gold. He has turned that money into brandy and doubled it without paying his fair share of duty, and that is something that even my father frowns on. It is criminal activity. We can call the customs men, of course. Even without the casks in the cellar there is enough information here to put your cousin out of circulation."

Helena helped him to gather together the necessary papers and replace the others. She was thinking furiously. Madame Relet's letter made clear what she had long ago surmised: Only Harry had the motivation to try to murder Richard. Garthwood might be a villain, but in spite of the smuggling and Richard's attempts to save some of the girls in Paris, he had no cause to harm the viscount. In which case, unless Harry was involved, that still left the attempts on Richard's life unexplained—as was Harry's friendship with Garthwood. Yet Richard had ignored that and would continue to ignore it. He had pursued Garthwood and done what he could to save the girls in Paris while shrugging off the attacks against himself. It seemed a terrible and incomprehensible bravery.

She was so preoccupied that the other letter almost slipped from her attention. One glance told her it was from Edward. She turned it over and looked at the front. It had been addressed to her! Why on earth should her cousin have kept one of Edward's letters and not sent it on to her? Without thinking, she slipped it into her pocket. At that moment there was a slight noise in the hallway.

Richard put a finger to his lips and signaled her to the place in the paneling where the hidden door to the underground passages still stood open. The light went out in his hand and they groped in the dark into the opening. Helena closed the door behind them and Richard put his ear to it.

"There's a peephole," she whispered.

The faintest glimmer of light shone into their hiding place from a pinhole in the wall. Richard looked through it for a moment. Then he took her hand and guided her silently back down the passage.

"It was only a servant," he said at last. "Though I'm not happy that he's about this late. I think we have enough to hang our friend, though not to draw and quarter him as he deserves. Let's get out of here."

They continued down the passage in the dark until they at last saw the dim phosphorescent gleam of water. They were almost back in the cave. It was some faint instinct, perhaps, honed by his years operating under the noses of the French army in the Peninsula, that caused Richard to stop just before he stepped out into the open, pulling Helena behind him. In the next moment there was a blaze of light as half a dozen torches were lit at once.

"And so we are nicely trapped," he whispered, and he

leaned his head back against the wall and laughed silently. "For as we noticed, they are stirring at the house as well."

"We can go back and try the other passage—the one to the lane."

And then she also heard the slight noise that Richard had already noticed. "No, I don't think we can. Someone comes down that very conduit behind us. I'm afraid, dear wife, that we have been outwitted. I can't tell you how sincerely I hope you aren't a party to it."

Helena had been clinging to his hand, but she forced herself to let go. If it came to a fight, Richard would not want to be encumbered with her. As for his last comment, there was no time to think what he might have meant. The noise of footsteps in the passageway behind them was getting louder. She peered around him and looked into the cave. There were several rough-looking fellows climbing out of a boat that lay bobbing in the water. None of them were men from the village or anyone she recognized from her childhood. Nigel Garthwood sat alone on a barrel. His head was cocked to one side as if he were listening.

"You might as well come out, my lord," he said softly. "I have loyal servants in every pathway, and there is no escape."

"Do you suppose we should go out and face him?" said Richard. "Or continue to skulk in the dark? It's obvious which would be the nobler course, but in spite of carrying the blood of earls, I'm damned if I'm feeling terribly noble."

The light from the opening danced for a moment across his features. He was grinning! Helena thrust herself back against the wall as Richard drew out his pistol and looked around.

"Stay here," he whispered, and he began to run up the tunnel they had just left, back toward the house. It was a slim hope, surely, that he could avoid their pursuers. Clinging to the damp wall, Helena saw his faint silhouette as he sped up the passageway, then he jumped and seemed to disappear. A moment later the outline of a man carrying a torch appeared in the same spot, the flame leaping over the rough, glimmering walls of the rock. There was one darker shadow lost in the recesses of the roof, which suddenly dropped and knocked the torch to the floor. The scuffle was entirely silent except for a sudden grunt and a dull thud as the pistol cracked into a skull and the man fell back unconscious. Helena ran to Richard's side.

" 'Once more unto the breech, dear friend,' " he said, and taking her hand began to run with her back up the passageway to the house. They were too late. More men began to pour into the conduits from the study and the other passageways until they were surrounded. The men stopped at the sight of Richard's pistol.

"Don't I recognize you from London?" asked Richard with a polite bow in the direction of an unpleasant-looking ruffian who had thrust a torch in their faces and was grinning at them. "Decided to take up full-time employment?"

There was obviously no hope of escape, even if Richard were to start shooting. The men were also armed to the teeth. Helena thought for one dreadful moment that her husband was going to try to fight his way free against impossible odds, but instead he tossed his pistol to the floor in the direction of the man with the torch and laughed.

"I surrender, sir," he said. "I trust you won't take any unseemly action in front of the lady?"

His answer was a blow across the face that sent him staggering backward.

"Mr. Garthwood wants a word first, my lord," said the man. "Otherwise it might be unseemly enough. You left one of my friends dead back there in the city."

They were jostled back down to the cave and thrust out into the blaze of torchlight. Helena was allowed to sit down on an outcropping of rock, but Richard was dragged between two of the men to stand before Garthwood.

"So you came down to make your claim, my lord?" said Garthwood. "I should have thought you'd have come in the day with your man of business. This is rather a havey-cavey way to go on for a member of one of England's first families, isn't it, breaking into folks' houses at midnight?"

"Alas, as you no doubt noticed at Acton Mead, sir, I have appallingly sorry manners." What did the man mean—make your claim?

"I tried to find the unfortunate document there, of course, but you had it hidden, I suppose. After that it seemed simpler to get you out of the way."

"What are you talking about, Mr. Garthwood?" said Helena. "Do you mean to tell me you came to Acton Mead before and were looking for something there?"

"He hasn't told you, has he?" said Garthwood. "I thought not."

"So it was you," said Richard with a smile, "who searched my room in September? Whatever for? I suppose I must commend you for having the nerve to enter my home in broad daylight. Can you ever forgive me, Helena? I must have been out of my wits."

"I forgot it long ago, my lord," said Helena. Instead, she was thinking that this meant she had been wrong too. It hadn't been Harry.

"I'm sure a great many people think the world would be a better place without my insufferable presence," said Richard to Garthwood. "But why you in particular?"

"Who else can Helena turn to if you should meet with some sad accident?" said Garthwood. "Like a stray bullet in the wood, or a fall from a horse, or even an unpredictable elephant at a fair? She would be left destitute and alone in the world once more. Perhaps then she would accept my suit? To put you out of the way seemed the best first course of action."

"But she would not be as penniless as you seem to imagine, sir. Lady Lenwood will inherit Acton Mead and a considerable independent income upon my sad demise. Whether she would entertain your suit I cannot say, but she would be under no financial compunction to do so."

Helena looked at him in amazement. "But I thought Harry would inherit from you?" she said. This was getting more confusing by the minute. Garthwood still wanted to marry her. Was he insane? And did Harry know about Richard's will? Harry might eventually get the earldom, but there would be no immediate financial benefit. In which case, what was his involvement?

"Did you, my dear? I should have told you." Richard's cheek was beginning to color where he had been struck. "Until I married, he was my heir, of course; but didn't you realize that I would change my will to provide for you? Harry knew I had done it."

"I never thought about it," she said. But the knowledge seemed to light a small fire of courage. He had cared enough to leave her Acton Mead! She looked from him to her cousin. She would far rather Richard stay alive, than she inherit anything! "But I can't see, Mr. Garthwood, why you would have wished still to marry me if you thought I brought no dowry."

"I have to admit, sir," said Richard, "that I am wondering the same thing."

"Are you, my lord? I can hardly believe it, and that is why you have to die, and your knowledge with you. You are otherwise no more than a nuisance. It's been a devil of a task to keep track of you these last few months. The dye was a clever idea. Madame Relet eventually saw through it, of course, but by then you had already left again. Do you suppose you lead a charmed life? I think finally that has come to an end, don't you? But I shall not leave my poor cousin alone very long. It was a difficult day for me when you whisked her away from this roof and left me to my wounded sensibilities. You seem to forget that she was considering my offer at the time."

"Please don't pretend there is any affection between us," Helena interrupted with considerable heat, "for there never has been and never will be. You are wasting your time to kill Richard if you are under any insane illusion about my feelings, for I will never marry you!"

"Thank you for that, at least," murmured Richard to Helena, and one eye closed in a small wink.

"I had thought of that," said Garthwood, ignoring him. "In which case my cousin will have to follow her husband to his watery grave."

"So that Harry can inherit after all? Is that what this is all about? Harry has been your accomplice from the beginning, hasn't he? Did he promise you a share of the proceeds from Richard's wealth? Aren't you satisfied with the profits from your unconscionable racket here?"

"It is my—I prefer to call it a business venture—my business that I wish to protect, dear Helena. Richard understands."

At which Viscount Lenwood began to laugh out loud. "I'm damned if I do, sir! Madame Relet doesn't seem to think I'm worth bothering about, yet you've gone to a considerable amount of effort, it would seem, to murder me."

"It's on this end that I can't have you interfering, of

course," said Garthwood, and he turned to the men who held Richard's arms. "Kill him!"

The man standing at Richard's left elbow had produced a long knife. As he swung it and Helena screamed, Richard tore from their grasp, then dropped to the rock floor and rolled, kicking hard as he did so. The two men fell and tripped over each other as Richard spun away from the reach of the knife. As others surged toward him, he was on his feet and had leapt back toward the shelter of the rock at the entrance to the tunnel. He was almost there when his pursuers stopped uncertainly in their tracks and Richard was arrested as if he had run into a wall. The passage was guarded. The man who stood there smiled and raised a pistol.

"I hope I'm in time, dear brother," he said, and tossed back an errant lock of black hair that had fallen over his forehead. "You seem to have the parti-colored look on your cheek this time. How the hell is the family's name for elegance to be kept up if you will keep appearing in public brindled like a cow?"

Helena ran toward them. It seemed that she was in a nightmare. She could never run faster than a bullet, and not only Harry had a weapon trained on Richard. One of the ruffians had also raised his gun and was taking aim at Richard's back.

"For God's sake, Helena! Stay back!" cried Richard as the cavern resounded with the sound of two pistols fired at once, then seemed to explode into a cacophony of gunfire. Men were appearing out of the dark passage behind Harry and pouring into the cave. There were yells and grunts as flesh thudded into flesh and screams as bullets found human targets. At the arrival of the newcomers, the smugglers had tossed most of the torches hissing into the sea. The result was that the air seemed to fill with smoke and noise, and nothing could be made out except dark shapes and leaping shadows. There was only one thing that Helena saw clearly before chaos took over. The ruffian who had been aiming at Richard's back had dropped like a stone and his bullet struck harmlessly into the rock as he fell. Harry's expert aim had found its target. It was Harry who had killed the marksman and saved Richard's life.

"Take care of her this time," said Richard's voice. "And for God's sake, stay out of it. You've done your bit already, rather well, as it happens."

"Yes, my lord!" cried Harry. "Though I admit it was a damned close-run thing. Thank God I went back for the revenue men."

And Helena was thrust into Harry's arms and pulled to safety out of the battle.

"You shot that man!" said Helena. "The one who was aiming at Richard's back!"

"Well, I'm damned if I'm going to let some rickety fellow like that shoot down my brother. He would probably have half missed and made a mess out of it. It's the one advantage of having decent eyesight. You've a slightly higher chance than the next fellow of hitting your target cleanly. Are you all right? You won't faint, will you? Richard will skin me alive if anything happens to you."

"Will he?" said Helena as they climbed behind the shelter of an outcropping of rock. "No, I won't faint. Who are all these men?"

"His Majesty's excisemen, of course. I told Richard about Garthwood seeming to have an inexhaustible source of rather excellent liquor; I have been buying some from him, as a matter of fact. It was just a hunch that he was using Tre-thaerin for bringing in brandy. Thank God it was the case, or we'd have looked like fools! As it happens, after getting thoroughly lost in your damned Cornish lanes, I came across a tidy little string of pack ponies hacking up the headland. I saw where the ponies were hidden and watched where the men came in, then I thought I had better call in reinforcements. Seemed like too many fellows for Richard and me to take on single-handed. Here, get back!''

The cave was now filled with fighting men. As they moved into hand-to-hand combat, there was less gunfire. Helena saw Richard's yellow head among the others in the gloom. Somehow he had come into possession of a sword—dropped by a wounded excise officer, perhaps. He had taken up the one remaining torch in his other hand and was fighting over its possession with one of the smugglers. Others, including her cousin, were piling into the boat. If only they could plunge the cave into total darkness, there was still a chance that Garthwood and his men might escape. The man made another lunge for the torch. He was armed with a long knife and a wicked-looking cudgel. He swung the latter in a long arc at Richard's sword arm.

"Not again, sir," said Richard. His clear voice seemed the only sound that Helena could distinguish above the hubbub. "But then, I was alone in London, wasn't I? This time I have professional reinforcements. For God's sake, dispatch him, officer!''

The man glanced back for only a moment, victim of the oldest trick in the fighters' arsenal. It was enough. Richard neatly disarmed his assailant, and sent him to the floor with a blow from the flat of the blade. But then he had to give way before the combined onslaught of three other men. With her heart in her mouth, Helena watched him suddenly toss the torch high into the air. It landed with a hiss on the barrels of brandy, and the flame flickered and died for a moment. In the next instant the kegs caught fire and with a roar of blue flame the cave was lit like daylight with burning brandy and a shower of fiery barrel staves where more than one cask exploded. Richard then took up a flaming piece of debris and tossed it into the boat. The tar-soaked boards caught fire instantly, and several smugglers dived into the water. Garthwood stood and raised his pistol.

Harry determinedly pulled Helena farther back into their shelter. She fought back her panic. Richard had been right all along about Harry. How could she possibly make it up to them? "How did you know we were here?" she asked. Pray that Richard survive this night!

"Dickon left me instructions in his room at Acton Mead, of course. We had it arranged beforehand. I followed Garthwood to London and saw him safely settled in, or so I thought. When I realized he'd given me the slip and left the city, I went straight to Acton Mead and climbed the ivy. Didn't hit Sir Lionel this time, you'll be glad to know. Richard's note said you had come down here to check up on our hunch about the brandy. I got here as fast as possible. You have to admit it was splendid timing."

"I'd rather you didn't cut it so close next time, sir."

"Well, I admit I was expecting things to happen right after Christmas, when I first followed your nasty cousin to London. He left a man to watch Acton Mead, of course. He'd had a man watching me in Oxford before. Richard knew that. And we supposed he wouldn't move until he got the message that you and Dickon had crept away in the night."

"Or that Richard was dead," said Helena grimly. "You mean Richard knew that Garthwood would follow us here? He walked openly into a trap?"

Harry shrugged. "He knew it was a possibility. But if Garthwood had waited in London for a message from Acton Mead, as we expected, you'd have had a couple of days' lead. As it was, I suppose Garthwood got impatient and was already at your doorstep, then came down here on your very heels. Richard knew it might happen. But my brother is a man who loves risk, dear Helena. Why else did he marry a lady he had known for two days? Though I don't imagine he thought for a moment that Garthwood would harm you, or he'd never have brought you here."

"We couldn't come any sooner. There was poison put in the port you gave Richard for a present."

Harry listened in silence as Helena described how John and Williams had been taken ill.

"The man is a devil," he said fiercely. "I already know to my cost he has some depraved knowledge about drugs. I believe he slipped something in my drink the day I first met him, so that I would talk. No doubt I was garrulous enough, then I was sick as a dog."

"When you first climbed the ivy? I thought you were drunk, Harry."

"Well, it wouldn't be too out of character, of course, but actually, I was just ill. Richard nursed me most of that night. I'm sorry, Helena, but I'm going to have to leave you here and go put a bullet in your cousin."

There was a small noise behind them, and Helena whirled around.

"No need, sir. His Majesty's representatives have done it for you," said a familiar voice. Richard had climbed to where Harry had taken Helena, the fair hair lit from behind by the still-burning barrels. His breathing was slightly disordered and his coat seemed to be torn, but he was otherwise perfectly calm. "Nigel Garthwood put himself in the way of a stray ball of lead. I'm damned sorry, actually, because now we're never going to understand this insane coil."

Helena flung herself at him. "Richard! Thank God! You're not hurt?"

"Might I take it that you're really as pleased as you seem, sweet wife?" said Richard, and pulling her to him, he kissed her without mercy.

"What's left to understand, old fellow?" said Harry after a discreet interval.

"What Helena's role in all this is, of course," said Richard.

Twenty

They went together up the long rock passage and back into the study at Trethaerin House. Someone had been sent to see to their horses, variously left in the woods. The revenue officers had finally overpowered the smugglers, and the survivors were being led away. Garthwood's body had been trussed in a piece of old sail and carried out with the prisoners. Helena felt an overpowering relief that he was dead and yet that neither Richard nor Harry had killed him directly. He had been her cousin, after all, and in spite of everything she now knew about him, he had been generous enough to her when he first inherited Friarswell and Trethaerin from Edward.

Richard had spent some time with the commanding officer of the excisemen, and given him all the written records that they had discovered that proved the involvement of Nigel Garthwood in brandy smuggling. The records about the girls he kept to himself. They weren't relevant to customs officers' concerns.

"We still don't know," said Richard slowly once they were seated, "why Garthwood so wished for my untimely decease, except that it would appear to have been something to do with my wife."

He had poured them all a glass of the excellent contraband

that sat on the sideboard. Helena sipped very carefully at the unfamiliar liquor.

"You surely don't think Helena knew about all this, do you?" said Harry indignantly.

"No, Harry," said Helena instantly. "Of course I didn't, but don't you see? We have cleared up nothing really. Garthwood said he wanted Richard dead so he could marry me, but that's absurd. There was certainly no insane passion there; my cousin was as cold as a fish. What could he possibly hope to gain? He didn't even know that Acton Mead would be mine. In fact, he was counting on my being penniless and turning to him for help. And then he implied that if he had succeeded in murdering Richard and I had turned down his suit, he would have had no compunction in dispatching me too."

"If I had known that, I would never have brought you, my lady," said Richard. "You will believe that, won't you?" Then he turned to Harry. "He seemed to think that I knew something. Something more than about Madame Relet or about the brandy smuggling. Something to do with Helena or Trethaerin, obviously. What is it? The answer to that question is the crux of the whole issue."

"Helena doesn't know," said Harry firmly.

"Yes, Garthwood made that clear." Richard gave Helena a smile that threatened to break her heart. "But he thought I did. What knowledge could I have about Trethaerin that Helena would not?" He stood and began to pace the room. "Nothing in Paris or in England; before that, then? Something that he believed Edward might have told me, perhaps?"

"And what did Edward tell you?" asked Harry. Helena realized that Richard must have told his brother about Sir Edward Blake long before.

Richard smiled at them. "That's just it. Nothing at all. I

thought he was trying to tell me something when he died, but all he was able to say was Helena's name."

"And how would Garthwood know about anything between you and Sir Edward Blake?" asked Harry.

"Edward wrote to me," said Helena suddenly. "He sent a letter before he died, but Garthwood kept it. I found it in his desk." She felt in her pocket and took out the stained sheet.

"The devil! He opened it?" said Harry.

"My dear Helena," said Richard softly. "If you could bear to read it now? Only Edward, it would seem, can cast any light at all on this crazy web of intrigue."

Helena carefully unfolded the crabbed writing that had been so familiar from all Edward's Peninsular letters. "It's mostly just ordinary news," she said after a while. "No! Oh, Richard, listen to this!" She began to read aloud.

"I wonder sometimes if I shall ever see dear old Cornwall again. Although we all believe the war is nearly over and Boney stares defeat in the face, there are too many mishaps here waiting to trap a fellow. If anything should happen to me, dear cousin, I surely shouldn't want old Garthwood to get his hands on Friarswell. So I am taking the precaution of seeing that he doesn't. I have written a will leaving everything to you. I had a couple of the fellows witness it. I thought I'd give the document to Richard Acton for safe-keeping. You know what I think about him; if he were here right now, I'd have asked him to be a witness, but he's off on one of his clandestine adventures, as usual. Until he gets back, I'm putting the papers in the safest place I can think of: stitched inside the cover of my brandy flask. I'm a dab hand now with a needle, you know."

She stopped and looked up at them. "I don't think I can go on." And Helena laid down the letter and burst into tears.

Richard put his head in his hands and allowed Harry to

put an arm around her shoulders. "Don't cry, for God's sake," he said gently. "Are you all right?"

"Of course." Helena smiled bravely and wiped at her eyes. "I'm fine. Dear Edward!"

"Where is this brandy flask?" asked Harry after a moment. "Buried in France?"

"Not at all," said Richard, then he looked up and met Helena's eyes. "It's at my father's house, in the safe where I left it. Helena, I'm so very sorry."

"For what?" asked Helena.

"For everything," said Richard. "We had better get to King's Acton right away, I suppose, and see if this thing is a legal document."

"And if it is?" said Harry.

"Then Helena is mistress of Friarswell and Trethaerin in her own right, dear brother. Which means, incidentally, that she had no need at all to marry me."

"Well, you always were a gallant fool, Dickon," said Harry. "So that's what Garthwood was trying to get out of me: the whereabouts of the brandy flask. He searched for it at Acton Mead. Then when he failed, he followed me to the inn with the excellent oysters. He must have been in an agony over when you might reveal that you had it. No wonder he thought you'd be better off dead."

"He would have assumed it was why you married me," said Helena. What did it matter if she had been rightful owner of her old home all along if Richard didn't need her? "And then he thought if you were out of the way, he could keep possession by marrying me himself."

"And I was as ignorant of the will's existence as you were. Unfortunately, Garthwood didn't know my peculiar character. I suppose to the greedy, everyone is assumed to have the same motivation. If I had known of the will, of course, my reaction would have been the opposite of his. I wouldn't have married you; I'd have given the document directly into your hands and all of this could have been avoided."

"Why," said Helena, choking back her reaction, "did he not just murder me when he found out about the will?"

"Because he thought that I knew about it. He would always be afraid that I might reveal its existence, and as he said, 'make my claim.' Without Trethaerin, all of his operations would have been impossible. The man must have been in the most dreadful suspense since the day he read Edward's letter. When he couldn't find the brandy flask, what more straightforward act to a creature of his type than to see that I met with an accident?" Richard gave a wry smile. "I suppose I must be grateful that he was not more practiced in assassination."

"And not a decent shot," said Harry. "Nor familiar with your embarrassing prowess with horses and elephants." He stood up and yawned. "Do you dear creatures perceive that it's almost dawn?"

Richard rang the bell, and a bleary-eyed servant eventually appeared. Helena realized that the household staff had managed to sleep through the entire night's occurrences. Not a sound from the cave would have reached the house, and they had been quiet enough in the study.

"I want my chaise and four brought from the Anchor in Blacksands," Richard said, ignoring the man's dropped jaw at the sight of strangers in the master's study. "You may tell the innkeeper that the request comes from Viscount Lenwood. I shall trust him to pack for us, and give him this." He tossed a purse toward the startled man.

The servant looked past him at Helena. "Is that really you, Miss Trethaerin?"

"That's right, Potter, it's me. You won't see Mr. Garthwood again, I'm afraid."

"Then I'm heartily glad to hear you say so, ma'am. There's been the most fearful goings-on here since you left."

Helena looked down at her hands, thinking of poor Penny and the other girls, then she raised her blond head and smiled. "That's all over now, Potter. Please to send for the carriage as the viscount asked."

The journey to King's Acton went by in a blur. Helena slept for much of the way. She had not expected to feel so tired, but then, she had never experienced these various adventures before, including the secret that she still kept from Richard. As before, they didn't stop very often or very long. When she woke one time, it was to hear Harry telling Richard about the dramatic cold weather that had seized London before he left.

Helena heard Harry's account with indifference. Mixed with an enormous relief that Richard was now safe, there was still a dreadful apprehension. She, ordinary Helena Trethaerin, had an estate of her own after all. Richard had never needed to marry her. Would he now live to regret his generosity? Would he leave directly from his father's house for Marie's company in London? Her mistrust of Harry had helped to turn Richard against her, but that misjudgment could only have grown because Richard had never trusted or confided in her. She remembered what Charles de Dagonet had said: *Be patient with him.* But if Richard left her alone again at Acton Mead, she would never get the chance to redeem herself, and then Richard was as lost to her as if Garthwood had succeeded. The thought chilled her more than the cold of the ice-bound roads.

* * *

The Countess of Acton came out and met them in the hall. A moment later the earl appeared behind her and scowled at his sons.

"What on earth are you doing abroad in this horrid weather, children?" said the countess with her beautiful smile. "I thought I would be turned into an icicle on our own trip back from London, and apart from my little room, this place is as cold as the grave. Richard, did Harry give you that appalling bruise?"

"You must believe that I ran into a door, my lady," said Richard, kissing her, then turning to his father. "Your servant, my lord. I trust I find you in good health?"

Harry in turn kissed his mother on the cheek, but the Countess of Acton was gazing at Helena.

"How can you drag your wife about the country in her interesting condition, Richard?" the countess said. "Really, you men are about as sensitive as oxen. Come in and get warm, my dear, and have some food and something hot to drink. How long have you known?"

"Known what, my lady?" said Richard.

"Why, that your pauper wife is planning to present us with a next generation heir to Acton, of course. I have not borne six children only to be incapable of recognizing when a lady is *enceinte*."

At which Richard went quite white, as his father flushed a deep shade of crimson. "Is this true?" the viscount said to Helena at last.

She could not avoid his eyes. "Yes. I wasn't sure until recently, but yes, there'll be a new Acton in the spring. I meant to tell you, but there never seemed to be the opportunity. Are you pleased?"

Richard looked blankly at her. "Helena, for God's sake! You mean to tell me that you went all the way to Cornwall while carrying our child? And all those boisterous games with the others at Acton Mead? How dare you risk yourself? Are you deranged?"

"Of course she's not," said Harry quickly. "Congratulations, Richard and Helena. You realize"—and he gave Helena a friendly wink—"that this puts me out of the running for the earldom on a permanent basis, for which I'm very glad. And she's no longer a pauper, Mother. Tell them why we came, Dickon, because Father's long silence means he's about to have apoplexy."

Richard had taken Helena firmly by the hand. His grasp threatened to crush hers and she could feel the pulse racing through his fingers.

"My lord," he said calmly to his father. "It may please you to hear that we believe my wife to be the rightful owner of considerable property in Cornwall. If I might fetch that brandy flask that I left here after our last visit? Then there are some other papers that I wish you to see, which do not involve the ladies."

"Damn you, sir, for an irresponsible lout," spluttered the earl. "She's carrying the heir to my name and you have been dragging her about the countryside like a farm girl. Damn the property! I don't care if she has a penny to bless herself with or not, she's carrying the fourth Earl of Acton! Lady Acton, please see to this child!"

"I am in no danger, my lord," said Helena firmly. "I am young and as healthy, I trust, as any poor girl on a farm. It will be some time before my condition requires that I take any special precautions. I would very much like to see the brandy flask, too, if you would be so kind as to allow Richard to fetch it."

"There is really no reason why this interesting object cannot be examined in my own drawing room over tea, though, is there?" said the countess. "Before we all freeze to death in the hall."

Richard was forced to release his wife's fingers and allow his mother to lead Helena into the comfort of a private little room with a blazing fire and elegant spindle-legged chairs. He still seemed to be in shock when the men rejoined the ladies, and he silently handed to Helena Edward's battered leather case with its silver crest. She looked at it for a moment. Then, when Lady Acton gave her a pair of embroidery scissors, she carefully picked apart the stitching. She had wanted Richard to keep the flask, all those months ago at Trethaerin, thinking Edward's death a harder blow to him than to herself, but of course it brought him nothing but a painful memory and he had locked it away. And thus Nigel Garthwood had not found it at Acton Mead and instead had determined to kill his rival. A single sheet of paper lay between the cover and the flask. Helena unfolded it.

"The last will and testament of Sir Edward Blake of Friarswell, Cornwall," she read aloud, and silently scanned the rest. Then she handed the paper to Richard.

"It's all in order," he said at last. "These witnesses should even be possible to track down. Clever Edward! Helena, you are mistress without question of Friarswell and Trethaerin. This is what Edward was trying to tell me. If I hadn't been such a damned fool, I'd have guessed."

"And saved your regrettable involvement with me and my nasty cousin," said Helena.

"Oh, fiddlesticks," said the countess, standing suddenly. "And left Richard still wandering aimlessly around the world, no doubt. Now he will have a son to take care of. What will you call the child if it's a boy?"

"Edward," said Helena and Richard at the same time.

"Damn me, sir," said the earl. "I'm glad to see you do your duty by your house at last. Edward! It's very well. It was my father's name, of course."

"I think," said Harry, catching his mother's eye, "that it's time we left the viscount and his wife alone for a moment. Father, there is something that Richard and I wanted you to see. Brother Dickon, let me have those papers and you take care of Helena for a moment, there's a good fellow."

Richard laughed suddenly and handed Harry a sheaf of documents that Helena recognized to be those they had found in her father's desk: the sad lists of names of little girls sold into virtual slavery, and the records of the money that Nigel Garthwood had begun to make from the trade.

"If you are going to join your brother in cudgeling me about my political views, Henry, I won't stand and listen to your impertinence, sir."

"Come, my lord," said the countess, taking her husband's arm and leading him from the room. "Only Richard has the nerve to try and cudgel you. You know that Harry would never dare."

And Richard and Helena were left alone.

Twenty-one

"I am very happy about the baby," Richard began. "Are you sure you are well, that you put yourself in no danger?"

"None at all," she replied. "I talked with the midwife in Mead Farthing, a very sensible country woman who seemed to think that females have babies all the time. In her opinion I should carry on with a normal life and refuse to confine myself until the last possible moment."

"Why on earth didn't you tell me when you found out?"

Helena looked away from his dark eyes. "You have not exactly been very available, my lord. And then when John became ill, and Williams, there never seemed to be the right moment."

"When I think what was risked in taking you to Trethaerin!"

Her eyes flew up to meet his. "You couldn't have left me behind! I was already involved. Trethaerin was my home. And what about you? How can you dismiss the risk to yourself so casually? If you hadn't married me, you would never have had to face all those attempts on your life."

He shrugged, and then smiled. "Your cousin was a pretty paltry assassin."

"Did you suspect me?" she asked. Richard had begun to pace, but he stopped and whirled around. "I rather hope you did. It would have been only natural to wonder if I was in

league with Garthwood, and maybe it will even out my accusations against Harry. I couldn't think of anyone else!"

"I thought I did. And for that, I can never forgive myself.
But I couldn't maintain it. As for Harry, I should have shared
what I knew with you as it happened. What else were you
to imagine? I have been in the habit for years of trying to
protect him. It's a terrible affliction to be a favorite child,
you see. Harry never asked for it, but my father has always
burdened him with the force of an entirely selfish attention.
He must always do better than anyone else—at riding, at
shooting, all of it. Father made him practice until he was
exhausted. He had to creep away if he wanted to join me in
normal mischief like any other boy. Then it would hurt him
terribly when I alone was punished and he was not, which
was generally the case. Grandmama reacted like everyone
else and tried to make it up to me and the others by overlooking him. Which left Harry with no one else but me."

"I should have believed you," said Helena. Of Richard's
reaction to his father's preference for his brother, she could
say nothing. But how many children would have responded
as he had, with love rather than with jealousy?

"Should you? Why? What reason did I give you to trust
me? Helena, I have been a contemptible husband. You are a
woman of your own means now, and if you wish to be free
of me, I shall arrange it. I shan't try to impose on your independence. But there's a child to consider. What can we
save from this intemperate marriage?"

"I don't know, Richard." She looked back up at him. The
firelight gilded his face and struck sparks of light over his
fair hair. The bruise that he had been given in the tunnel
seemed to distort the clean line of his cheekbone. What did
he want from her? That she should stay at Acton Mead while
he rejoined Marie in London? She felt her courage begin to

fail her and she clenched her hands together. "Because I haven't been honest either. I told you when we met at Trethaerin that I didn't believe in pretending anything, but I didn't realize how hard that would be when I wanted something so very much."

"What do you want?" he asked quietly. "I have given so little thought to what you might need for yourself."

"You have been too busy staying alive!" she said with a wry smile. "You offer me my independence—I assume because you want yours. Very well. Our child should get to know Trethaerin as well as Acton Mead, so I can move between both places. I hope you'll want to see the baby often, but otherwise, I shall try to enjoy the freedom you offer me. Perhaps in time I will, but I can't pretend to want it." Whatever the consequences, she owed him the truth now. "What I had hoped, you see, was that if I kept quiet and made Acton Mead a place that would welcome you without reproach, you would still come and visit me there. I wanted your company. So I pretended not to know about Marie. Well, I do know about her. And I can't feign anymore not to care. I can't live with half of you, Richard. I'll take the gift you give me and make of it what I can, if you'll take mine. Take your freedom back too. Go to London."

"And live with Marie?" said Richard incredulously.

The gray eyes were fixed on his face. They were filled with a longing that Helena could no longer disguise. "If you love her."

Richard's voice was soft with emotion. "But I haven't seen Marie since September and that was just to say good-bye. I haven't slept with her for over a year. I have never, for one instant, thought I was in love with her. If it had not been for the wild efforts of Nigel Garthwood, I would never have left Acton Mead. How did you find out about Marie?"

Odd things began to flutter in Helena's chest. "From what I overheard your father say about your mistresses, and then Harry said . . ."

His face began to become suffused with laughter. "My father has always had exaggerated ideas about my adventures, dearest Helena. And my brother, though an honorable conspirator and a deadly shot, does not know all the details of my life. When he asked about Marie at Acton Mead, I had already given her up. Besides, she's a widow of independent means who makes a career out of entertaining lonely, single young men of sufficient wealth. A future duke is enjoying her company now, I believe. She would find a married man who was besotted with his wife a dreadful bore."

"But you aren't," said Helena. "Besotted, I mean. Only dutiful."

At which Richard came and knelt at her feet and took both her hands in his. His golden hair had grown just long enough to curl a little at the temple.

"I am besotted, Helena, word of an officer and a gentleman. I love you. I don't blame you if you despise me. Heaven knows I have done nothing to earn your regard, but if you will give me the chance to try, sweet wife, I will do my best to woo you. We never had time for a courtship, did we?"

"I suppose not. My cousin rather disrupted things, didn't he?"

"Then will you allow me three months? Helena, don't turn me away, and for God's sake, don't send me back to London. I know your sense of honor, but I also know your generosity. Can't you give a little to me? If you cast me back out to wander the world again, I'll no doubt survive, but I'm damned if I want to."

"Are you saying you would like to stay at Acton Mead with me?"

"I am saying exactly that. I told Charles de Dagonet a long time ago that I had fallen in love with you. But I won't coerce you. You are the one who has made Acton Mead into a home. You have entirely won over Mr. and Mrs. Hood, as well as the medieval princesses and my brothers. You have earned the right to turn me from the door if you want."

He had moved her hand to his lips. The golden light on his hair blurred suddenly. "But I don't, Richard. I want you there with me. I want you there when our child is born. I would want you there even if it were only once a month. Can't you see, my darling viscount, that I am helplessly in love with you?"

He gave a delighted laugh. "Then why, my lady, are you crying about it?"

"I am not crying!"

Richard leaned forward and kissed the tears away from her face. "Helena, I love you more than life itself. When I thought that you would be indifferent if Garthwood succeeded in his half-baked attempts on my life, I didn't really care if I died. If you will allow me to live with you as a husband, I assure you that you'll be tired of my company within the month and begging me to leave again."

"No, I shan't."

"You are my anchor, sweet Helena. Promise never to cast me adrift."

His anchor. That was what she had thought about him when he had first come to see her at Trethaerin and she had been tempted to take shelter in his strength. Now at last she was being offered an equal bargain. "I promise, Richard. Or if we are to be cast adrift, let it be in the same boat. Now I want to ask a favor."

He looked at her in surprise. "Name it!"

"Please kiss me in earnest, for I have been longing for you to do so ever since Christmas Eve."

Viscount Lenwood handed his wife down from the carriage at Acton Mead with the greatest care.

"I'm really not porcelain, Richard, just because I'm carrying our child."

"No, I didn't think you were. I think you are a beautiful, desirable woman, and intend to prove it as often as you will let me. But in the meantime, let me at least show you some simple courtesy and try to reclaim my title as a gentleman."

"A gentleman who would tease his wife with the beginnings of limericks that he never finished?" He looked at her and raised a brow. "In Exeter you began some rhymes and said you would finish them after we were married."

And Richard began to laugh. "They had no endings, my dear. I was making them up as I went. I just wanted to marry you so very much, and I was afraid you'd cry off."

They had left King's Acton in a remarkably good humor. The earl had declared himself delighted with his oldest son's marriage now that the fortune hunter had turned out to have property of her own and was about to create another generation of Actons, and all his prior rancor appeared to be forgotten. He had even, it appeared, given Richard and Harry a fair hearing over their concerns about the young girls and promised to think about it. It was more than either son had ever expected, and they had left the evidence of Garthwood's racket with the earl. The countess had kissed them all.

"You may, after all, be the saving of my impossible son," she had said quietly to Helena. "God knows he needs it."

Harry had claimed the right to kiss Helena soundly on the cheek, and declared himself bound for Paris. "Someone has to rescue that little maid from the Anchor," he said with a grin. "I can't leave all the derring-do to Dickon, can I?"

Mrs. Hood came out to welcome them home, the elderly butler hurrying at her elbow. "There's a gentleman and a lady here to see you, my lord," she said with a slightly disapproving nod toward the drawing room. "Hood let them in as if they owned the place."

"Yes, so I hear," said Richard dryly, for someone was playing cascading duets on the pianoforte. He went forward and flung open the door. "As I suspected," he said. "Who else but Charles de Dagonet? What on earth are you playing—Mozart?"

"The same, dear sir," said Dagonet, rising from the piano stool. "Forgive our rude use of your home. Like Odysseus, we find shelter wherever we are washed up. I believe you have already met my wife?"

But Helena had seen who was sitting at the instrument with him. "Catherine!" she cried, and, running forward, she embraced her old school friend who had once been known simply as Catherine Hunter.

"You're a damned dark horse, Dagonet," said Richard. "When did this happen?"

"When did Kate grace me with her hand? It's a long story for another time, my friend. But we are headed for Exmoor and wanted to stop and give you the news." He looked up at Helena and gave her a solemn wink. *"L'amour et le fumée ne peuvent se cacher."*

"And where there's smoke, there's fire? Let us take off our hats and then I shall insist on hearing all about it," said Helena, laughing. "Ring for tea, would you, Catherine? We'll be back in a moment."

* * *

Richard took Helena's hand as they went back into the hall. "I had forgotten," he said, "that you knew each other. Do you suppose they can possibly be as happy as we are?"

"I sincerely hope so. If it hadn't been for Catherine Hunter, who is now to my amazement Mrs. Charles de Dagonet, you would never have had the excuse to offer for me," said Helena. "I might even have married Mr. Garthwood."

"No you wouldn't," said Richard instantly. "My vow to Edward was most convenient, but I could never have left Cornwall without you. I wanted you then and I want you now. I was just too much of a damned fool to see it."

"Then prove it, my lord," said Helena as, moving up to him, she stood on tiptoe and kissed him on the mouth.

"You know, Charles," said Catherine, reseating herself at the piano stool. "Your friend Richard seems changed from when I met him on Exmoor."

"How changed, *ma chérie?*"

Catherine tipped her head to one side and allowed her fingers to stray idly over the keys. "I don't know; healed somehow, I think."

"It's because, Kate, he has found that he knows how to love and he has also found someone who loves him back, as, to my infinite surprise, have I. And I can think of no person who more deserves it than Richard Acton."

"Except for Helena Trethaerin," said Mrs. de Dagonet.

Author's Note

It was the fashion in the brothels of the eighteenth and nineteenth centuries for gentlemen to pay large sums to deflower virgins, and young English girls were often sold to Europe for this purpose. Girls were particularly vulnerable in France after the Revolution, since the *maisons closes* were regulated only by a corrupt police force without the backing of the courts. In England such exploitation was next to impossible to control when there was no child labor law in general. Legal restrictions on the employment of children began late in the Regency, but it was not until 1882 that an independent inquiry recommended that it be made a crime to lure British girls into foreign brothels.

Helena's recipe for black ink using the galls of Aleppo is genuine. It comes from a delightful book written in 1814, entitled *The Young Woman's Companion; or Female Instructor,* which belongs to my family. The medieval custom of killing a wren on the day after Christmas persisted into Victorian times. I hope readers are able to picture the Regency kissing bough. The Christmas tree did not become popular in England until introduced by Prince Albert in 1841.

Both Charles de Dagonet and Richard Acton were members of Wellington's Intelligence in the Peninsula. Such a group of scouts did indeed exist. The most famous of them, Major Colquhoun Grant, was described by Wellington as "worth a brigade to me." Without their work with the local partisans, the Peninsular campaign could never have been won.

The adventures of Dagonet and Catherine Hunter may be found in *Scandal's Reward,* previously published by Zebra. A big thank you to everyone who wrote to me about Dagonet! I will have a short story in *Flowers for the Bride* in May. Richard and Helena appear again in *Rogue's Reward* in November 1995, when Eleanor Acton meets dangerous Leander Campbell, the bastard son of an earl.

I love to hear from readers. I may be reached at P.O. Box 197, Ridgway, CO 81432. A stamped self-addressed envelope would be much appreciated, of course, to help defray the costs of reply.